CW00970749

To and Fro Upon the Earth

A Novel

Markus McDowell

RIVERSONG
BOOKS

An Imprint of Sulis International
Los Angeles | London
www.sulisinternational.com

TO AND FRO UPON THE EARTH: A NOVEL

Copyright ©2017 by Markus McDowell. All rights reserved. Except for brief quotations for reviews, no part of this book may be in any form or by any electronic or mechanical means, including information storage and retrieval systems, without written permission from the publisher. Email: info@sulisinternational.com.

This book is a work of fiction. Names, characters, places, and incidents are the product of the author's imagination or are used fictitiously. Any resemblance to actual events, locales, or persons, living or dead, is coincidental.

Riversong Books
An Imprint of Sulis International
Los Angeles | London

www.sulisinternational.com

Cover photo ©2013 Markus McDowell.
Cover design by Sulis International.

Library of Congress Control Number: 2017902803
Paperback ISBN: 978-1-946849-01-4
eBook ISBN: 978-1-946849-10-6

The lyrics in Scene 9 are from "No One is to Blame" by Howard Jones, ©1986 by Songs of Kobalt Music MUSIC PUB OBO HOWARD JONES MUSIC AMERICA. Used by permission.

The poetry quoted in Scene 75 is from "An Essay on Man" published by Alexander Pope in 1734. Public domain.

The quote in Scene 75 is from *The Gulag Archipelago*, "Part I: The Prison Industry, Ch. 4, The Bluecaps" by Aleksandr Solzhenitsyn. Public domain.

Scene 77: "Disobedience to conscience makes conscience blind" is from C.S. Lewis, *A Preface to Paradise Lost*, ch 2. "The secret of all failure is disobedience." is from W.P. Livingstone, *Mary Slessor of Calabar: Pioneer Missionary*. "Justice is truth in action" was spoken by Benjamin Disraeli in a Speech in the House of Commons on 2 February 1851. All are in the public domain.

In scene 87, the writing "non est ad astra mollis e terris via" is from Pliny the Younger, *Hercules Furens*, line 437, spoken by Megara, Hercules' wife. Public domain.

To Lisa,
My gude-sister and anamcara,
who shares my fascination with the
inscrutability of life and faith.

"Life was an urgent struggle to make sense of what was happening."

—Esther de Waal
Seeking God: The Way of St. Benedict

Part One

TO AND FRO

1

"That's one small step for man," I said under my breath as I stepped out of the van and into the light of day.

The other men climbed out behind me, but I paid no attention to them. Two buses sat idling in the broad parking lot, like sleeping monsters gently snoring. The sign on the front of the closest read "San Bernardino-Los Angeles Union." The other was "Phoenix-Tucson." Besides the two buses, there were three cars, parked apart across the asphalt expanse, like vehicle outcasts. Afraid to get too close to anyone else.

I took a deep breath of the warm morning air. My plan had been to return home, despite how different it would be. Many of my contacts would still be there. Still alive. But that *other* emptiness might be more than I could stand.

I heard a female squealing. One of the men was hugging and kissing her. She was not attractive and looked far older than him, though her bawling sounded like a child. The man was delighted. They stopped kissing and began to talk with animation. I watched as she led him to one of the lone cars.

Another who had been with me, a black giant of a man, lumbered over to a pickup truck where an elderly male leaned against the driver door, arms crossed. They shook hands. The larger man opened the passenger door. The truck rocked as he struggled to get in.

It was a bus for me. Phoenix? I had visited a few times on business, but had no real contacts. I knew nothing tell each other our ideas for decorating. No debate or discussion right now. On and on, until we have been through them all."

"Even the closets?"

"Even the closets."

"The wine pantry?"

"The wine pantry."

"Then what?"

"Then, we take our time—months if need be—to discuss, decide. This house is the result of many years of hard work and integrity. It should be decorated with care and order."

She shook her head. "I'm not sure I can be patient! But I'll try."

"Good! Everything always works out as it should, anyway, right?"

"Indeed it does, my dear Jay. We are living proof." She looked at the door. "Let's do it!"

Jay laughed at her playfulness. It had been a great year. A great ten years.

He turned the key in the lock of the large wood and wrought iron door, and threw it open with a flourish.

3

As I waited for the bus to leave, I thought about the tasks ahead. It was a puzzle, I decided. A puzzle with missing pieces, pieces that do not belong, and no picture of what the completed puzzle should look like. Someone created the game by tossing random pieces into an empty box.

I have money enough for travel, food, and lodging—for a little while. I need to speak with Mr. Munro. He might have some good ideas or contacts for me. Maybe even some work, for a time. But every time I had tried to call, he was out of the office or with a client.

The last time I had spoken with him was over a month ago. I had been ordered over to the central office to take his call—a call I had not expected. As I walked over, wondering what it was about, I had a panic attack. It was too much like my last visit to the central office, nine years earlier. Yet when I had gotten there, it was good news, and he had seemed genuinely happy for me.

Since then, I had tried to call three times. The last time, a week ago, it had not gone well.

Sitting in the bus seat, waiting, I replayed the call in my mind. The office assistant asked me if I wanted him to call me back, and I had to remind her—again—that I could not receive calls. She got testy, and I hung up. As I stood there, holding my little notebook, a man standing nearby—Jon something—asked if I was done with the phone. I told him yes and got up, but he said he had heard I was leaving and wanted to know if I had plans. I had said, "not really." It's wasn't his business.

"You should look up my old boss," he had said. "He's always willing to give a guy a chance—takes me on every time I need work. Runs a commercial fishing operation out of San Pedro."

I told him I had no experience, but he said it didn't matter. Despite my insistence that I wasn't interested, he grabbed my notebook and pencil and wrote the name and address. I remember being offended—it wasn't proper to touch other men's personal property in there.

Thinking back on that conversation made me snort. If I end up on a fishing boat, it will mean that the puzzle pieces are useless cardboard.

4

"If you can donate another five or more before December, I could get this taken care of. The sooner, the better. It can be any charity."

"I'm happy to donate more, Jocelyn. But I've given a good amount already. What's the goal?"

She spread her hands out. "True. You have donated far more than most clients. But five thousand more and I can get a significant tax advantage for you. It's just an accounting and tax law issue."

He smiled. "Anthony recommended you as the best tax accountant, and that's why I asked for you. But here's the thing—" Jay leaned forward. The fine leather squeaked. "I will happily donate more. But not for a tax break."

Jocelyn thought *Oh no, another self-righteous, bleeding heart with too much money*.

"You keep working on my finances. In the next month, an opportunity might present itself. If it is a real need that I can meet, and it's the right thing to do, I'll do it. It might be more than five thousand; it might be less. *If* that happens, I'll let you know. If not, that's how things work out. As they should."

Yep, she thought, *another fabulously successful man salving his conscience by pretending to have integrity with his opulent wealth*.

She spread her manicured fingers before her on the desk. Bright red nails. "I understand. But it's just numbers. Give another five or ten to some organization you've already donated to. They'll be happy, and you get the tax break. It doesn't matter."

"Ah, but it *does* matter. It is *not* just money. It is action and life. Everything works together; everything has an effect. I will not donate for a tax break. It may not make sense to you, but it does to me." He smiled.

She nodded. "Of course, Mr. Adam. I am here to serve you." *And now that you've made your show of integrity, you'll do as I ask with a clean conscience. I've seen it a thousand times. I can wait.*

"Good. And stop calling me Mr. Adam. I'm Jay."

"Uh, yes…okay…Jay. Thank you."

He shook her hand and left the office. As she began to shift through the papers on her desk, a knock came at the door.

"Come."

A head appeared around the jamb. Close-cropped hair. Tanned skin. "How'd it go?"

She nodded. "Good, good."

He stepped in and adjusted his tie. "But…?"

"He gave me the old 'no, I-don't-want-to-give-to-charity-just-to-get-a-tax-break' speech. But how he described it was strange."

He laughed. "That's Jay Adam. And it was not a speech. He lives it. He'll hemorrhage money rather than go against his beliefs—even when it would be ethical and moral and legal! But you won't find a more successful businessman. Or a better man."

✳

A few hours later, a vase of flowers and an envelope were delivered to her office. The envelope contained a generous gift certificate to the Goldenrod Club. She flipped the card over.

Jocelyn, you are the best. You and Ephraim enjoy this dinner on us.

Jay and Stella

5

The bus bounced and banged along the freeway. The eight passengers were dispersed like shy children on the first day of school. Periodically, a particularly alarming *bang!* shook the bus. I hadn't been on a bus for over a decade, but I remembered that it was a social convention to ignore both the noises and the other passengers.

I stared out the window at a world that was familiar in some ways, but foreign in others. Sand, dirt, and scrub brushes spread out on either side of the freeway. A dirt access lane raced along behind a short fence. A perpendicular road appeared and flashed by. Arrow-straight, it cut through the brown-yellow land as if cut with a laser, until it reached the vanishing point. The dust and dirt on it belied its lack of traffic.

Ahead, a collection of buildings caught my eye. As we drew close, I saw it was a tiny community: about ten clapboard houses and a few rusted mobile homes. Old cars were parked nearby. Some were heaps of rust, with missing tires and hoods raised. There was no activity. Was it abandoned, like the road? As we passed, I spotted three small figures running around in a dirt backyard. I guess it was inhabited, despite its condition.

It wasn't a town or even a village. It wasn't a temporary camp for road or railroad workers. It had been there a long time. Did it have a name? Were the people outcasts? Maybe they just preferred a small one-horse community to gleaming skyscrapers or manicured housing tracts.

A few miles down the road was another. This was even smaller—just three or four obviously-abandoned structures. The desert scrub had obliterated any sign of yards, roads, or landscaping. Smashed windows and open doors gazed like dead eye sockets, passing judgment on speeding vehicles. Graffiti covered every external wall. The last building had a caved roof. Who had lived or worked there last? I wondered how long it took for natural creation to reclaim the human-made.

A column of black smoke caught my attention ahead. I thought it was on the freeway, but as we approached, I could see it was off to the side, near two small buildings. Soon I spotted small flames around the base of the thick column that billowed straight up into the sky. A bonfire. It was strange to think that, out here, far away from population centers or even farmland, people lived, worked, loved, hated, and died.

As we drew closer, I saw a figure, outlined by the fire, standing with hands on hips. Unmoving, the person appeared as if toasted black. How could one stand so close without cowering?

I craned my neck to watch the watcher as we passed. Just before the window frame blocked my view, the figure appeared to drop its arms and walk straight into the fire.

6

Jay woke and tried to remain still so he wouldn't wake the kids. The television was still on, but the game was long over. He wondered who won.

Keren and Ally were sprawled over him as he lay on the couch. Both were fast asleep in that free unconsciousness that only children experience.

He heard footsteps in the hall. Stella was home.

She entered the room and said, "Jay—" before clapping her hand over her mouth as she spotted the children.

"Sorry," she whispered, admiring the scene. Jay smiled. He loved the joy she found in their family.

She pulled her purse from her arm and set it on the ottoman, then sat next to it.

"How'd it go?" he asked.

She nodded. "Good. Good."

He knew that tone. "Not convincing, love."

"No, it *was* good. The committee is doing some good work." She scrunched up her face. "Jenny made a strange comment."

"Yeah?"

"We were standing with Kathy, and Kathy asked about the work we are having done. The addition, the arboretum, the stone oven—everything. Jenny said, 'some people get it all! I need to hang around you more, so some of that good luck will rub off!'"

Jay waited.

"I've always thought that all the good stuff we have—the things that happen to us—is because we work hard and try to be decent people."

"Well, that's true. We do."

"I know we do. But is that why we're successful?" She paused again. "Are we a lucky accident?"

Jay began to laugh but caught himself. "Most definitely not. We plan like crazy people."

Keren shifted at Jay's side. She gave a little three-year-old's sigh and went still. Her long eyelashes remained closed.

"So you don't think it's all random? Right place at the right time?"

"Maybe there's some luck. But those who plan are prepared to take advantage of chances that come their way. Good work ethic. Responsibility. Accountability. That's a formula for success and a good life."

"But don't you think that sounds kinda trite sometimes? Why did I get appointed to this committee? Why were you asked to join the Board of Directors of Allied last year? We didn't earn those things."

"Sometimes things come because a person is already successful. It's proof of worthiness, based on past efforts."

"So where did it start? What was the first success that led to another? And why the first success? Merit? And what about lazy and mean people who succeed?"

He grinned. "Wow, slow down. I always knew you were smart, but it's a little late for discussing the philosophy of existence…"

His levity failed to have an effect. He reached out his hand. She looked up and took it in hers.

"Where's this coming from, Stella?"

She shook her head, like a horse shooing away flies. "I don't know. Her comment just made me wonder."

"It's not that complicated, Stella. Work hard. Be decent. Perhaps some luck. Bad people do prosper sometimes, but not for long. Everything works out as it should."

She sat, staring at the floor, as if in a trance. He wondered if she would say that his words sounded "trite" again.

With a thin smile, she came back to the present. Leaning over, she kissed his forehead. "I'm fine. Silly thoughts." She nodded at the kids. "We need to get them in bed."

"Yes, and us, too." He sat up with care and reached for Ally. Stella stood and picked up Keren.

"Let's get some sleep," said Jay. "Everything's fine. You'll see."

Stella sighed, then smiled. "I'm sure you're right. You always are."

7

A bang and a bounce woke me. Again. I peered out the window. No change. Desert. Dirt, sand, and scrub brushes. Electric poles. The occasional structure dotted the forsaken land. Had I slept ten minutes or an hour? It looked no different outside.

It was bright and sunny, though. The sky was so blue it almost hurt. No clouds. I took that as a positive sign from the universe.

I should feel some joy. I had inhabited a foreign world for almost a decade. A world where everything was the same. There was order, but it was meaningless order. Punctuated once or twice a month by moments of chaos.

At one time, I would have been thrilled with the opportunity for a new start. A clean slate to draw upon, to impose my will through careful choices. I thought I could draw anything I wanted on that slate. I had always figured I was in control.

The bus hurtled down the arrow-straight road. Trucks and car flashed by on the other side. Was this Tuesday? Yes.

I had the absurd idea to just stay on the bus. Go all the way to the end of the line. Buy another ticket and ride back to Phoenix. Repeat. I could be the Sisyphus of Greyhounds.

I don't suppose the bus line would allow that. Besides, I have a lot of choices in front of me, though not unlimited. I can't bring back the dead or undo the acts of others. But there must be a lot I *could* do. I had done it before. I just need to keep working on the puzzle.

Which reminded me that I needed to call to find out how many more insurance payouts are left. They took most of it, of course.

8

The phone beeped.

"Yes?"

"Mr. Adam, Mr. Zohn is here to see you."

"Send him in."

Jay turned back to the report he was reading. Excellent news. It meant more capital for next year, among other things. He could expand—

A motion at the door was Edward Zohn hovering outside, as if delay would make it easier.

"Zohn? Come on in." Everyone called him 'Zohn.' It suited him.

He looked worse than usual. Disheveled. His bad haircut was especially bad today.

"Hey, uh, boss, can I talk to you?"

"Of course. Have a seat." Jay knew why he was here.

Zohn shuffled to the chair in front of the desk and sat. He leaned forward as if he might need to jump up and run away at a moment's notice. His unfocused gray-blue eyes looked at the floor, to the surface of the desk, then back to the floor.

Jay noticed that the two lines which ran from either side of his nose to the sides of his mouth were deeper than usual. There was a cranberry-colored scrape on his temple.

"Well, boss…" He glanced at Jay and then back down. "I screwed up again last night." He grimaced and let out a sigh of disheartenment.

Jay knew he could relieve his anguish, but thought it better to wait a bit. Let him unearth his failure. Zohn was a good guy, but he never seemed to learn from experience. On some days, Jay thought he might gain that skill. On other days, he was sure he never would.

Jay also knew that Zohn hated to disappoint him, though not enough stop him from repeating his mistakes. Every couple of months. On schedule.

"I screwed up," he repeated. "I—I wasn't going to do anything, but a friend came into town, and we went out to just get a couple of drinks. That's all. I…" he dropped his head. "I screwed up again."

Enough. "Zohn, I already talked to the Chief. The officer called me last night when he took you in. Who do you think bailed you out?"

He nodded and grew sadder. *That's a good sign*, Jay thought.

"We'll get it straightened out, Zohn. But you need to learn where your boundaries are." They'd had this discussion before.

"I know boss, I know. I will."

"Good. You can't this keep up—I might not be able to help you someday. Now, go on back to work. We'll talk later."

Zohn stood and put his hands in his pockets. His height amplified his discomfort and awkwardness. "You're a good boss."

"Thanks, Zohn. Happy to help."

The phone rang. Zohn bobbed his head and ducked out.

It was Stella. She had just come from a luncheon at City Hall for one of her civic projects—a reading program for children of single parents, he remembered. She was involved in so many projects it was hard for him to keep track. He asked how it went.

"The luncheon went well. We gave awards to the Pedersons who donated *so* many books last year, and then the mayor talked about the fundraiser and the new opportunities. He was quite happy with the project."

"That's excellent. Not surprising, of course. But congratulations."

"Thank you, love. But that's not why I called. I have some exciting news. The mayor told me he wants *you* to run for city council. He says you would be a shoe-in—he's already talked to other board members, the chief of police, the—"

"That's quite kind. And intriguing. Work is awful busy though." It did make him feel good that the mayor thought he could contribute.

"I know, Jay. He *said* you'd say that. He said that it wouldn't require a lot of your time—they'd even make exceptions for meeting attendance. They want your *wisdom*—that's the word he used."

Jay smiled. "It's quite a compliment. I suppose I'll have to consider it. I'd like to help, but it's politics. I hate self-promotion."

"Well, he also said you'd say *that*, too, and that's *exactly* why they need you. You'd put the city first. He mentioned when you paid to have that playground built, and that charity you set up after the earthquake. He wants you to call him to discuss."

Jay was silent. It would be nice to do more than merely contribute money for the common good.

"Jay?"

"Sorry, I was thinking. I'll give it some thought."

"Of course," Stella said.

Jay was pretty sure she already knew he would accept.

9

"Kinder words have not been spoken."

I opened my eyes. The speaker was a man sitting on the bench seat across the aisle. He had not been there before. Facing sideways, his legs and feet were in the aisle. His head looked like a boiled egg: shaved head and face. Even his eyebrows. He did have kind blue eyes but sported a ridiculous grin.

I was pretty sure he had boarded the bus when I had. Which meant he had been in the white van with me, too. I didn't remember.

I had no desire for conversation. Not from someone on a bus.

"What?" It came out like a croak from my dry throat.

He made an "O" shape with his mouth and flipped both hands up as if feigning surprise. "I'm so sorry. You were sleeping. I thought you were just looking out the window." He waited as if he expected me to say, *Oh, that's ok*.

"Oh, that's ok." It was out of my mouth before I knew it. My discipline was weak. I was a bit groggy.

He smiled—a big, missing-teeth, happy smile. "I said, 'kinder words have not been spoken.' Don't you think?"

"I don't know what you are talking about."

"The radio. On the radio. The news report."

I became aware that music was playing. Tinny, crackly music. The driver must have turned on the radio while I was asleep. I didn't recognize the song. Male singer. Some pop-electronic song, perhaps from the 80's.

> *Some break the rules*
> *and live to count the cost…*

I took a deep breath and shook off the cobwebs of bus sleep. "That's a song, not the news."

"Yeah. Good music. Before the music. They were talking about assisted suicide. Somewhere made it legal. I don't know where. Never heard of the place. They passed a law. Said it was legal. A doctor said, 'when a person is ready to die, it should be their choice. Why should someone tell them their story is not over?' Kinder words have not been spoken, don't you think?"

> *no one, no one, no one ever*
> *is to blame…*

I wanted to tell him to get lost, but I had no idea how long we'd be on this bus together. Even on a bus, there should be some social rules. "Yeah, I suppose. If someone wants to die, let them die." I'd never really thought about it. I'd prefer a law that made it illegal to kill people who did not want to die.

> *You can see the summit,*
> *but you can't reach it,*
> *it's the last piece of the puzzle…*

"I've thought of dying," he continued. "I have a bank account. Been racking up interest. I could use it. Travel to that place. Find a doc and do it. I think my story is over. I don't have anymore."

"Didn't you just get out?"

"Sure." He shrugged. "But there's no more story to write." He nodded enthusiastically, inviting me to join along. "Don't you agree?" He grinned even bigger.

No one grins like that if there is a sound mind behind it. Why did he choose me out of all the men on the bus? I had no need for chit-chat. Or necro-philosophy.

"How do I know, you ask?" Still grinning.

I shook my head. "I didn't ask."

"How do I know my story is over? Because *I* am the author!" The grin morphed into a triumphant cackle. "The author knows!"

He held up one finger. "*Some* say that stories take on a life of their own once they exist. The author is a fallacy; the story an artifact." He pulled himself up. "I disagree!"

A mental case educated in literary theory. Good for me.

He frowned and looked down at his feet. His mouth opened, then closed. His eyes bulged. He seemed to be struggling. I sat up straight. I had experienced too many instances of the violence that could erupt from the most seemingly gentle of men by the most innocuous trigger. "Volatile," the officers called them, who then pepper-sprayed and zip-tied their arms as the body writhed on the ground screaming.

He raised his gaze. His eyes did not show crazy. Intensity. But not insanity. "I don't think it's correct. Is it?"

I shrugged. "Maybe not. I don't know." I hope this ends soon.

Another song was playing now. I knew this one. Older. The Beatles? No, McCartney solo, I think. Didn't he have a band with his wife? "Venus and Mercury" was the name of the song.

The man stared at his feet. He seemed quite sad now. I felt a bit sorry for him, trapped in a mind that stutters and coughs like an old engine. "You know, it is your story. You can write it however you like."

He looked up with an expression of confusion.

"*My* story?"

"Yeah, your story. You can write it how you like."

He frowned and his face reddened. "Oh, I'm not a writer. I write some letters. Not very often."

Great. "I meant the story of your life. How you live your life."

"Oh!" He grinned. "I have plans. I have a bank account. Been racking up interest. I could use it. Travel to New York, I think. Maybe Europe."

I nodded. "Sounds like a good plan." Despite myself, I felt sorry for him. Were his mental problems from drug use? Or genetics? Still, I was sure he could have made better choices. And still could. There are always options.

"Yeah. I have heard that they have assisted suicide there. I'm going to find the radio doctor and—"

Mercifully, the driver interrupted over the loud-speaker. "We are approaching our first stop. Desert Center in about twenty minutes. A forty-five minute stop if you want to get a bite to eat or stretch your legs."

"You getting off at Desert Center?" he asked.

"Maybe." *Not if you are.*

"I have to get to El Centro. That's where my bank is. I have plans. For the money. Some radio doctor is going to help me finish the story."

10

Jay took his seat in first class. As the plane had reached cruising altitude, he picked up the flight phone beside his seat and dialed the office.

"Cristy? It's Jay."

"Hello, Mr. Adam! Are you in Dallas already?"

"No, on the plane headed there—just took off."

"How did the presentation go?"

"Fantastic—that's why I am calling. They loved it. We got the contract."

"Oh, that's great!"

"You know how much chaos we endured while putting this together! But it worked out as we planned. This is going to put us on the map, Cristy. I want to celebrate."

"One of our famous parties?"

"Yes. This Friday. I've already got Joleen working on the catering. I'd like you to send out a memo. I'll email you the details of the deal itself so you can share it with everyone. We'll stop all work at noon that day, and the celebration will begin at four. I want them to bring their families, too."

"The project team and their families?"

"No, *everyone*. We're all part of the team for something this big. I am so pleased with everyone—they deserve it. Lots of food, lots of drink."

"Got it. That'll be nice. We haven't done a company-wide party in a while."

"Call Joleen to coordinate. Spare no expense, Cristy. I want this to be our biggest one yet. I'll call you tomorrow after my meeting, and then I'll be back around noon Thursday."

"Okay. I'll get right on it. Let me know if you think of anything else."

He hung up and pondered the joy he felt from a job well done by a team.

His good humor abated when he glanced at his phone. An email from the Nashville interest. They had screwed up another financial filing requirement. He sighed. They were a good group of young men and women, but they needed more direction from him than he had been able to provide. Their enthusiasm sometimes overshadowed expediency and forethought. Some of their mistakes could have been costly.

Ah well, he thought. *I'll spend a few days with them after next week.* He didn't want to be away from Stella and the kids again so soon, but planning ahead always made things work out better.

Frustrating. He wanted a diversion, so he scrolled through the available movies on the screen in front of his seat. *The Tree of Life* by Terrance Malick came up. It had won the 2011 Palme d'Or. Plugging in headphones, he tapped "play," and settled back in the large leather seat.

11

The light began to brighten. A white, sun-like glow. The sound of airplane engines faded away. It was so quiet, every sound dampened by bales of cotton. So silent that I wondered if I had gone deaf.

I shifted in my seat and found it was no longer a first-class chair, but a throne of cloudy whiteness. Yet I felt no fear. It seemed reasonable, though part of me knew it wasn't.

A movement to the left caught my attention. Two figures floated in the cloudy distance, one small and one large.

A thin voice broke the silence. "Read the story to me, Mommy, read the story again!"

"Okay, okay." A woman. Laughing.

"Once upon a time there was a small child who lived in a great kingdom. The kingdom was ruled by a kind queen. But the Queen had no King, no children, and no family. So she adopted the people as her family."

Each day, she went about her kingdom giving food to the hungry, clothes to the destitute, and comfort to the sick. Each time her subjects thanked her, she would smile and say, "*Do ut des, do ut des.*"

There was a small child, a little girl, who had no mother or father, just an old grandfather who took care of her as best as he could.

"Yes, yes," shouted the little child, "Keep going!"

"One day, some people came to her school and told her that her grandfather had died. They said she had to come with them to live in an orphanage."

"She didn't want to, did she, Mommy? She had heard bad things about the orphanage, hadn't she, Mommy?"

"Yes, she had."

"Keep reading, keep reading."

"But the little girl had heard how children were mistreated in the orphanage. How they were locked up in a dark closet for being bad. How their knuckles were rapped when they answered incorrectly in class. How the food was thin and bland. So she ran away from the school and hid in an old shed by a blacksmith's shop. She knew the people would look for her, so she snuck during the nights to get scraps of food from behind the market stalls."

"But they caught her, right, mommy?"

"They did, dear. One day, as she lay sleeping on some old dirty blankets, there was a great ruckus. Men broke into the shed, grabbed her, and took her before the Queen."

※

The Queen sat on her throne, gazing down on the poor child. Dirty, thin, and disheveled, the Queen felt compassion for the child with no family.

"Little girl? Can you hear me?" The Queen's voice was always clear, bright, and commanding.

The little girl nodded, trembling as she sat on the cold stone floor, knees up, head down and cradled in her arms.

"Your grandfather died?"

She nodded again.

"And you did not want to go to the orphanage?"

The child mustered up some courage. "No, Queen! I have heard bad things."

The Queen pursed her lips. "Yes, I have heard those bad things, too."

Without turning her head, the little girl peeked up at the Queen with one eye.

The Queen nodded. "I understand why you ran away. Perhaps we can find *someone* who might take you in. Someone who has no family. Who has no children of her own." She smiled.

The girl raised her head and looked up at her monarch. "Like…like the Queen?"

The Queen allowed herself a small laugh. "Yes, like the Queen."

The little girl wiped away her tears with a grimy arm. "However."

The girl cocked her head.

"However," the Queen continued. "You trespassed. You stole from others. Food. Shelter. Clothes."

The child dropped her head.

The Queen raised her eyes and shouted, "Attend!"

The child jumped at the harsh command. The doors to the throne room crashed open. Marching feet made echoes around the throne room, stopping beside the little girl.

The Queen nodded at the soldiers, then turned her head away at the sound of blows, breaking bones, and screaming.

"*Do ut des*," she whispered to herself.

12

"Jay?!"

"By the fire pit!" he shouted back.

Stella breezed through the triple-wide French doors at the back of the house, thrown open to invite the warm summer evening. Jay watched with appreciation as she walked down the cobbled stone path from the house above.

She held out his phone. "You left your phone upstairs. Looks like Anthony has been calling you."

He placed his book face down on the cushion beside him and took the phone.

"Thanks, love."

"Come in soon?"

"Yes, after this call."

She winked and left. Jay dialed the number. The bank receptionist put him through without delay.

"Anthony, this is Jay returning your call. What are you still doing at the office?"

"Just finishing up. How was your vacation?"

"Fantastic. We had a great time. Thank you so much for suggesting the island. So peaceful, and the weather was great. Keren and Ally got so tan we didn't recognize them."

"Laucala is one of our favorite places…Listen, I don't want to keep you, and I need to get home. I am sorry to bring this to you, but I have a problem."

"Sure, anything you need."

"It's a bit awkward. Do you recall the loan you co-signed last year? For a guy named Peter Foucault?"

"Yes, of course. One of my employees. Still is."

"I know you wanted to help him out. And if you remember, after we did some research, I told you it was not worth the risk. But you insisted."

Jay smiled to himself. "I did. And he has defaulted."

"Well, not yet. We would have, but…it was you who co-signed, and I wanted to give him a little more time. He still hasn't responded, so I told my people to hold off so I could talk to you first."

"I appreciate you trying to protect me. But you should not treat me any different than anyone else. Tell you what: I'll pay the amount necessary to bring it current, plus a month. Send me the details."

"Jay, as your banker—and friend—I have to tell you this is not a good idea. I know you are trying to help him, but—"

"Thank you, but I know his situation. I am not concerned."

He sighed. "Very well. I understand your desire to help people. But if you ever expect anything in return—even kind words—don't. People don't value what they get for free."

"No worries, Anthony. I know what I am doing. It'll all work out."

13

The bus slowed to a crunchy halt in a dusty parking lot, sighing as it stopped in front of the concrete and aluminum bus station. Dark film sheets had been stuck inside the glass windows to keep the desert sun at bay. White-gray bubbles dotted the film here and there. Some of the corners had curled up. A white sign with red letters pronounced that the bus station was OPEN.

I rose, lugging my bags behind me—I wasn't leaving them on the bus while I ate. I set them down beside an old wooden bench outside the door of the station and waited for the other passengers, and the bus driver, to file inside.

Across the street was a truck stop. A gas station sat on the opposite corner—maybe a Chevron, I couldn't see from here. Just beyond that was a café, with the inspired name of *Desert Center Café*. It made me think of an old western saloon. I hoisted my bags and trudged across the street.

As I entered, I half-expected the waitress to say, "Howdy," as the slatted doors swung shut behind me. "You ain't from around here."

"Gimme a whisky," I'd say.

Stop it. Too much whimsy. The universe doesn't deserve any playfulness at the moment.

The wall of the diner on my right was covered with worn wood paneling up to waist level and windows the rest of the way to the ceiling. Discolored aluminum posts divided the large panes. Cheap blinds hung from above—some closed, some open, all askew. Booths lined the wall under the windows. All were occupied, except the one closest to the door.

Across from the booths, in front of me, was a long countertop. Bar stools, affixed to the floor, were all occupied. To the left was a little dining area with three or four tables, also occupied. I supposed this was the most popular (only?) feeding hole in the area. For all I knew, the whole population was here.

I found myself taken aback by the busy hum of voices and the clacking of plates and cups. It wasn't the noise— it was the tone. Different than what I was used to. More lively. Not as somber as a mess hall. I wasn't sure I liked it.

A middle-aged woman stood at the cashier's station, counting money and working a mechanical cash machine. Her black and gray hair was pulled back in a bun. The dark color of her skin and the lines on her face belied a long life in the desert.

I saw myself from above, a lone scruffy figure standing motionless as a beehive of activity buzzed all around, like synchronized swimmers.

The cashier saw me, bringing me back into my body, and gave me a quick nod at the empty booth. She turned and disappeared into the kitchen through swinging doors.

I shoved my bags into the seat and slid in beside them. Facing away from the rest of the booths, I felt a mental itch. As if someone might tell me I should not be here: "Move along, mister."

The cashier came out of the kitchen, bearing a coffee pot. She pulled four laminated menus from the rack near her station and dropped them on the table in front of me. She poured me a cup of coffee.

"If you're eating alone, and a bar seat opens up, I'll have to ask you to move. We don't sit singles at booths, but that's all there is right now."

"Sure."

The menu consisted of one laminated page, front and back, crowded with text. Lists, boxes, circles, and headings. Sizes and colors differentiated each dish. "Daily Specials!" "Best Grilled Cheese in the West!" "Our Enchiladas are To Die For." Much of it was the same food offered up in different ways. An abundance of possibilities with rice, beans, tortillas, beef, and chicken. Variations on burgers, sandwiches, and soups. Ten different salads. Eggs in every form known throughout history, along with other breakfast foods "Available All Day!!!" as if the patrons would be three-exclamation-point surprised at such a bizarre turn of cuisine chronology.

The front door opened and a waft of hot air blew over me. A woman walked to the cashier's station, fumbling in a large purse. She was so intent on her digging that she did not notice the cashier station was vacant. Her appearance told me that she didn't fit here any more than I did—for different reasons, I was sure.

There were slight wrinkles around her eyes—a clue that she might be in her forties, not thirties as I first assumed. She had natural blonde hair, as near as I could tell, with skin and body tones that bespoke a stereotypical "California girl."

She was dressed well—not opulently so, but enough to show she was well-off. Designer sunglasses, perched atop her head, and a gold watch on her thin wrist revealed that she had enough to spend on luxuries. Her choice of couture made a contradictory statement that she was both delicate and tough.

She held a few items in one hand, with her bag crooked over that arm, while pawing through the contents with the other hand, seeking an elusive piece which refused to cooperate.

She let out a puff of exasperation and looked up. Seeing no one at the counter, she scanned the room. Her eyes lit on me so quickly that I did not have the time to look away before our eyes met. I shook my head in apology and looked back down at the menu.

She came over and set her bag on the opposite seat. "Do you mind? I am trying to find my wallet and having a terrible time of it." She glanced around, her blonde bob swaying once then twice. "This place is packed, isn't it?"

"Sure. Yeah." I hadn't had a chance encounter with anyone in a long time—except for the suicidal man on the bus. I felt like an awkward schoolchild.

She began taking items out of the bag and piling them on the table. A package of gum, a travel toothbrush, three lipstick cylinders, a brush, two hair clips, a small notepad, some wadded-up pieces of paper—

"Ah!" She held up a brown leather wallet, twice as big as her hand. A sparkling bracelet slid down a tanned arm. The wallet threatened to burst open: every pocket and slot was stuffed with papers and business cards. "Here it is."

The treasure hunt over, she sighed and regarded me as if for the first time. "Thank you."

"No problem."

She looked around again.

"Do you mind if I sit here?" Her confidence stood in stark opposition to my incertitude. "I need to eat lunch

28

and get back on the road. I'll be glad to pay for your lunch in return for the imposition."

Panic grabbed my belly and rose up my esophagus. I was not sure I knew how to chit-chat or act with a stranger. In the last ten years the only women I had interacted with wore uniforms.

"Oh, well…I—" I began.

"Oh!" Her face burgeoned with realization, manicured eyebrows raised, eyes wide. Despite my discomfort, I noted that her makeup application was expertly applied and understated. "You're waiting for someone. I'm sorry!"

I shook my head. "No, no, I'm not. It's fine." I wasn't sure it was fine. "I was just…I've had a long day. You can sit." I felt my face heat up.

"Oh, good. Thank you." A shy smile. "I know strangers don't do this sort of thing often…" she laughed an honest and open laugh. "I promise I'm nice."

I managed a polite laugh. "I'm sure you are. There's no need to buy my lunch." I was calming down. Her honesty and genuineness helped.

She pushed her bag across the seat and slipped in beside it.

"I insist. It will make me feel better about being so forward and interrupting your solitude."

I pondered the word "solitude." I had experienced so much unwanted solitude. Now that I would have opportunities for interaction, I was not sure that I wanted them. At least it would be my choice from here on out.

"My name is Ellie." She held out a white, delicate hand.

"I'm Jay." I took her hand briefly and shook it, falling quickly into social traditions. I had come to think that these societal machinations, oiled by pleasantries, belie self-centeredness and self-preservation which lay below. It made sense —platitudes are easier than philosophizing; papering over easier than exploration. Still, it now felt awkward, unlike in my past. I used to be such a glad-hander—sincere, but a gregarious social navigator. Now I was suspicious of accepted norms. Even those that seemed harmless.

"Nice to meet you, Jay." Professional. Polite and friendly, with no hint of flirting or neediness. Good. I am not sure I'd trust her if she were too friendly or kind. There was always a selfish agenda, I feared.

As I struggled to think of something else to say, she spoke.

"So what brings you to this lovely oasis?"

14

He hurried out of the meeting and through the lobby to the street. His driver was already waiting. Once they were on I-35E, he called Cristy.

"I won't make it for the party, Cristy. Rhodes and company are in crisis."

"Oh, no, I'm sorry. You're going to Nashville?"

"On my way to the airport now. Everything ready to go for the party?"

"Yes. Joleen and I have everything lined up. I'm so sorry you have to miss it—we've outdone ourselves this time, if I say so myself."

"I have no doubt. Did you think about getting rides and drivers available for after for those who might need them?

"I already called SoCal Chauffeur and requested a few limo vans, with drivers to bring our cars home."

"You're the best, Cristy."

"It's my pleasure, of course. Call me if I can do any-thing else—even over the weekend."

"Thanks, but you've worked above and beyond the call. Enjoy the party and the weekend. I'll see you Mon-day morning."

He hated missing the celebration, but he'd make sure to thank them all in person later. And he'd give Cristy and her husband a weekend trip.

Maybe he could address the Nashville problems and take a red-eye back tomorrow. That way he would make it in time for Keren's recital.

The driver turned onto the John Carpenter Freeway. Jay took a deep breath. It was not a catastrophe. Not yet, anyway. Of course, if some busybody at the SEC wanted to cause problems—

No reason to go there yet. If need be, he could call the authorities himself and explain what happened. Being honest and pro-active usually went a long way.

Everything would work out.

15

"It's a long story. Pretty shocking."

"I've been around," she said with a shrug. "I'm not easily shocked. I travel all over as a sales consultant for a medical supply corporation. I volunteer at local shelters when I am home. I've got three brothers—one's been in and out of the hospital and jail because of drugs. I've seen it all."

I doubted it. "Sounds like an interesting job."

"Sometimes. I like it because I'm in an industry that helps people. I didn't have the patience to become a doctor or nurse."

The waitress came over with a cup for Ellie. We ordered. She ordered a Cobb salad and an iced tea. I wanted a thick burger, double fries, and a shake, but since she was paying, I ordered the same. The waitress took our menus and left without a word.

Ellie steepled her arms on the table, clasping her hands together under her chin. "So tell me your story."

I kept it brief and to the facts. I had found that inserting my commentary and interpretations often brought suspicion, as if I "protesteth too much."

I had always thought I hadn't protested enough.

She sat in silence as I spoke. It made me nervous, but I told myself it didn't matter. She's insignificant, and I won't ever see her again after this.

I finished and gazed down at my coffee cup, fingering the handle. Even a brief and intellectual recitation beat me down. Squeezed my heart. Drained my life.

Her silence made me look up. She was regarding me with what seemed to be tenderness. I looked away. Sympathy might be nice, but when it stared me in the face I found I didn't like it.

"Wow. That *is* quite a story," she said, almost in a whisper. "Now what?"

"I don't know."

"Where are you headed?"

I exhaled. "Good question. I'm taking a bus back to where I used to live."

"Job ideas?"

"Just some vague one, based on what I did before." She looked sad. It irritated me. Maybe I did want sympathy, but I had no use for pity. "I'm going to contact some old friends. And my lawyer might have some ideas."

"Do you have money? Because…" I had hoped she wouldn't go there. That's the worse kind of pity: salving one's conscience by writing numbers on a check. I jumped in.

"Yes, there's money from the life insurance payout." I didn't tell her that most of that account had been sucked dry by restitution. Which reminded me, I needed to call and check the balance. And call Munro again.

Part of me wished she had never sat down. But something else was stirring inside me, like nascent bubbles in a pot of water on a stove. For the first time in a long time, I felt a hunger. I wanted to *accomplish* something.

She startled me by suddenly leaning forward. Her eyes were smiling.

"May I tell you something? I think this is…what's the word? Opportune? No, that's not it." She looked to the side, then back at me. "I think we've ended up meeting here for a reason. I've been reading this book on my trip—" She turned and rummaged through her bag, pulling out a thin, worn paperback. Strips of paper were stuck between the pages here and there.

"It's called *Man's Search for Meaning*." She squirmed a bit in the seat, her speech coming faster. "I don't understand all of it—the author is very smart—a survivor of a Nazi camp, and he wrote this while there, hiding bits of paper—he says that if you are a good person, and you are suffering, there is some meaning in it. So you need to figure it out."

That sounded trite. But since she was being nice, I decided to play along. "How do you know I'm a good person?"

She sat back and smiled. "I can tell. I'm good at reading people."

I tightened my lips. "Okay. Well, for argument's sake, I'll say that his book doesn't ring true. The whole problem with Holocaust sufferers was there *was* no reason for it. Just evil. Meaningless. What was that phrase? 'After Auschwitz, no one can believe' or something like that."

She was undeterred. "Well, he was *in* the Holocaust. He was a psychologist or psychiatrist, and I'm not, but I am pretty sure that's what he is saying. If you are a good person, then your suffering is for *some* good purpose. If not, then you suffer because you haven't been a good person."

"That seems neat and tidy."

She fell silent. Maybe I'd offended her. So what. She didn't seem bothered, though, and went right on.

"I was reading it the other night—it had been a long day, and a lot of frustrating stuff had happened with the head office and my customers. I mean stuff that makes one think of quitting. Really giving it all up, no matter the consequences. I've worked so hard for so long—doing what I loved—that I had no time for a husband or kids or even friends outside of work—giving up my career would be a huge step. But I was so unhappy. So I was reading this book, and I fell asleep."

Please don't tell me about a dream you had.

"I dreamed I was floating in darkness like I was in space. The week before I had seen that movie about space, the one about a trip to Jupiter or Saturn? Kubrick, I think. Anyway, I was floating like that spaceman. I wasn't wearing a spacesuit, but I could breathe. It was funny, though—it felt normal. Then something like a ghost flew past me and around, coming to a stop right in about Tucson. Maybe I should head out to parts unknown. *Really* start all over. In every way.

With an attempt at dispassion, I decided that the known was better than the unknown.

I want some order to this puzzle that is my life.

2

"I'm scared."

Jay laughed. "Of what?"

She shrugged. "It's such a big house. It's more than a house. It's a…mansion." She whispered the last word. "Did you ever think we would own such a place?"

"No. Not really."

She stepped close to his side and laid her head on his shoulder.

"Truly? You are such a *planner*. All those years, you never dreamed of this house, those cars, the success?"

He laughed again. Taking each arm, he turned her toward him.

"Stella, you know me. I plan. I work hard. I don't dream."

She leaned in to give him a quick kiss. "True. And you know I loved the house from the start. But it belonged to someone else and was full of their furniture. Now it's big and empty and *ours*. A little overwhelming." She smiled. "But I'm excited. You got the key?"

He pulled it from his pocket and held it up. She feigned a serious expression.

"Are you ready to enter our new home?"

"Yes, yes!" she shouted, giving a little clap. "Let's!"

"Ok. Since I'm a planner, here's the plan. It's now empty. It's ours. So let's visit each room, and in turn, we front of me. I got all goose-pimply in the dream, and suddenly I *was* scared."

I picked up my mug and took the last sip of tepid coffee. It tasted better than listening to someone else's dream.

She went on. "Was it a person, or the light playing tricks? I didn't know. Then I heard its voice, though I couldn't see any mouth. It was deep and loud." She mimicked a deep voice, speaking slowly. "No one is perfect."

Dumb, I thought. She even seemed a bit embarrassed. Her eyes flitted down, then back up. Blue, blue eyes. She gave a quick shrug with one shoulder.

"Maybe that sounds silly, but when I woke up, it had a *profound* effect on me. It's *true*. No matter how hard we try, none of us are perfect—me, my boss, my co-workers. I probably make life difficult for others sometimes and don't even know it. I don't know what others are dealing with. We are all like...like the walking wounded. So...I was in a really bad place, and that dream helped me to relax and wait it out."

I failed to see any connection between Holocaust suffering and the dream, and couldn't muster any sympathy for office politics. It was not that her sincerity was lost on me. If such mindless musings made her feel better, good for her. But her words made me angry. I wanted to stand up and walk out. Was I overreacting? I wasn't sure. And that made me mad, too.

She wore comfortable sandals that might get an occasional pebble in them. I wore boots filled with salt, with spikes and a vice inside that slowly crushed my bones.

16

"Jay? It's five in the morning." She was half-sitting, twisted up in sheets and bed covers, blinking at him across the room.

"Go back to sleep, hon. I need to go to the office."

She flopped back onto the pillow. "It's Sunday."

"I know." He finished buttoning his shirt. "I need to make sure everything is okay in Nashville."

"You were just there."

He laughed. "Yes, and it was a mess. I'll be back within a few hours."

"Ok. Love you." Her eyes drooped shut.

❄

The large meeting room was a mess. "Must have been a great party—wish I'd been here," he said to the large, empty room. Trash cans overflowed. Bags of trash sat beside them, many open and leaning sideways as if they were ill and about to vomit. It looked like someone had started to clean up and gave up. A few plates of food were stacked on the tables and floor. Half-empty bottles and cans were sitting about. There were even a few forgotten jackets and a pair of shoes.

Jay laughed. It made him happy to know his people could celebrate with abandon for a job well done.

The janitors would clean it up early tomorrow. But he couldn't refrain from helping some. He took the trash bags out to the big dumpsters in back of the facility, wiped down the tables with a wet rag from the janitor's closet, and dragged them into the supply closet.

He surveyed his work. *Good, he thought. That'll make it a little easier on them.*

He'd already been here over an hour. That took longer than he thought. Once seated in his office, he found ten emails and three voice messages from Nashville. As he reviewed them, he began to wonder if his visit had been a waste. He made notes and started checking numbers, documents, and filings on the computer system.

After another hour, he sat back and sighed. It was worse than he had thought. They'd hadn't disclosed everything to him when he visited. Markham was new, but he should have known to check with the accountants and lawyers first. This was the kind of thing that administrative agencies loved to pursue. Jay understood—it could *look* like an attempt at tax and investment fraud. And the practice nowadays was to assume guilt and investigate later. What Markham did looks like he tried to cover it up—though he was probably just trying to fix it. Stella often told him that he gave his employees too much rope to play with. "That's a good way for people to learn," she'd say, "but it's also a good way for someone to hang themselves. "

He called Stella to apologize because he'd be longer than he thought. "I'll make it up to you guys, I promise."

He took out a pad of paper. He was good at this. Even in a severe crisis, it was almost like a game. It was fun. Brainstorm the issues, problems, possible solutions, contingencies, and unintended consequences. Map out some strategies. Diagram and outline. Detail the plan, and set it in motion.

He'd have to go through the entire account history. Resolve what he could from here. For the rest, he'd send emails to Markham, the accountant, and the attorneys. Then call the proper administrative agencies (which ones?) and notify them of the problem and what he had done to resolve it. It was always better to be proactive and honest. They might just let it go. At worst, they could levy a fine. *I can live with that.*

∗

He had been sitting for hours without a break. He'd made two calls to Nashville, which he hated doing on a Sunday.

In such a vast and wide-ranging business, with so many people involved, things went wrong sometimes. The complexity of company and government regulations can make even innocent mistakes look bad. He'd get it worked out. There were always answers, always solutions.

He stood up, stretched, and went to the cafeteria. The staff refrigerator contained a chocolate bar, some yogurt, two bottles of beer, and three cans of Coke. He ate the yogurt while standing in front of the open refrigerator. Thinking.

He turned to leave and spotted three empty beer cans sitting on the table. The trash cans were full, so he took them with him to the bathroom. Not only were those trash cans full, too, but three half-empty liquor bottles sat on the sink counter. *Wow, they really did celebrate!* he laughed. He gathered up the bottles went in search of an empty trash can. As he walked down the hall, he heard his phone ringing in his office. Hurrying inside, he dumped the cans and bottles on his desk and grabbed the phone.

"Hello?"

"Jay? You okay?" It was Stella.

"Yes, of course." He glanced at the clock. Five-thirty. Wow.

"I called a few minutes ago and you didn't answer."

"Sorry, I was in the cafeteria."

"How's it going?"

He sighed. "I've figured out what they did and fixed what I could. Just a few emails and calls to make."

"Good. How much longer?"

"Maybe an hour? I'm sorry."

"I understand. See you soon."

✳

Jay drove out of the parking lot while mentally reviewing his plan and actions. He was confident that by tomorrow afternoon it would be cleared up. A conference call with the Nashville team and the attorneys tomorrow morning would put the final touches on his plan. The only outstanding issue was how the agencies would respond. Should be okay, though.

He wondered if he had set the alarm before he left. He had been on the phone with Stella. *No matter, the janitors will be there in seven hours.* In the dark, he turned his the car onto the 5 Highway and home.

17

I'm at a funeral home. I float above the scene, watching people, dressed to the nines, mill about. Somber faces. Occasional whispers.

I descend like an eagle, touching down light on the shiny floor. I'm wearing one of my finest suits, all black with a white, crisp shirt. A light blue tie. She loved this suit and tie.

The room is filled with family, friends, and acquaintances. Black dresses, black pants, dark jackets. All quite concerned. Sympathetic nods. Reaching out to touch an arm. A brief hug. "I'm so sorry."

Of course, I wasn't there. I wasn't allowed.

Mary blamed me. "If I hadn't gotten caught up in it all, I'd have been there, and it would never have happened." I guess James thought the same, though he never said a word to me. Ever.

Someone must be to blame.

In a memory I did not have, I listened to the quiet, respectful murmuring. Vapid words of comfort. Glances they thought I didn't see.

The silence begins to gnaw inside my bowels. It grows, like an angry lion who refuses to be tamed. I clench my fists. I cannot hold back.

I scream and every body in the room jumps. Every head turns. I yank my jacket off and rip my shirt open, the buttons popping and bouncing off black skirts and dark pants, clattering to the floor.

Wailing, I fall to my knees, beating my chest. Those closest to me retreat with haste, hands to mouth. As the circle opens, I fall to my face in the arena, sobbing without restraint.

18

Shock spinning black noise *crash*! lights red yellow white *crash*! noise streetlight wheel noise glass metal.

Quiet.

Breathe. *Breathe!*

Let go. Pain. Hands. Flex. Skin. Shards. Look down look up look left look right.

Danger? Turn key. Pull keys. Drop.

Lean back. Seat belt. Where?

Knock. Knock. Silence. Knock knock. Lights flashing. Knock knock. Window. Cold air.

"Are you okay, sir?"

Nod. Seat belt. Where? Trapped.

Hands arms groping pulling. Look right, look left. Face. Officer.

Asphalt glass metal voices. Cars bicycle. Running people. Yelling lights red white green. Motor running. Tires squealing.

Arms pulling. "Let me help you out, sir." Arms out both sides stumble pain. Car door open crunch broken glass.

"Sit down here, sir." Distant voice. "Sir, right here."

Hand up palm skin broken skin on skin.

"Can you tell me your name?"

Gotta wake up. Wake up. Sitting on curb. Gutter. Hand down. Dirt. Crushed Coke can. Paper wrapper. Reese's? Oil. Garbage. Head hurts. Spinning nonsense balderdash gibberish claptrap blarney, hogwash baloney tripe drivel, bilge bunk poppycock. Hooey. Tommyrot.

Sirens. Loud. Flashing red lights. Flashing blue lights. Cars. Bicycle. Crying. Was I driving? Did I get home? Dreaming? Wake up! Left office turn off lights locked door toss cans and bottles. Garbage refuse rubbish. Here. There.

Driving home? Driving home. Good plan. Everything ok? Yes, thinking. Red lights, green lights, yellow lights. Everything okay.

"Sir, can you hear me?"

Flashlight. Badge reflecting red light.

"Sir, an ambulance is on the way. Can you tell me your name?"

Name. Jay. Always Jay. Not Jason or James. Just Jay. "Jay Adam." Left shop, keys in back pocket. Don't usually keep them there. Set alarm. Did I? Driving home. Stella. Keren. Ally. Everything will be fine.

Face in hands. "Going to check your…just a moment…injuries?…just going to check…" *What?*

Arm grabbed tight rubber squeezing flashlight eyes hands groping.

"…hold still, please…that's good, sir…you're going to be okay…"

Screaming. Sirens. Red fire truck. White ambulance. Parked at an angle. Police cars fire truck cars trucks disobeying the rules.

"He's in shock, but vitals check out. Cuts on hands and face. One bad."

New voice. Strange voice. Far away. "The one on the bike?"

"They're putting her in ambulance now."

19

She raised a delicate, manicured finger. "I think you will look back and see the good in it. Everything happens for a reason. But right now all you want is stability. And you will have it soon. I know it." She sat back. A bit triumphantly, I thought.

It's been ten years. I haven't seen good in *any* of it. But I kept silent.

"Do you believe in prayer?"

I snorted mentally. Bringing up religion or politics between strangers make people nervous, but that didn't stop them from doing it anyway.

"I'm not a stranger to prayer, nor do I have anything against it."

"What was the last thing you prayed for?"

"Death." I instantly wished I'd kept *that* to myself, though it did stop her for a moment. And gave me a bit of pleasure, I admit. If she wants to talk religion, then I'll talk death.

The silence that followed was that particular silence when a conversation with a stranger turns intimate, and neither one knows how to back out of it.

"Well, Jay, I hope you will take heart. I can't say I've been through anything like you, but I know people who have. One of my brothers was a doctor, very successful, had a huge house built. Their dream house. Then they started finding problems in the construction. Turned out the contractors were corrupt—cutting corners, bribing inspectors—a bunch of homes were affected. The structural problems were so bad people had to move out. The lawsuits went on for years. The lead contractor committed suicide. The stress was so great, it affected my brother's marriage and they divorced. He closed his practice and went to work at a clinic. He still hasn't recovered. Just devastating."

Devastating? *House* problems? Divorce over stress? I was speechless. Rather, I had plenty to say, but chose to keep it to myself and not cause a scene. What blathering insensitive nonsense!

I considered that I shouldn't be so hard on her. She *was* sincere. And she wasn't simple. She was a deep thinker with a lay philosophic view of life that seemed to serve her well. She appeared to accept people with ease, no matter their station in life. Like me.

She had firm ideas of what was proper and right, but I also detected a desire to occasionally step out of that ordered world and paint where one should not paint.

It was clear that my view of troubles made her uncomfortable. She didn't like that I thought her approach was trite. To be honest, I *didn't* believe it was trite. It was in-depth and thought-out. It just didn't work in real life.

"Well," she said. I realized she had been talking and I hadn't heard a word of it. I felt a twinge of regret at my private reverie in the face of her sincerity.

"Sorry. Just thinking about what you said."

"That's ok. I didn't mean to cross any boundaries. Just trying to share some of my own frustrations with life. I hope it's helpful."

"It is. Thank you. You are quite kind." It was curious how meaningless pleasantries came rolling out of my mouth after so many years of disuse. But isn't that what we do? The purpose is not to communicate truth, but to avoid discord.

She dipped her head. "You're welcome."

I looked up at the clock. "I need to get going—I don't want to miss the bus."

I argued about the lunch bill again, but she was insistent. As I stood up and gathered my bags, she said, "Jay, remember what I said. Just be patient. It's all to teach you something, I'm sure. It'll be fine, you'll see."

What a stupid thing to say. She had no way of knowing it would be fine.

"Thank you, Ellie. Good luck on the rest of your trip."

"You, too, Jay."

✳

It was blistering hot outside. I walked to the side of the cafe and took a deep breath. Maybe the heat would sear my alveoli and I could suffocate.

20

"Hey, did you take my cash box over the weekend?"

"No. Why?"

"It's gone."

Jay followed Cristy to her desk. He had not spent the night at the hospital—over their objections. But he was quite stiff and sore this morning. And his hand hurt pretty bad.

She showed him where she kept it—lower drawer, back behind the files.

"You are sure you didn't take it out and leave it somewhere?"

"I never take it away from my desk. No reason to."

"How much?"

"Three thousand, four hundred and eighty-seven. And seventy-five cents."

Jay thought for a moment. The janitors? Unlikely.

They both searched her office, the reception room, and the bathrooms. Nothing.

"Call the janitorial service and report it—"

She frowned. "Jay, we've worked with them for eight years, and it's the same crew who—"

"—I doubt it's one of them, I'm just covering all the bases. Call security to come search the building. Then set a conference call with Nashville for this morning. In an hour or so."

"Okay, will do. By the way, Zohn hasn't shown up yet. Again." She didn't think much of Zohn, and never passed on an opportunity to let Jay know.

He nodded absently and headed down the hallway to his office, stopping short in the doorway.

His computer was gone.

✳

Another search of all the offices found five other computers missing, as well as three televisions, other electronics, and some smaller items (personal items and cash). Jay called the Chief, then told Cristy to have everyone take rest of the day off.

Cristy blinked. "Won't the police want to interview everyone first? I mean, I doubt it was anyone here, but that's procedure."

Jay nodded. "Yes, you're right. Ok, hold off." He paused. "It's probably my fault, anyway. I may have left the door unlocked last night."

She didn't seem to know what to say.

"Alright, let's get to work. We'll let everyone go as soon as we can." He turned back to his office.

"Hey." She reached out and touched his arm. "Are you okay? It happens, you know."

He smiled. "I'm fine. Just had a lot of important work to do this morning. It's just equipment and money."

✳

He was still at his desk, writing a summary of the conference call when the Chief appeared at his door. "Jay?"

"Yes, Chief? Anything?"

"You need to come see this."

❊

Zohn's body was behind the dumpsters. Jay shuddered. *Was he there when I dumped all the trash?*

Jay identified the body for the officers. He felt like he was dreaming. *This can't be real.* The officers steered him back into the building. Inside, they commandeered a conference room and sat him down. Cristy hovered outside the door, a stunned look on her face, until they told her to go away. They'd call her in when they were ready.

Jay answered their questions like automatons. *When did you last see him? When did you last talk with him? Was he suicidal? Did he say anything that might…*

21

Dark hall. Long. Narrow. I stumble forward. The hallway lurches to the right; my arms fly up to protect me as I stumble against the wall. Now a lurch to the left. Earthquake? I grab the edge of a nearby doorframe for stability. Behind me are gas lanterns, fixed on alternative sides of the walls, flickering. I try the door latch. Locked.

I continue with one hand touching the wall, just in case. Looking down, I see my shoes are black, shined to a gloss that reflects the unsteady light. The carpet is a thick pile, cheap, with a red and gold pattern. Faux royalty. Worn. Dirty.

Another door on my right. Also locked. I peer through a small window set at eye-height. A long hallway, with doors on either side, spaced alternatively left and right.

All closed. A tray sits on the floor beside one door. Piled with dishes. Hotel?

Peering forward, I see a doorway at the end of the hall. Open. Thick frame, raised threshold. I creep forward. Stairs lay just beyond, reaching up into darkness. I hasten my pace, still sliding my right hand along the wall.

The hallway tilts to the left. Slow. Like a plane making a long, banking turn. I jump through the doorway and grasp the stair's railing with both hands. The slow lean stops, and begins to tilt back. Not like any earthquake I've ever experienced. Maybe it's the Big One they keep talking about.

I wait, holding my breath, and look back. The hallway levels out, but keeps going in the other direction. Not as far. Then back again, still less. Like a pendulum. Had I been drinking? No. I remember. I ate yogurt and drank water. Then I went home. Didn't I? Home to Stella and Keren and Ally.

A horn sounds. Muffled, from above. I hear a voice. Quiet and tinny. I can't make out the words. It was crackling and faint, like the radio sat on the credenza in my parents' living room. A big, wooden radio, with two large plastic knobs, each with a needle pointing to numbers on a gauge. I wasn't allowed to touch the dials. I wanted to. At night, I lay on the floor, playing with my toys, while they listened to music. Jazz, perhaps. Then, under the music, thin static noise grows, threatening to obliterate the music, horn by horn, guitar by guitar, drum by drum. My dad makes a "harumph" sound, lifts himself from his chair, and goes the radio, turning a dial back and forth, like a thief cracking a safe, and then—

I jump at a loud ringing. Alarm? It seems to come from everywhere. A red flashing light begins a fast cycle, making the hall look like a scene from a horror movie. Fire alarm?

I hear a *whoosh* behind and look back. Yellow flickering light. I see flames.

I leap up the stairs three at a time. At the top are double doors with handles. I throw them open with both hands, then almost fall as my feet nearly slip out from under me. The floor is slick.

Not a floor. A deck. Not a hotel. A ship. People are running and screaming. Men, women, children. Running towards the bow as the ship begins to tilt back—

22

He jerked in his sleep, woke up, and groaned. Stella, still awake reading a book, reached out and touched him lightly.

"Are you hurting? Need another Percocet? It's been long enough, I think."

"No, it's fine."

"You're kind of restless. Are you worrying about something?"

"No. Not at all."

She placed her book face down on her lap. "Well, love, I am. Can you talk to me about it?"

Jay turned over and raised himself up with a grunt, and positioned his pillow so he could lean against the headboard. He reached over and took her hand.

"The Chief told me that night that he was pretty sure there'd be no charges. It wasn't my fault. What's bothering you?"

"The other thing we discussed. When a car hits a pe-destrian, it's always the driver's fault. That's what I've heard."

"Usually it is. But she rode right in front of me, against the light, in the dark. The streetlight was out. I was not distracted—the radio wasn't even on. It's all in the police report. It was a terrible accident."

"But Jay…she's *dead*."

He dropped his head. "I know. I feel horrible. I can't fix it, but you know I had John reach out to her family and offer to pay all expenses. And more. It's the right thing to do."

She grimaced. "*That* worries me, too. It might look like you're trying to pay them off."

"No, it won't, because I also had John tell them that offer to help was not contingent on anything. If they felt they needed to file a civil action, they should do so."

"I know you have gone above and beyond. You always do. But not everyone thinks that way. Some people want revenge."

He waved a hand. "Bah. It doesn't matter. They prob-ably wouldn't win, but even if they did, a judgment would probably be less than I'm offering. It's the right thing to do, even though it was just an accident. Bad things happen sometimes. It's life. We just keep on doing what we do. Being *us*. Everything works out in the long run."

She nodded, still looking down at her lap. He reached over and poked her in the ribs.

"Stop, Jay. This really bothers me."

"Ok, sorry. Honestly, love: it will be fine."

23

Send me back stop the business stop the loan stop the school stop the ideas no child no marriage no childhood no parents no birth

They can't be gone. They can't*!*

Storms, mistakes, accidents, death. The way of humans. But all of this…so much…

The clouds close in. Dark, menacing, full, and ominous. Dark, dark, dark. Take me away, darkness.

I hear demons laughing. My mind plays tricks on me. Overload, overloaded, overwhelmed. Too much pain too much.

It happens. It will be okay. Bumps in the road. It works out.

A figure, in all black, appears out of the dark, striding towards me. Trousers, robe, and cowl flowing with the wind. Beyond the figure, I see piles of rocks. Further out still, an ocean. Small choppy waves, crawling all over larger choppy waves, which rise and fall in larger swells. Swaying back and forth, crashing into each other. They rise toward me and break upon the black rocks. *Crash.* Spray.

I reach out my hands to either side and place my palms down. Grass. Wet grass on either side of me. I clutch at the turf. The mage-like figure lifts its robed arms high above its head. The face turns up to the stormy sky, and the cowl falls away. I see a ring of shaggy white hair lit from behind by a blood moon.

My fingernails grip more tightly into the grass, reaching dirt. I jump at a thunderclap. Lightning crackles, far out to sea. A flash of light exposes a shape rising out of the water. A whale? A torpedo?

I strain to see, looking past the mage. The red light reveals a murky shape, rising up, up, up out of the dark angry water. Spray flies from its black bulk like rats escaping a storm drain in a downpour. Silver rivulets, reflecting the red moon, stream down its sides like blood from a thousand wounds.

The monster's ascent slows and stops. A pregnant pause. A calm before the storm. A fermata before the coda.

The top of the massive shape tips, gaining speed as it falls. The water parts beneath its massive bulk with anger and speed to the left and the right. A foamy double arc of watery chaos.

Coming right at me.

24

"With all due respect, these rich people get money, status, success—and then they forget. They are in a bubble. They are protected by all the people they know. After a while, they forget what matters. The end justifies the means. They get lazy."

The D.A. leaned back in his chair. "Interesting theory, but there are plenty of wealthy people who don't break the law."

"Only because you don't know about it because they are protected, like I said."

The D.A. laughed. "You can't prove an argument with a negative, Paterson. Let's stick to the facts. What do you have?"

The detective leaned forward in his chair and opened the folder which sat on the desk.

"Two eyewitnesses say he was drunk. Four beer cans and three bottles of liquor in the trash can in his office. Spills on the desk. Front door to the offices unlocked. No skid marks at the scene. He attempted to leave the scene. When they detained and questioned him, he had no explanation for what happened or his behavior. And he immediately lawyered up—with Goulden."

"That doesn't mean anything. Goulden is one of the best."

"Come on, boss, that's what these guys do when they are guilty—hire the big guns instead of waiting for charges to be made."

"Sobriety test?"

"You know what happened."

"I know what the summary report said. Officers failed to administer one."

"Yes. They were short-handed because of that fire and robbery downtown. They were dealing with a *death*. With lots of people around. It wasn't pretty, and they had too many things to deal with."

"I understand. But you can't prove he was drunk."

"We have plenty of circumstantial evidence."

"Did anyone *see* him drinking?"

"Not yet, but the two at the scene said he was drunk. One of the officers was sure of it. No employee statements yet."

"Paramedics?"

"Nothing definitive. Still interviewing them. Boss, there were no skids marks! He plowed right into her!"

"Forensics support that?"

"Haven't gotten the report yet, but they will. I am telling you, boss, this guy's dirty. He's been getting away with stuff for a long time."

"Oh, come on, Paterson, this is *Jay Adam* you're talking about. *Maybe* he got drunk and went driving and had an accident. Though even that seems unlikely to me." He frowned. "Why was he at his offices on a Sunday?"

"Don't know. Seems suspicious."

"People work on Sundays sometimes. You don't know him, but I do. He's one of the most charitable business-men we got. Popular city councilman. There is nothing nefarious here."

"Exactly—you know him, you know his *public* image, so you don't look behind it. Did you know that he got a warehouse built in an area not zoned for it? Somehow he got a waiver. A few years back, he added a significant extension to his office buildings, and there's fishy stuff about *that*. Did you know he supported the mayor in his last re-election—to the tune of hundreds of thousands of dollars."

"Alright, stop with the conspiracy theories. There can be reasons for all of those—and contributing to a political candidate is not a crime. We got involuntary manslaugh-ter at best, it seems."

"It's not a conspiracy if it's true."

The D.A. rolled his eyes and sat back. "My problem is that you have a view—which may sometimes be true, I admit—so you might have trouble with your objectiv-ity."

"And with all due respect, boss, you have pre-con-ceived notions, too."

His boss drummed his fingers on the desk. He was a fair man, trusted his people, and was always willing to listen. They were a great team.

"Who was the lead officer?"

"Rodriguez."

"Did you do the investigation alone?"

"No. Stacy and I."

"She agrees with you? What about Rodriguez?"

"Yes, both agree."

He let big sigh. "Okay. Move ahead. But I'll be surprised if you find anything more than a tragic accident."

The detective slapped the folder shut and jumped for the door.

"Paterson?"

He turned back from the door. "Yes?"

"I want to see see the *full* investigation details before we file charges—if you get that far."

"Of course. You'll see. I'm right."

25

I don't know where I am. I think I'm outside, but it's like I'm floating above the ground.

I hear a voice like it's inside my head. *The dawn is coming. See over there, those two bright little stars?*

That's Venus and Mercury. The heralds of a new day. New beginnings. Warmth and light coming out of the darkness.

Another voice, outside, whispers, "But not today."

Being angry is okay. Bad things happen sometimes. The rain falls on the rich and poor alike. The good and bad. The happy and the sad.

"Not like this. This is not hope. This is death disguised as hope."

A parent who breaks a child's arm to teach a lesson.

The doctor who says, "I have some bad news."

A tsunami that washes away thousands of lives as instruction on suffering.

"I don't believe you!"

I see lines of people streaming together. They come from all corners of the earth. They are angry.

"We are tired of pretending this is fair!"

"We have found our voices!"

"You will no longer rule our lives!"

They climb up the pillars of the earth, a great mob, screaming and crying. They brandish shovels, baseball bats, and rocks—anything they could find. Venus was closest and they reached it first.

Beating kicking throwing yelling bashing.

Its light wavered, flickered, dimmed, and went out. Forever.

They climbed again, a roiling humanity, yelling and cursing. Swinging their shovels, baseball bats, and rocks—anything they could find. Mercury was next.

Beating kicking throwing yelling bashing.

Its light wavered, flickered, dimmed, and went out. Forever.

Darkness. Silence.

26

The bus was nowhere to be seen as I hurried over. A dirty, disheveled man sat on the wooden bench outside the door. A bottle, in a paper bag, sat beside him. Stereotypes come from somewhere, and here was one.

I thought he was asleep, but as I approached, he opened one eye.

"Did the bus leave?" I asked.

"Bus?"

"The bus that was parked here."

He coughed. "Well, it ain't here, so I guess so."

I hoped the driver just went to get fuel. Inside, however, the clerk informed me it was gone. I started to argue that it left early, but my heart wasn't in it. What difference did it make?

I scanned the schedules. The next bus to Union Station was in three hours. Another went to San Bernardino in ninety minutes. The clerk said that buses left from there to Union every hour. I bought a ticket.

There was a pay phone on the far wall. I fished coins and my little notebook out of my bag. Time enough to work on some puzzle pieces. The natural first call would be to Stephen, of course. He had been my business lawyer through almost all the failures and successes. But he'd died in an alcohol-fueled drug overdose seven years ago—two weeks before he was going to visit me. I had been devastated. He wasn't an addict, though he did drink a lot. He used to tell me that lawyers had the highest rate of substance abuse and suicide of any profession. I'd hoped it was an accident.

Munro was still my first choice. Easiest, because he knew every detail of my situation, and knew I was on the move.

"Good afternoon, Law Offices of James R. Munro. How may I help you?"

"Hi, this is Jay Adam again. I'd like to set up a meeting with Mr. Munro."

"Mr. Munro is not in at the moment. Would you like to leave a message, or shall I have him return your call?"

"I'll be in town tomorrow. Can I set up a meeting?"

"His calendar is pretty full this week."

"Next week?"

"He has a trial next week, and then a tentative vacation. I can schedule you for…let's see…Tuesday, October 30. Or you can check back in a few days to see if he postpones the vacation."

Three weeks? My hands started to sweat. What to do?

"I guess I'll call back."

I felt out of control. Anxious. Scattered. I took a deep breath and flipped through the notebook.

Stella's mother and father. Not an option. I had not had any contact with them at all.

Cristy. She had moved to South Carolina about a month after I left. I need to call her eventually, but not now.

Business friends and connections made more sense, anyway. At least for now. Jocelyn. Anthony. Rodrigo. Chief Pomero. Mayor Austin—ex-mayor now.

I knew my anxiety was because I had not heard from any of them. It dawned on me that I didn't *want* to call any of them. Sure, it had been ten years. But they'd been my people. People who always came together for a someone in need. That's what communities do.

Right?

27

"How in the world, Jay? How does this *happen*?" She didn't look good. Worn. In shock. It worried him—she was always so even.

He shook his head. "I don't know. It was an old coffee pot. I don't know why it was back there. I guess in the commotion it got left on. All weekend. Firefighters said a pack of filters probably caught fire and it spread from there. Doesn't make sense to me. A coffee pot?"

"I can't believe it. Are we cursed? All this…and *Zohn*—" her voice caught. She raised a hand to her mouth.

He stared at the floor. "I know. I can't—I can't believe it."

She dropped her hand. "How bad is the damage? Do they know yet?"

He took a deep breath. "Fire damage to the whole back area, cafeteria, break room. The worse part was it destroyed the IT closet and filing storage. Lost a lot that wasn't backed up off-site. Smoke and water damage in the offices."

"Do you have to shut down?"

"They say we can get back into the offices in a few days. The rest will be at least a month or more."

Stella turned away, placing a hand on the dining room table as if bracing herself. "*What* is happening, Jay?"

He got up, went to her, and placed his hands on her small shoulders.

"I don't know. It's just life, I guess. Good things happen, bad things happen. We'll get through it."

She spun around. "This is *not* just ups and downs, Jay! The Nashville thing is getting worse, the accident, the robbery, then Zohn, now a *fire?!*"

"Calm down, Stella, it will—"

She pulled away and turned to face him. "How can you be so calm?! This is not *normal*." Her voice was shaky.

"You think someone is out to get us? We're not part of the underworld, Stella."

"Maybe someone *is* out to get us!" she said, perhaps more out of frustration than belief. Jay understood that. It was a lot to deal with all at once.

He took her in his arms. She acquiesced, but turned her head away.

"Look, I know what you mean. What do they say? 'Bad things come in threes'?"

She spoke into his shoulder. "This is five things."

He laughed. She began to giggle. They both stood for a moment, enjoying the moment of lightness. He held her at arm's length.

"People go through much worse than this. We have freedom to deal with it, we have our health, and we have our kids. The company is robust enough to withstand these setbacks."

She nodded. "I know. It Just seems like the universe has turned on us."

He sighed. "Yeah, it might seem like it, but the universe is not malevolent. It's just the way of things. We can't revel in the good things and then complain when it gets tough."

"It scares me."

"I know. But we'll get through it. You know that, right?"

She pursed her lips and nodded. "Yeah, I guess."

It *was* an unusual run of disasters and problems. The SEC problems, the accident, the robbery, Zohn, the fire…

Still, he was sure it would all straighten itself out. It always did.

28

Dark figures jump the fence and steal through the cemetery, running together in groups of three and four. When the first group reaches the nearest headstone, individuals peel off and begin digging. The other groups spread out across the graveyard.

I watch as dirt flies into the air, occluding the stars that spread across the deep of night. Muted thumps as shovelfuls hit the ground nearby.

One group is rocking a low headstone back and forth, shouting something I can't understand.

Farther down the gentle slope, five or six other teams are at work. Some use sledgehammers on large memorials: *thock…thock…thock* as marble and stone shatter. To the right, one of the vandals is trying to break into a mausoleum.

Should I do something? There are so many of them.

I place my foot on the bottom strut of the iron fence, grab the top and hoist myself up onto the crossbar. As I swing one leg over, I hear a loud cry to my left. Someone had broken the lock on the main gate and now hundreds stream in, shouting with glee as they run.

I drop to the ground as the group nearest me cheers and drop their shovels. One of them, holding a crowbar, jumps inside the freshly-dug pit. With each creaking and splintering sound, more cheers rise up. The crowbar flies out of the pit, and the figure emerges, dragging a body shrouded in black.

I watch as he makes the desiccated corpse dance and jump while the others laugh. I want to vomit.

A shout nearby tells me that other remains have been disinterred. A corpse's arm is pulled off, bringing more cheers and laughter. Just beyond that group, two dark figures walk together with a child's body, each holding a stiff little arm in a macabre image of a family. The white nightdress of the thin body shines brightly amidst the darkness.

I find my voice. "Stop! Stop! This is wrong! Let the dead lie in peace!"

No one hears me above the shouting and laughing.

I close my eyes and scream. "*Leave them alone!*"

A voice at my right startles me. "Sir, please keep your voice down."

I turn to the speaker and see it is a nurse. I am in a bright white room. A bed is nearby, surrounded by medical equipment. A man lay upon it. Tubes and instruments run from all parts of his body. Liquids pulse through many of them: reddish, like blood, or translucent yellow, like plasma. Or pus. And bodily waste. I felt the urge to retch.

The monitor above his head displays a heart rate of 65 beats per minute and blood pressure of 108 over 63. I don't know what all the other numbers mean.

I turn to the nurse. She stares at the patient with a satisfied smile.

"Who…who is this?" I ask.

Without turning, she says, "Oh, you don't know him."

"What's wrong with him?"

She points to screen. "See that? It's the brainwave activity."

I peer at the straight line. "He's brain dead?"

"Yes."

"Is there any hope?"

She seems confused. "Hope of what?"

"Of…of regaining consciousness. Of going home. Being normal."

"Oh." She cocks her head, still gazing at the patient. "No, of course not. He's been this way since the accident, many years ago. Even if, by some miracle, he awoke, there is so much damage he would be a slobbering fool. A useless sack of meat and blood. A drain on society."

I am shocked at her language, but say, "Why not let him die if there's no hope?"

Now she is shocked. "Why would we do that? We can keep him *alive*. Are you a monster?"

She shakes her head and storms out of the room.

29

Manicured lawns and trees in neat lines. Verdant grounds, blue sky. It was comfortably warm. A light breeze touched his cheek. He was staring at eight feet in front of him.

His phone rang.

He remained still.

Riiiing.

Still looking ahead, he reached inside his suit jacket for his phone.

"Yes."

"Jay?! Jay! Where are you? Are you okay?"

He came to life, as if awaking from hypnosis.

"Stella. Yeah. I'm fine. Sorry."

"Where are you?"

"Bellevue."

"Bellevue?"

"Bellevue Memorial."

Silence. "Your mom."

He walked forward and bent down next to the tombstone.

"Jay? Are you okay?"

"Yeah. Just needed to…come here. Not sure why."

"I understand, love. Just wish you'd told me. I was so worried when you weren't at work and didn't answer your phone."

"I'm sorry. I'm…just…overwhelmed at the moment."

He heard her sigh. "I know. It's a lot. The adjustors called, and they are coming out to assess the damage. Pedro came by, too—he was hoping to see you. He said they could start the demolition as soon as the insurance okays it. They are so busy after the storm. Everyone has damage. But he's making us a top priority. That's good news, right?"

"Yes, it is. Sorry, love, I got lost in myself for a moment. I'm on my way home."

They said goodbye. He tucked the phone back into his jacket and placed his hand on the top of the gravestone.

"You always told me life was a cycle of being born and dying. Everything we do is either one or the other." He blew a kiss at the stone and turned away.

The manicured grounds made him think of the contrast with the chaos in his own neighborhood. His home. He couldn't get those scenes out of his mind: the news reports of the storm, warnings of serious flash-floods and mudslides. In the past, the damage was never as severe as predicted. This time it was worse. When the police came through to evacuate everyone, he knew there was going to be a lot of damage to the property.

30

I can see the doctor in the delivery room through the glass, though equipment blocks some of my view. I cannot see the woman.

Two nurses move quickly and expertly, adjusting knobs, grabbing instruments, all with great purpose.

They were all speaking, but I only see lips moving. I press up against the glass, trying to see better.

The doctor barks something, and the medical dance stops. He frowns as he looks down. He speaks a few more words, and the nurse on his right nods and moves out of my vision.

The door to my right bursts open and a kid wearing an old-fashioned newspaper boy outfit rushes out. He has a bag slung over his shoulder and holds a newspaper aloft.

"Get it here! Latest news about the birth!"

I grab him by the collar as he flies past, spinning him around. He catches his balance.

"Hey, Mister! Watch it!"

I snatch the paper from his hand and flip it around to read the headline.

Stillborn!

I look back at the kid. His eyes are wide with fear.

I smile. "Good work kid. Keep it up. Tell everybody."

I slap the paper against his chest and he clutches it in astonishment, staring at me as I walk down the hall, whistling.

I lay face down in the dirt. The surface is cold and hard. *How did I get here? I'm supposed to be…supposed to be…*

Someone is yelling. Screaming. Sobbing. Different voices. I push myself up and gasp at the terrible pain in my thigh. Rolling over, I see an arrow protruding from just above my knee. A dark iris begins to contract my field of vision.

I look away. I take a breath.

I am on a hill. Bodies are strewn up and down the slope. Some writhe in pain, crying out. Others are quiet and still. The closest, about twenty feet away, is a bloody mess.

I look back down at the arrow. I can see the end of the shaft where it meets the back of the arrowhead. It looks like bronze. Metal, against which no flesh can stand. Perhaps it hit the bone; otherwise, it might have gone further and caused much more damage.

Should I pull it out? No, I think I'm supposed to leave it in until I am ready to staunch the blood and bandage it.

How did I get here? I am supposed to be…doing something….

I lie on my back, the arrow protruding toward the sky like a white flag.

With my arms near my sides, I push up into a half-sitting position with my legs still out in front of me. There does not seem to be a lot of blood.

I look left and right, as much as I can without moving my legs. Rolling hills. Carnage everywhere. Far away, down in a shallow valley, there are groups of people running about. Running away? Fighting? I can't tell.

How did I get here? I am supposed to be…

"Hey, you!"

A voice behind. I turn as much as I can but see no one. "Help!" I shout.

No answer. I shuffle my legs and arms to the side, trying to turn my body. The pain is tolerable.

I see no one. "Hello?"

As turn my head back, I see a rock hurtling at me.

⁕

I jerked and almost fell out of the chair in the station. Did I make a sound? I looked over at the desk. The bus station clerk was not there. I glance around the small bare room. Empty. She must have gone in the back.

I sit up straight and rub my back. The plastic chair was not meant for even short naps.

A television, mounted on the wall in a corner, plays with the sound muted. The close captioning below shows the words being spoken. Black and white footage of people running through a muddy field. They look poor, disheveled, and scared. The camera pans back and shakes as explosions erupt nearby. Fire and smoke appear in the distance.

I squint to read the text. *…villagers are fleeing once again as the government began renewed bombing…whether they are the target or not matters little to these poor farmers…forced to give most of their food to others, their sad but peaceful lives are upended by a conflict they have no part of and no interest in…yet they suffer the most…*

The clock tells me that I have twenty minutes more. I stood, stretched, and went to get some water from a fountain near the bathrooms, but it wasn't working.

I collected my bags and stepped outside.

"Ha, ha, you have no idea. Ha ha, right or wrong." It was the man I had spoken to when I came in. He wasn't speaking to anyone. Except perhaps the voices in his head.

He sat next to the bench on the ground, with his back against the wall of the station. He had a baseball cap pulled so low I could hardly see his face. His dark beard and long mass of tangled hair added to the stereotype.

He jerked and raised a hand out of the too-large military jacket he wore, pointing up.

"God is good…God is good...let us now prey…our father who aren't in heaven…hollow be your name…"

I wondered about *his* community. Who are his friends and acquaintances? The people he encourages and supports. The people who laugh with him. The people who help him when in need.

I went back inside and sat down with my face in my hands. I need to make some more calls. I sighed. I'll do it when I get to San Bernardino.

31

"With all due respect, sir, the evidence is there. Fraud, DUI, a fire set from within, a suicide...it all adds up. These kinds of guys think they can get away with anything. And often they do, because they have money and power and high-priced lawyers—like Goulden."

The District Attorney leaned back in his chair. "Why do you think those things are connected and not a stream of bad luck? Show me a motive. It doesn't fit."

"You're not seeing the timeline and the little details like we have."

The D.A. laughed. "You seem to have it in for him, so you see a pattern. I don't, so I see some bad luck and maybe some bad decisions. But the DUI manslaughter— I am with you on that. Sad. And not like him. But yes, the circumstantial is strong. Convince me it's connected to the rest."

The investigator leaned forward in his chair and opened the folder sitting on the desk.

"Okay. So why was he drinking so much that night— at the office? Because he had just found out about the financial improprieties in his Nashville division. We know he was calling and emailing the employees, the director, lawyers, accountants, trying to get it covered up. It looks like an elaborate fraudulent transfer scheme that—"

The D.A. waved his hand. "I don't care about that. It's not our jurisdiction. You reported it to the Feds. We aren't even allowed to use it in our case, unless and until he's found guilty."

"I understand. But it's the grounds of everything else. Stuff goes wrong; his plan is in danger of being found out. He drinks, he drives, kills someone."

"Manslaughter, at best."

Paterson plowed on. "Then the fire. A fire which destroyed paper records and the office backup systems."

"Forensics said it was started by a coffee pot and a filter."

"Yep, could be an accident. Could also be an easy way to destroy evidence. And in light of the other evidence, and Zohn's death—"

"Ruled a suicide by our own department—"

"True, but without a deep investigation into the circumstances. Even if it was a suicide—why? Adam had been tracking and working with Edward Zohn—outside of work—in secret. Why would the CEO of a massive company deal with a low-level, uneducated employee who has a history?"

"You think he was part of a coverup and Jay killed him? Come on; Jay is known for his philanthropy and helping troubled people."

"The last time Zohn was arrested, Adam bailed him out and called the Chief and no charges were filed. I still haven't gotten to the bottom of that."

The D.A. frowned. "Okay. That's a bit of a concern."

"Then the robbery and Zohn dead? Sounds like a set up to me."

"Or a robbery gone wrong."

Paterson leaned back in his chair. "I agree that any one of these things by themselves would raise little suspicion of foul play. I'd rule it a homicide and leave it at that. But it's the big picture. Did you see where he had his lawyer offer the DUI victim's family a significant amount—"

"Patterson, there is nothing suspicion about that. That's the pattern of Jay's life."

"I know." He sighed and leaned forward. "I just get a strong sense there's a lot of misdeeds here. If this all raises questions, what else has the guy done we don't even know about?"

The D.A. tapped the report in front of him. "I don't know. Yes, I agree some of it looks bad. But looking bad isn't enough."

"I'm well aware, boss. Just trying to convince you to let us dig deeper, so I can make the case. Fraud and panic, drinking, DUI, cover up, payoff money, deceased employee, questionable fire, robbery—all in short time. Let us open a larger investigation."

The D.A. drummed his fingers on the desk. The investigator waited with an eager face, still leaning forward.

"Boss, I hate to bring it up, but he is a friend of yours. Just to avoid the appearance of favoritism, you should let this play out."

The D.A. snorted. "I don't think you hate bringing that up at all."

Paterson waited.

"Rodriguez and Stacy agree with you?"

"Yes."

The D.A. let out a sigh. "Alright. Move ahead. But by the book. I'll give you a week to show me something solid."

The investigator slapped the folder shut and jumped for the door.

"Paterson?"

He turned back from the door. "Yes, sir?"

"I hope you are wrong. Because if not, Jay has pulled the wool over all our eyes."

Paterson nodded. "I know. But I'm not wrong."

32

The television was still playing in the corner. A talking head mouthed words and then cut away to "our reporter in the field." Soldiers trudged along in the mud, heads down, loaded with gear.

Fade to commercial. A woman sits at a loom, weaving a beautiful tapestry. She comes to the end of the spools and looks up with a laugh at the camera. (What is she selling?). Then there is a special salve, with men and women squeezing out lotion and spreading it on red rashes, dry skin, cuts, and scrapes. The children smile beatifically as the soothing cream miraculously eases their pain.

Back to the news. A man with an eye patch in a hospital bed, speaking to a reporter about the accident/explosion/attack. Now a scene of earthly devastation with a blazing sun; another at night with the moon high above.

An advertisement for a documentary. Blue, blue ocean. Rays of light shoot and dance through the marine world. Out of the murkiness, a dark shape grows and resolves into a whale. Two divers swim near it. If we didn't know anything about whales, we might fear for the poor, tiny creatures nearby. So frail and weak. But the whale had no interest in the humans who ventured out of their warm, dry homes to explore the watery depths.

Still, a mighty swipe of the tail, an untimely gape of the mouth, and those divers would die just the same if the whale had been a sea monster. It would have no inkling of the suffering it caused. It would hear no cries of injustice, no wails of loss, no demands for retribution.

33

"How did this *happen*, people?!"

He gazed with fury around the table. No one looked up, except the medical attorney at the Administrator's right side.

"The President asked me if my staff is completely inept. This is not only hospital policy—it's the law!"

The Director of Hematology finally spoke. "We're still investigating, but so far it appears to me more of a clerical, one-off issue than—"

"You're sure?"

"I'm sure. It was a mistake that is almost a—"

"As I see it, we have three issues. First, how did it happen and are we sure it won't happen again, as we sit here embarrassed at our utter incompetence. Second, we need to know the patients—current and past—who might have been affected, and contact them for testing because we don't know how to do our jobs. Finally, we need to know our liabilities and consequences."

The attorney took the last point as his cue, jumping in with confidence. "As you know, both State and Federal law cover all blood donation, transfer, storage, and transfusion processes. On this set of facts, we are concerned with FDA regulations and directives, Title 42, the FTCA, and medical negligence laws of both—"

"Stop it. Liability?"

Abashed, the lawyer lowered his voice. "Ah, well, the penalties depend on the causal elements of collection, testing, storing, distribution, and tracking through the entire process. For example, if we got the tainted blood from an outside blood bank, they are usually held liable—"

"Excuse me—" interrupted the head of Emergency Medicine, sounding a bit offended, "—but this does not seem to be a problem with a bank, testing, or selection. During the storm, when we lost power, we had to move the stores to other refrigeration units. We think one bag that had not been tested was misplaced."

"—okay, okay, well that's negligence but perhaps not gross or reckless. Certainly, the storm emergency is a factor, but courts are not kind to—"

"Other liabilities?" The Administrator again.

"Civil, of course. Each victim—assuming more than one—could sue on a variety of causes: negligence, gross negligence, medical malpractice, and could ask for treble damages. Maybe more. Won't know until someone files."

"It appears he is the only one," said the Head of Hematology. "An isolated case. We are double-checking."

The Administrator sat, tapping his fingers on the desk. The others waited.

"Hematology, finish your investigation. Get Patient Services on board if there is anyone else possibly infected. Stan, work with our Compliance Department to find out our *specific* liabilities as best you can as soon as Hematology and the blood bank give you enough information. Until we know, do not use any blood from our bank. Get to work. I'm going to go meet with PR to see how we handle this catastrophe you have all created."

✳

Rodriguez burst into Paterson's office without knocking. She dropped a folded newspaper in front of him.

"Check out the headline."

A smile crept across Paterson's face as he read. "Wow."

"Yeah, wow. Who'd have thought? It's like you said, with these guys, you keep finding more and more."

He snorted. "Yeah, but I'd have never thought *this*. What is it? Drugs? Sex?" He looked up. "Not that this has *anything* to do with our investigation."

"Oh, of course not. Wouldn't want a backlash. But it helps us. Taints him." She looked back down at the paper. "Poor sap."

"He brought it on himself." He picked up the paper and read aloud, "City Council Member and Businessman Jay Adam, Under State and Federal Investigations, Tests Positive For HIV."

34

I was the only new passenger. Climbing aboard, I saw that the bus was crowded. I would have to sit next to someone. I walked down the aisle, assessing each candidate. I settled for a spot next to a middle-aged man in a rumpled business suit. He looked tired and grumpy—like he wanted to be left alone to doze in misery. Perfect.

I tilted my seat back and closed my eyes as the bus pulled out of the station.

❋

Someone pushed at my shoulder. My eyes opened to the sweaty businessman in my face.

"Need to get out. My stop."

I sat up and slid my legs to the side. He grunted and squeezed past. The electronic sign at the front of the bus was blinking. "Banning."

A nice irony. Maybe I should disembark here, too.

The bus pulled out, and we were back on the freeway. I slid over by the window and watched until I saw:

San Bernardino
30 miles

I gazed out at the desert. It might be nice to be lost out there. I could walk until I collapsed of thirst and exposure. There are better ways to die, of course. But at least I'd be alone, and no one would ever find me.

A ton of bricks landed on me. My heart was pounding so hard I was sure the others could hear it. I leaned forward, face in hands. I felt I might vomit. Was I having a heart attack? Was this death?

No, I knew what it was. Post-trauma. Emotional triggers. I had been told all the words. Didn't make it any easier.

After a few moments of deep breaths, I calmed down. I guess I don't really want to die. Not yet, at least. Not until I figure this out. Get some answers and get back in control. Create some order.

And I'm pretty sure they wouldn't want me to die.

A memory flashed to mind. "Maybe someone *is* out to get us!" Stella had said. I made fun of her for it. "We're not part of the underworld."

I squeezed my eyes shut. My heart was pounding. I felt the cool sweat on my neck, hands, and face.

I can't go there. Stay in the present. Breathe.

A sinister plot to arrange events and decisions to smash Jay Adam out of existence? Did I think that, too? It made no sense.

No, the universe was just a random collection of infinite combinations of atoms. It might seem vindictive and unjust, but that's just coincidence. Which means I can wrest control back and impose an order of my choosing.

Right?

I sat up and wiped my eyes, and gazed out the window at the desert speeding past. Flashes of sand, dirt, rocks, dry plants, and brush. It seemed like the desolation never ended. Yet maps and experience say it does. Humans build roads and buildings. Run power and water and sewers. We bring order out of chaos.

My task is only a small puzzle in the universe. I just need to examine each piece, determine where it goes, and build the scene.

I was owed some order.

Right?

35

She was sitting on the bed, sobbing, as he came into the room. He went over and put his hand on her shoulder. She turned her face up to him, a suffering visage of wet skin, tangled hair, and smeared makeup that she hadn't taken off last night.

"They fired me, Jay. Fired *me*."

"What? What do you mean?"

"The committees! They *fired* me." He had rarely seen such anger in her.

"But…but you don't work for them. It's volunteer—"

"Okay, they told me not to come back. Is that better, Jay?!" He knew she was taking her anger out on him. It still hurt.

"Sorry, sorry. Which committee?"

"All of them, Jay! *All of them!*" She flung herself away from him, lying across the bed. Jay sat down and laid his hand on her hip.

"Did they say why?"

She spoke from beneath an arm thrown across her face. "Why? Because of you. Because they said it was not good PR to have the wife of a council member and business leader who is under investigation for a bunch of crimes and has HIV."

"They said 'HIV'?"

She growled in frustration. "No! But they think it."

He sighed. "It's not an investigation. They are looking into irregularities. It will be okay when they see the paper trail. Or what's left of it. And the accident was…an accident. I wasn't drinking." He sighed again. She knew all that.

Stella sat back up and faced him, speaking through fresh tears. "Do you think they care? It doesn't matter. You killed someone, you committed business fraud, and you have a disease! No one wants you around!"

He drew back and remained quiet. Perhaps they did feel that way.

"Jay, I know what happened, but it doesn't matter. It is like someone out there is setting us up." She stood and walked to the French doors, staring at the desolation that used to be a beautiful expanse. "I know that sounds crazy. But *you* explain it." She ran a hand through her disheveled hair.

"I know it's bad, Stella. Really bad. We just have to continue to do the right thing and be honest."

She whirled on him. "Really? And where has that gotten you so far?"

He threw up his hands. "What do you want me to do?!"

"I don't know! Fight! You have money and connections and power. *Use it!* Get the mayor to put pressure on the police. Have the detective fired. Put the newspaper out of business."

"You don't mean that."

"I don't know what I mean anymore, Jay. We have lost so much—and yeah, maybe we survive. But what if it gets worse? What if the insurance company comes after you next? What if the blood treatments don't work? What if that idiot detective won't let go of stupid Zohn's suicide?!"

"Don't talk like that, Stella. I won't respond in kind to them. My character matters."

"Does it?! Well, enjoy your character when you have nothing. When the kids and I are suffering—enjoy your character!"

She stormed out of the room, slamming the door behind her.

36

"How are you doing?"

Jay nodded. The two men sat across from each other at an old wooden table. Jay examined the surface: stained, scratched, and distressed from long years of use.

The slats in the back of the wooden chair dug into his shoulder blades. This was the first time out of the cell in a week.

Anthony wore an elegant Brooks Brothers suit—his favorite. His tie was power red. A bit old-fashioned. *That's Anthony*, thought Jay, *the classic banker*. He was freshly shaven. He smelled clean.

Anthony tried not to show his shock at how thin and sickly Jay looked. "Well, good. I'm glad to hear that. How are the treatments?"

"Fine. A cocktail of drugs. They say because they caught it immediately, it might go into remission."

"Good. What did the lawyer say?"

Jay lifted a hand from the table and looked at it, palm up. The scratches and cuts were healed for the most part. Just some scarring where the skin had been scraped off. Skin on skin.

"Said it didn't look good. Perfect storm." *The employees all testified that no one had taken alcohol into the offices during the party. Which was true.*

Anthony did not seem surprised. "Stella and the kids will be okay."

Jay looked up at him. "I know."

Anthony nodded. They had decades of a personal and business relationship, but it seemed he had run out of words. Jay felt no need to break the silence. *This feels like a wake.*

"It's not true, is it?"

"What?"

"The drinking that night."

"No."

He shook his head. "Terrible bad luck, my friend."

❊

"How are you holding up?"

Jay nodded. The two sat across from each other. Jay looked at the far wall. Painted with plain white-wash, patches and cracks could be seen under the top coat from many years of use. The slats in the back of the wooden chair dug into his shoulder blades. He hadn't been out in seven days.

Jocelyn's hair was cut and styled in a modern but professional look. Her jewelry was understated but classy. She took a lot of care with appearance because she thought she would not be taken seriously otherwise. *She underestimates herself*, Jay thought. He could smell the fresh scent of soap and a light dusting of perfume.

She was trying not to show her disdain at the cold and decrepit surroundings. Though Jay wore a standard jumpsuit, he looked out of place.

"Good. How did the hearing go?"

Jay rubbed his temple with his right hand. The treatments had begun, and the medication gave him a headache and made him feel quite sick.

"Not good. All circumstantial. But *so* much of it."

Jocelyn did not seem surprised. "Your business will weather this."

Jay looked up. "I know."

Jocelyn nodded. Their families had known each other for many years; Jocelyn and Stella had taken all the kids on outings. She had been invaluable to Jay with her financial skills. But it seemed he had run out of words.

"I can't believe all these things happened at once. The blood transfusion, the accident, so much death, the fraud." She paused, uncomfortable.

This feels like a funeral.

"It's not true, is it?"

"What?"

"The fraud."

"No. It's not true."

"Gosh, Jay. It's almost like a setup."

✳

"How are you feeling?"

Jay shrugged. The two sat on opposite sides of the table. Jay was staring into space: he had not eaten or slept much. The medications were helping, they said, but it didn't feel like it. He hadn't been out in seven days.

Cristy had on a typical outfit: a flower-print dress with a light sweater over the top. Conservative but attractive, just like her personality. *A stable, dependable person,* Jay thought. He could smell the fresh scent of soap and a light dusting of perfume.

She was trying not to show her great concern at his demeanor. Jay was always enthused, work or play. Now he looked like all the joy had been drained out of him.

"Good. What…what is going on with the insurance company?"

Jay shifted in his seat. He was nauseous from the medications. The assured him the treatments were working, but there could always be setbacks. In any case, he'd be taking the cocktails for years. Maybe for the rest of his life.

"They decided to pursue the lawsuit."

Cristy did not seem surprised.

He and Stella had met her while he was getting his MBA. She had been by his side ever since, first working part time until she took over as his executive assistant.

Her input was always sound. But it seemed she had run out of words.

"I just can't believe all these terrible things have come at once." She paused, uncomfortable.

This feels like a memorial.

"It's not true, is it?"

"What?"

"The fire. I know things were bad, and insurance money—"

"It's not true."

"This is a nightmare, Jay. Like someone is trying to break you."

37

The desert burns my feet. Hot, hot, hot. I try walking faster. I try walking on the outer edges of my feet. The first doesn't make it any cooler, and the latter was uncomfortable and slow. I look ahead, shielding my eyes from the glare. The mountains in the distance are a hazy mix of grays and greens and whites. I see, just before the foothills, a shimmering black lake. Parallel lines of white and blue appear and shift and fade. It is not water. I know a mirage when I see one.

There are no clouds in the clear blue sky. The sun is directly above, beaming rays of heat on my head like some god is holding a blowtorch a few feet over it.

I see a series of small silver stakes far ahead, perpendicular to my path. Far away. They appear about three inches tall from here, all the same height, in a perfect line stretching from right to left. Every once in a while, a flash appears. Sunlight momentarily reflecting from glass or metal, perhaps.

I drop my hand and continue marching along a faint path. Whether made by animal or man, I do not know.

How did I get here?

Where is my beautiful wife? Where is my beautiful house? sang a song in my memory. *Letting the days go by let the water hold me down.*

There is no water here. But there might be when I get closer to the mountains. Maybe there is water underground. Perhaps in the morning I can find some when the sun begins its return from the Underworld and the temperature change causes dew to form on some of the smoother surfaces. There is enough for the flora and fauna that grow and live here. But probably not enough for a human. For a solitary man. For any length of time, anyway.

I sang out loud to the desert.

> *And you may ask yourself*
> *Where does that highway go?*
> *And you may ask yourself*
> *Am I right?...Am I wrong?*
> *And you may tell yourself—*

A tall plant blocks my path. It is about ten feet tall. Spindly, with broad leaves at the middle. It is brown and dry. The leaves curl into themselves, like an insect between a window and its screen that has dried up. Looking close I see that, near the base, there is still some green.

"Are you dead?" I ask, startled at how slurred my voice sounds. Like a homeless man at a bus station.

"I am," the plant says.

My face makes an expression of surprise—exaggerated, like I am on a stage playing a role in a bad scene. I am not surprised that a plant can talk. My reaction is scripted. Here, in a bone-dry land that can miraculously support exotic desert plants, insects, and animals, it seems unlikely but not impossible.

"What happened to you?" I'm not concerned. Just curious. I have always been curious. Or used to be.

"It is an old, familiar story."

"Sorry I asked."

"I came here as a seed on the wind," the plant says. "I rode upon Ninurtu and disembarked here. It was a spot that was quite moist. A keen eye will note that this area is a bit of a depression. A shallow bowl to capture the morning and evening dew, and the rare rains." It spreads a few of its thin, outermost leaves, indicating the slight, shallow dirt bowl in which we stand.

I nod and purse my lips in thoughtful consideration. Do I appear erudite? I hope so.

"During that season, Enlil had won freedom from his imprisonment, and so the rain came. Not often, for Enlil's attention was always elsewhere. But the edges of the storm brought moisture. Sometimes Enki visited. It was not much, but enough for my sustenance. I grew. I was proud. There were others with me, but none as strong or tall as I. I had chosen the perfect spot."

"But something went wrong?"

"Alas, it was the perfect spot, just not forever. I should have kept going. I should have ridden the wind to the mountains, where water always flows. But I was lazy. I had thrown in my lot with Enlil. And a great battle ensued, and Enlil was defeated once more. No more rain. No more water. No more moisture."

"I don't know of whom you speak. But maybe this…Enlil?…will escape again and bring you water? And you will be revived."

"No. And it is no matter. It is the way of things. There is no effect without cause. I linked my destiny with Enlil and reaped the result. Good at the beginning, tragic at the end."

"Do you speak of Fate?"

"No. There is no Fate, only choices and consequences. My choices led to this. We reap what we sow. We make our bed and lie in it. Our destinies are perfectly aligned with our decisions. As it should be."

The plant falls silent. I wait, but no other phyllo-philosophy came forth. The heat bakes the hair on my head. I run my fingers through it and fluff it up. It burns the skin of my fingers. Holding them in front of me, I see that they are brown and curling. I don't care. Maybe I should sit down here with the plant so we can wither and die together.

"As it should be?" I ask.

"Yes."

"I agree actions have consequences. But sometimes things just happen. And sometimes there is injustice."

"No."

"Well, bad things happen sometimes and no one is to blame."

"Incorrect. You just don't know where the fault lies. Perhaps it was a mother. A grandfather. An ancestor. Somewhere along the line. Every effect has a cause."

I am not convinced, but I am pretty sure I will not prevail against the plant. It is rooted too deep.

I raise my gaze, locate the line of silver stakes, and walk again. I cannot see the path any longer, but that's okay. There are not many obstacles between me and my destination. Just sporadic small, dry plants and some rocks and pebbles along the way.

❋

I am on my hands and knees. I shake myself, as if I had been sleeping, and raise up. I lay in a small, dry gully. I remember that my journey had become a mesmerizing pattern of step…step…step and endless desert. I had stumbled and cast myself down into this dead stream bed. It is deep enough to have a bit of shadow at its edge. I suppose the gully had been created through the work of Enlil, long ago, before the return of Utu, or Ninurtu, or some other person I don't know.

I lean back again the sloped edge and try to scrunch myself into the shade. The soil upon which I sit is cool. I get my head and half of my torso into the shadow, but the rest is in full sunlight. I cannot stay long.

Across from me are two large boulders. They sit with defiance against the opposite slope. Between them, in a shadow of their own making, is a gossamer web. Perfect in symmetry, it is a stark contrast to the desiccated disorder around it. I consider the meticulous work and the engineering skill that went into the construction of the web. As I watch, I see there is a large, brownish-white spider hanging just off center. As if a spider-arrow had been shot from a spider-bow and the spider-bowman had just barely missed the bullseye.

"Are you alive?" I ask. The sound of my voice broke the heated air of the desert. It startles me, like the shout of a drunk man in the midst of a *molto pianissimo* passage.

"Yes, quite so," the spider says.

"There is so much death. I was not sure."

"I will not be here long."

"No? Why?"

"Because I entice my prey with pretty strands, I lure them here with the hope of shade and coolness. They become stuck fast in my web of deceits. I embalm them to keep them alive, and then, at my pleasure, I devour them. It is an evil which I enjoy."

I am taken aback. In my experience, those who practice evil are not so forthcoming about it.

"Well, it is how you survive."

"I am a skillful deceiver. I am proud and victorious. But my wickedness has its price. My web, built from guile, is neither permanent nor reliable. A strong desert wind, from the right direction, destroys it all. An animal, searching for morsels, tears it away without even knowing. A human, happening by…" The spider turns to focus a multifaceted eye on my images.

"Yes, I get it. But surely that alone doesn't make you evil? It is simply the nature of spiders."

"Linguistic gymnastics. Logical poppycock. Excrement of excuses. I have heard such arguments. I made them myself, long ago. No longer, for I have gained wisdom over the years. Actions have consequences. There is no effect without cause."

"Do you speak of Fate?"

"No. We reap what we sow. Our destinies are perfectly aligned with our actions."

A gust of wind blows, like someone had turned on a furnace. I flinch at the searing heat and see the spider do the same. My skin feels like it is curling up.

The desert becomes still again.

"It is a terrible heat!" I wail. "Nothing can survive here long, can it?"

"No. But there is still hope for you. If you are not a deceiver, you might be able to escape. If you do not rejoice in using others for your own ends, you might live.

Since actions have consequences, *good* actions have *good* consequences."

I shake my head. "I don't think that is always true, either."

"Of course it is. It is logical. It is fair and just."

"But is it true?"

The spider does not answer. I wait, but no other arachnid acumen is forthcoming. The heat bakes the skin on my arms. I rub my hands on opposite forearms and cry out as the skin of my palms burn. Holding them in front of me, I see that they are made of ash, and the desert breeze is blowing everything away.

38

They called him out of the block after dinner. "Adam, report to the officer's station." They handed him a blue pass and told him to go to the main office.

He walked across the empty yard. He'd never been called to the office before, though he'd only been here a year. But he knew that no one got called unless it was bad.

Is my condition worsening? They said the antiretroviral therapy worked, but it could always relapse…

Am I being transferred? Sometimes that happened, for no apparent reason. But I've only been here a year…

Did something happen in the Federal case? Surely I would have gotten a letter from the attorney…

He reached the door and pulled it open. He was taken aback by the number of officers lounging around inside. One sat at a desk, three or four in chairs, one leaned against a small table, and two others stood against a wall.

Their conversations died as he entered. All eyes turned on him.

"Adam?"

"Yes, sir."

He held his hand out. Jay handed him his card. The officer glanced at it and handed it back.

The room was stuffy, like a medical tent in a disaster zone, where a surgeon has terrible news for the newcomer. The onlookers wonder how he will respond. *How terrible, but it happens.*

The officer fixes his eyes on Jay and says, "I have some bad news."

✳

Swirling, spinning, sickening. Receding, reeling, retching. Everything went black, but he could still hear voices.

Mute.

Numbness.

Disorientation.

✳

"I don't *believe* you!" he screamed.

Someone was at his side. Two people, holding his arms.

"This is someone trying to get me! Is it the Feds? The detective? Zohn? Who is doing this?!"

Blur.

Struggle.

Yelling.

Pulling.

"Get him to medical!"

✳

"Condition?"

"Unresponsive, doctor, BP quite low with elevated heart rate. Some arrhythmia."

"This isn't a recurrence of the infection, is it? He stopped ART a while back, just before he was incarcerated. Pronounced functionally cured."

"And have we monitored it?"

"Yes, though he's only been an inmate for a year. Poor guy—he's got nine more left."

"So this incident is probably acute stress reaction?"

"I think so. They just told him his wife and kids were killed in a car wreck."

Part Two

UPON THE EARTH

39

My tailored suit is new—it had cost almost a million dollars. Along with the dress shirt, shoes, pocket square, cufflinks, and tie, it came to well over two million. It seems extravagant, but quite necessary to give the impression that I am successful when I argue cases. It's part of the game of justice.

Ideally, I would have a different suit for every day in court and never wear the same one twice. That would show I was one of the *best*.

I sit at the defense table in the courtroom. I wasn't sure where it was located. Not even sure if it's on land. In fact, I don't even recall how I got here. But that's all irrelevant: someone will answer for all the losses and suffering.

I review my neatly typed brief. My staff and I had labored over it for years, night and day. We researched every relevant statute and tracked down every case that even mentioned the issue. The Table of Contents is structured and balanced like a carefully constructed bridge over troubled waters. After the Introduction and Summary of the Case, there are three major headings:

1. The Error of Effects That Violate the Scope of the Prior Cause

2. The Injustice of Reaping a Different Crop Than Was Sowed

3. The Misapplication of the Law of Merit and Destiny

I take pride in the parallelism of the three headings, and the rhetorical twist in the third. Each of the three sections contains well-structured and convincing arguments supported by copious citations. Each had been reviewed and edited by six thousand different researchers. It will lead the judge down related branches that join at the end into one, powerful trunk rooted deep in the soil of justice. Beginning with the seeming chaos of leaves and twigs, it ends by revealing an imposing Sequoia that leads to one, unassailable conclusion.

I flip to the end of the brief, a Summary and a Request for the judge to reinstate the defendant and return all property, status, losses, and those who died. It begins, of course, with "Therefore With All Great Respect to Your Honor…."

There are three main questions addressed in the Summary, each of which leads to one conclusion.

First, does anyone gain from the extreme suffering of the defendant? The answer, of course, is "no." No one learned a lesson, no one was educated, no one was reformed, and the world was not a better place.

Second, is the system so short-sighted that it cannot see the injustice foisted upon my client? The prosecution might argue that any punishment must fit the crime— but in this case, it surely did not. Indeed, a footnote proclaims that the loss of this fine person who had done so much good for others makes the world *worse*.

Finally, was the system so small-minded that it believed that the universe required the suffering of this one little life—which only had a few decades left, anyway?

Not bad. Of course, I anticipate the counter-arguments. But since the facts are on my side, they can only be arguments of *reductio ad absurdum* and *argumentum ad an-*

tiquitatem. I expect some *dicto simpliciter* and *circulus in demonstrando.* Perhaps even some *ad hominem* arguments—always a sign of a losing cause. I argue the intent of the law, public policy, equitable relief, and other legal phrases that we all understood but did not mean much to anyone else. Except for the judge.

I look at the clock. Its black arms read nine-twenty-three. As I watch, the large arm clicks to nine-twenty-four. The dark-paneled room, with its deep blue carpet and scrolled furniture, holds no one but the bailiff and myself.

I raise my hand and call out—too loud in the soft, quiet room. He nods and makes his way over to me from his desk at the front side of the courtroom.

"Yes, Mr. Adam?" I notice his name tag says "C. Rahab." "Officer Rahab, am I correct that the hearing was to begin at nine?"

"Yes, sir."

"Neither the prosecuting attorney nor the judge has arrived. Is there something I should know?"

He shrugs. "Not anything out of the ordinary. You have never appeared in this court, have you, sir?"

"No, this is my first case."

"Local rules, as you know. Here, the prosecuting attorney and the judge are the same. So, if the judge is late, then, by the laws of nature, the prosecuting attorney will be late. Following from that, if the prosecuting attorney is late, then, by necessity and from the utmost—"

"Yes, yes, officer. They are the same person?"

"Why, yes, of course."

"Doesn't that violate the rule of law and provisions about fairness or due process or…"

"Not at all. It is *part* of the Law."

"No law I ever heard of."

95

"Nevertheless, it is the Law. I am quite certain, sir. I am a Bailiff of the Court."

"By whom was this law drafted? What legislature debated and passed it by a majority? What judicial system has tested it?"

"The judge, of course." He seems as confused by my questions as I am by his answers.

"Are you telling me, an officer of the court, that *one person* legislates, judges, and prosecutes? If I proceed to ask who enforces judgments and laws, will I be disappointed in your answer?"

The bailiff stood back and pouted. "I see no reason for sarcasm, Mr. Adam."

"Apologies, my good man. Shall I rephrase my question in a more polite manner?"

"There is not much reason to ask a question for which you already know the answer."

I say nothing, staring into his eyes until he looks away.

"The other parties will arrive when they arrive, Mr. Adam."

"What a pleasant tautology."

"Will there be anything else?"

"No, officer. Thank you."

Officer Rahab returns to his seat.

The papers in my hand had flopped over so that the top of the pages are resting on the table. It *is* a good argument. Perhaps, however, *in propia persona* is not the way to proceed. I am out of my element and courts love to humiliate out-of-towners. I need someone to intercede, but I am afraid to ask the bailiff for suggestions because I think I know what he would say.

I toss the brief into the waste basket and walk out.

40

I had forgotten how unpleasant San Bernardino could be. It was just as hot as Desert Center, but with the addition of cement, asphalt, and far more people. Moreover, the city planners did not seem to care for aesthetics.

It was almost dark when I arrived, and I was still sixty miles from "home." I did not want to make the calls I needed to make. When did I become so reticent? So weak? Was I afraid that every call would be like trying to contact Mr. Munro? That's silly.

I discovered that a bus left for Union Station in two hours. From there I could transfer to a bus bound for Mission Viejo or Laguna Hills, and then a taxi to anywhere. A hotel, for now, I guess.

However, that would put me in after 10:00. I did not want to arrive that late at night with no place to stay. A fresh start tomorrow would be better. Which meant I should stay here.

I left the bus station and saw two motels within walking distance. Hoisting my bags, I headed to the closest, which proudly displayed a faded sign that read "The Nighttime Inn."

The lobby smelled of disinfectant. It was small, with a chest-high counter across one end. The floor was linoleum, the lights were fluorescent, and the drapes were dingy. It should be cheap.

There was no one at the counter, but a door leading into a back room was open. I walked to the far side of the counter to peer in, but only saw a messy desk with a typewriter and a phone. Someone had pinned maps to the walls. By the looks of their yellowed edges, they had been there a long time.

I tapped the bell on the counter and waited. A wooden rack on the counter contained brochures describing all the things one could do in and around San Bernardino: "The Original McDonald's Site and Museum," "San Manuel Amphitheater," and "Norton AFB Museum."

A man's face peeked out from around the door frame. "May I help you?"

"Yes, I would like a room for the night. Single, the cheapest you have."

He opened a large ledger to a marked page and ran his finger down the right-hand page. "102 is available—no, that's a double…121 is a single." He looked up. "Forty dollars for the night."

Prices have increased quite a bit since the last time I stayed in a hotel.

"I'll take it." It would not put too much of a dent in my cash. I reminded myself that I still needed to check my account and insurance payments.

He pulled out a sheet of paper and retrieved a pen from his shirt pocket. Bending slightly, he began writing.

"Name?"

"Jay Adam."

"Address?"

"I don't have one at the moment."

He straightened up. "Do you have I.D.?"

Well, that's one puzzle piece I should have taken of first thing. "No."

He put the pen down. "I am sorry, sir, I cannot rent a room without I.D."

"I have cash." I took the envelope out of my pocket and opened it, showing him the stacks of ten dollar bills. "I am traveling and in between residences."

"I'm sorry. I can't let a room to someone without some form of ID. Security."

I took a deep breath. "Look, I've been on a bus all day. I haven't had time to get my ID yet. I just need a place to stay for tonight, and then I am on my way."

"Why don't you have an ID?"

I took a deep breath. "Well, I don't have a home or a job yet, no car so I don't need a license—"

"—I'm sorry. No rooms. Security reasons."

"But...I'm not homeless." As I said it, I realized how stupid it sounded. I *was* homeless, at the moment. "I mean, I am on my way to find a place to live and get a job."

"Sorry. No ID, no room. Security reasons." He turned and went back into the office.

I was so taken aback that I just nodded and left. I stepped outside and leaned against the building. My heart was pounding. Years ago, I would have been calm, reasonable, and done my best to connect with the man. To show understanding for his position and to demonstrate my humility and sincerity. A human connection often leads to compromise, if not beneficence.

But I gave up. Like a dog who had beaten too many times.

So this puzzle is more complicated than I thought.

I gathered my emotions and crossed the street, walked one block down, and entered the second motel. It had a larger sign, brightly lit by a little row of spotlights: "Charles Worth Inn." I didn't know who Charles Worth might be, but it seemed a bit more upscale, and therefore more expensive.

The inside, however, was almost a doppelgänger of the last. A large man stood behind the counter. He wore a Hawaiian shirt, and his hair was a tousled mop of dirty blonde, as if he had just toweled off from a brief swim.

"Good evening. How may I help you?"

"Do you have any single rooms for the night?"

"We do. Price is fifty-nine ninety-nine per night."

"I'd like one, please."

"Payment up front, some form of identification, and the make of your car."

"I don't have any identification nor a car. I'm down on my luck, no job, no place to stay, but headed back to where I grew up. I just need a place to stay tonight."

He pursed his lips and frowned. "We don't let rooms to people without identification. We've had problems in the area with gangs and other low-lifes."

"I assure you I am neither. I had my own business for many years and lost it all. Can you help me?"

He glanced back at the door behind him. "I'd like to. No one ever said Saul didn't help the down 'n' out. But…"

"It's just one night." I adopted what I hoped was an innocent expression.

He sighed. I could see he was struggling. I almost had him.

"Why don't you got no ID? Down on yer luck, sure, but don't you have *something*? A food stamp card?"

"I do have ID, but my wallet got stolen." I was surprised how readily I lied. It had always been a point of pride with me that I tried not to mislead people.

"Then how you gonna pay?"

"I have cash." I could see the holes in my lie.

He glanced down at my hand on the table. Too late, I knew he was looking at the tattoo between my right thumb and the forefinger. He looked back up at me.

"You an ex-con."

I sighed. "I just got out today. I'm not a criminal. It was a car accident. Let me tell you my story and maybe—"

"Get out!" The change in his demeanor was like whip-lash. "One of your type held me at *gunpoint* and robbed us! Said he just got out, then he put a gun to my head!" His hand fumbled at the desk and he lifted a tan phone receiver like a weapon. The coiled cord flipped papers into the air. "I have mace! I'll call the police!" The papers drifted slowly to the floor.

I left, cursing Charles Worth and his Inn. I cursed his wife, his children, his employees, and everything he owned.

41

I found myself standing in front of a bar and restaurant. I was still shaking. I hadn't eaten anything since breakfast with Ellie. Maybe that was why I was out of sorts.

The place was dim, lit by cheap chandeliers casting a yellow light. Ten or fifteen four-person tables dotted the square interior. At the back was a long bar. At one table, three men were drinking and playing cards. Two people sat at the bar; far enough apart to show they were alone. A man and woman were in a corner booth, sitting on the same side together

I took a seat at the bar. The bartender came over.

"Give me whatever your best-selling beer is." I didn't care about my limited cash at the moment. "Are you serving food?"

"Sure, 'till ten." He turned to the bar behind him and retrieved a small menu from a stack.

When he returned with my pint, I ordered a ham and cheese sandwich and chips. He took the menu and left.

I drank the beer in a few gulps. It had been over a dec-ade, yet it tasted like no time had passed. Some things from my previous life seemed distant and hazy; others as clear as yesterday. I ordered a second.

As he returned and set it down, the man to my left turned to me.

"Hi there. I'm Zig. You from 'round here?"

His speech indicated he was already on his way to drunk. I should have sat at one of the corner tables.

"No, just traveling through." I took a sip of beer, staring straight ahead.

Drunks lose the ability to detect social cues.

"Ah, good, good. Welcome to San Berdoo!" He slid over one stool to bring his bulk and breath into closer proximity. He reached out a hand.

I set my beer down and shook his hand. "I'm Jay. Just getting a bite to eat, then I need to find a place to stay." Maybe he'd have some ideas. A YMCA or a shelter, even. I don't care.

"Good, good. Where are you from?"

"I've been in Arizona for the last ten years, but headed back to L.A. now."

He picked up the beer glass in front of him, which was almost empty. He gazed at it as if trying to figure out where the beer went.

"I've lived here all my life. It's not as bad as people say. At least not in the north area. But I'm getting out, and I'm celebrating!" With a flourish, he downed the rest of the beer and set the glass on the bar with unnecessary force. "I've been offered a job in Sacramento. Last week, I sold my house. Yesterday, my divorce was final. I am a free and happy man—and I'm celebrating!"

I smiled as seemed appropriate. "Congratulations, Zig. You look quite happy."

He leaned in. "You don't know the half of it. I was a good employee and a good husband. Did everything right. But I got tired of my wife, my boss, my co-workers. All soul-sucking money-grubbing *users*!" He slapped the bar to get the bartenders' attention. "Hey, bring me a couple of shots of bourbon. What's you got?"

"Jack Daniel's, Maker's Mark, Jim Beam, Wild Turkey. Think we still have a Georgia Moon left."

"Georgia Moon? What's that?"

"It's a classic corn whiskey from Tennessee."

"Let's try it." He turned back. "Drink with me. My treat. I finally had the guts to do the right thing!"

I wanted to eat and leave. But I needed a place to stay, and here was someone who might help. Gregarious people are often happy to help others in need.

I nodded. "Sure thing. Thanks."

My food arrived and I began to eat. I stopped long enough to toast Zig when the bourbon arrived. He didn't like the corn whiskey (though he drained it). He ordered another for each of us—Jim Beam, this time. I ordered another beer to finish my meal.

"I was the best husband to her. *Doted* on her. She never cared. Just wanted stuff. Money. Jewelry. Stuff for the house. Didn't know how to love anyone."

He continued with his story as empty shot and pint glasses lined up in front of us. Zig regaled me with stories of his wife and of San Bernardino (I was not sure which he thought less of). He was a salesman for a company that sold and rented professional audio equipment and systems. According to his own assessment, he was the best. He wasn't asking about my family or my work, so I was happy to play the sympathetic listener and let him patter on.

After a time, I glanced up and down bar. It was now full of patrons. My dishes were gone. I must have finished eating, but I didn't recall. What did I have? A sandwich? Zig was still talking.

"—the reason our sales shot through the roof. He knew it, of course, but he took all the credit. And he knew I knew. I knew he knew—"

It was dim and noisy. The lights sparkled off the mirror and glass shelves behind bar through shelves of bottles. My tolerance was low, and I had drunk too much. But it felt nice to let go. Hadn't done that in a long, long time.

"Hey! Jay, you still with me?" Zig laughed with a roar. A flash of faces spun across my vision. I held still until his visage came into focus.

"Yes, yes, still here. What were we saying?"

"Well, I was telling you about my terrible marriage and outrageous boss, and you were telling me about your car wreck and your prison time."

I told him? Wasn't I just thinking how nice it was that he was doing all the talking? I looked down the bar. Where were the two motel clerks? It was so tall I could only see the top of their heads. Both grabbed the forward edge of the counter and pulled themselves up and towards me so that they could peer down at me. In the bar mirror, I could see the floor behind the counter where their feet dangled as they hung from their hands, bellies pressed against the bar top. They screamed, "Are you contagious? You look *disgusting*! Get away!"

I shook my head. That wasn't right. I'm in a bar. With my new friend, Zig. I looked down and saw a pint of beer in front of me, half full. I picked it up and took a gulp. I should ask for some water. Oh. There was a water glass in front of me. It was full. I put down the beer—with care—and picked up the water. Both glasses seemed heavier than they should.

"What was I saying, Zig?"

"*I* was telling *you* that *you* gotta apologize and change your ways."

"What?" I tried to focus on his face again.

"I mean, you'd been living a bad life and it caught up with you. That's how it works. You can't live a bad life and get away with it forever."

I frowned. "No. I wasn't. I did good—"

"But you got drunk and killed someone."

"I wasn't drunk. They *said* I was drunk."

Zig put his hands up. "Okay, whatever. You putting the juice away pretty good now! But what I'm saying is that it's *karma*. All the bad stuff happened 'cause you were living bad. Maybe not drunk driving. Other stuff. Maybe in *secret*. Otherwise why all this bad stuff happening to you?"

I shook my head. "It's ridiculous to think my *family* died because I wasn't a good person! I worked hard. Helped people. Was responsible." The last word was hard to pronounce.

"Ah…" he wiped away my protestations with a beery gesture. "We all done bad stuff no one ever knew about. Maybe even *you* didn't think it was bad."

"No, I didn't deserve this." I grabbed my beer and took a drink, sloshing some on my shirt.

"Stuff like that doesn't happen to someone unless they got it coming. That's how it works. Karma." He leaned back with triumph. I don't think he even knew what "karma" meant. But drunken philosophy is the most profound at the time.

He took a swig of his beer. Zig took a swig. Big Zig took a big swig. Like a pig did Zig swig.

He leaned forward. "Did you hear me?"

"Nope. Was writing a poem about you drinking."

He laughed. "I'd like to hear it. But this is important." He leaned in further, a bit unsteady. "You did bad stuff, you paid the price—" he held up his hands "—I know, I know, you said you didn't. Just stay with me, this is the important part."

He leaned back and set his glass down with care, then pushed it back about six inches. He took a bar napkin and wiped the moisture from the table in front of him. I could tell something important was about to happen. Or he thought so. He turned on the barstool to orient his entire body towards me.

"What matters is now is that you say, 'I lived wrong. Not going to be that way anymore. Straight and narrow from here on out.' Then you get a clear conscience and a good life." He picked his beer up and raised it high. "Like me!" He held it towards me for a toast.

I did not return the gesture. "I *had* a clear conscience and a good life!"

He set his beer back down and shook his head. "Okay. Maybe stuff happens that isn't our fault. Like my wife and boss! Not my fault, but I suffered! 'Member that bad earthquake a few years back? My good friend lost his family and his home. Not his fault. But he still did some wrong, even though a good guy. Had to be some stuff, or none of that would have happened to him. Might not be related, but it's karma. Worse you do, worse it is."

He leaned in so close I thought we might bump noses.

"You gotta be honest, buddy. Admit you been a bad guy. Tried to tell my wife the same thing, she wouldn't listen, either."

I felt an explosion coming to a boil inside me. Coming fast. The gasses and molten rock had been down there a long time under extreme pressure. Trying to find a way out, but always blocked. Now there was a weakness in the strata, and it was flowing to the surface at incredible speed.

"You *idiot*! Can't you hear? I worked hard and I was good! I'm not perfect, but I didn't deserve *this*!" Glass shattered on the floor. "You don't know!" I spun around at the room. Smiling faces, grimacing faces, shocked faces were moving in and out of focus and spinning around. "You talk like you know something but you know *nothing*!" I hurled the last word out at the whole room, screaming it as loud as I could. It felt good. Really good.

Scuffling talking yelling I stumbled forward more faces Zig beside me arm out.

"No!" I screamed. I shrugged away from Zig's arm and fell back against a stool, then righted myself. I stuck a finger in his face.

"You think it's all so simple so easy...so neat and clean." Zig was beside me again with both hands on shoulders. "Take it easy Jay, sit down it's okay I didn't mean anything" bartender in front me weaving and waving grabbed on all sides it seemed like a whole group of people pulling I said stop but I couldn't move and it went on and on and on and on

42

I sat on a bench, head in hands, bent over. Cement. Cracked. Dirty. My head was spinning. Motion to my left. Zig sat beside me, holding a mug. Had I been saying something?

"Here," Zig said. "Drink some more." I took the mug and sipped. Coffee. No cream, no sugar. Was this a dream? I took a deep breath and looked around. Outside the bar, I think. On a bench in front of the parking lot. The air was warm, even though it was nighttime. I took another sip of the coffee. I don't think this is a dream.

It came back to me like a bucket of ice water over the head. I leaned over and vomited between my feet. Mostly liquid, but some chunks that were, perhaps, ham and cheese. Splatters on my shoes and trousers. Zig handed me a napkin. I wiped my mouth.

"Sorry, Zig."

"No problem, buddy. I should've known you couldn't handle all that once I learned how long it had been."

I grunted. "Yeah. Me neither."

We sat for a moment in silence. In the distance, I heard vehicles on the freeway. Off to the right somewhere a woman yelled, then laughed hysterically.

"Did I make quite the scene in there?"

"Yeah, pretty much. But that's not unusual for this place. You aren't even close to the top twenty."

I took another sip. "Well, that's something, I guess."

I had no idea what time it was.

"Thanks, Zig. I'm okay now. I have a bus in the morning, so I'm going to sleep inside." I nodded towards the station.

"Inside the station?"

"Yeah, it's clean, and I should get an early bus. It doesn't bother me."

"Well, it bothers me. I've been staying in a friend's unused mobile home. You're going to sleep on my couch. Least I can do for a guy getting a new start. Come on."

I didn't have the strength to argue. Or get up on my own.

We stumbled to his car, his hand on my upper arm to steady me.

43

Zig's couch was the most comfortable spot I had slept in for many years. I floated in and out of awareness, a drunken sleep punctuated by a throbbing headache and moments of wondering where I was.

I told Zig that I was sure there would be a lot of buses to Union Station so time was not a factor. He said he needed to go at 8, and then loaded me up with aspirin and a jug of water. He left me on the couch with a stack of blankets.

The streetlights outside made a regular pattern of light on the thin curtains of the living room window. The shapes shifted as the wind stirred the trees. My blurry eyes saw the outline of Europe, a bottling machine, and then a friendly bear. The bear seems to be singing. Is he playing a guitar or ukulele? Like the country bear jamboree at Disneyland. I'd heard it had closed while I was away, so perhaps he is a refugee. Wound up in San Berdoo to ply his trade on the streets at night.

I must have invited him in because he looms over me in all his animatronic glory.

"Jay," he says in a deep, bear voice. "I have some people who want to talk with you."

"Go away. I've had enough talking. Need to sleep."

"Oh, but you'll want to hear these people. They are your friends."

He backs up, shuffling his considerable bulk out of the way to reveal three shadows shaped like humans. I peer into the dim light. Is that Ellie on the left?

"Hi, Jay."

"What are you doing here?"

"I just wanted you to know I am thinking about you. Be strong, and it will all work out. Things always work out for good people."

The figure next to her stirs, and I hear a dry, rustling sound. It has multiple arms. I can't make out a face, and its voice seems to come from everywhere.

"Choices have consequences. Make good choices, and everything will be okay."

Another voice speaks—smaller, more distant. I can't tell where this voice is coming from either. "We reap what we sow. We lie in the bed of our own making."

The third figure looks like Zig, but is way too large. The bear? No, the bear is still towering behind the three (four?) with an unblinking stare, looking somewhere over my head.

"There is punishment for misdeeds, Jay," says the bulky figure. "It's all pretty straightforward."

"This will make you stronger."

"You'll be a better person."

"Good things come to those who wait."

"Take responsibility for your actions."

"It's all part of the plan."

I swing my feet off the couch and sit up. My head is surprisingly clear. I feel energy coursing through me like a warm elixir is spreading through my bloodstream.

"Get away! I don't want you here! You have no idea!" They do not move.

"I mean it! Away with you and your insipid pronouncements!" As the last word leaves my mouth, the bear comes to life and moves forward. The others shift aside to allow him to pass, then move back together. His bulk obscures them.

I think he is going to swipe at me, to punish me for my outburst. Instead, he begins to play his ukulele. I recognize the tune, even though I have never heard it.

The bear nods, and I sing. My voice is beautiful, sonorous, and captivating. The lyrics are poetic mastery. I sing of the eccentricity of the world. Of its complexity and mystery. The chorus is strong, both musically and lyrically, bemoaning the fact that there is no moral purpose to the workings of life, and those who think so were fools or children. The second stanza is like the first, but offers examples of the randomness of life. I repeat the chorus, then enter a bridge section with a plodding and pointed rhythm in a minor key. I sing mindless clichés and platitudes with as much sarcasm as I can muster.

After the third chorus, a brief coda closes the tune. Slower, more melodic and melancholy than the rest. I sing the words, but they sound like gibberish.

As the last notes die away, I straighten up. I feel triumphant. The song captures what I had struggled to tell them. Perhaps it is harsh, but they need to hear it. They have nothing to offer, and they need to leave me alone.

"Do you hear, all of you?" I wave my hands, trying to get the bear to move aside so that I can see the team of useless counselors. The bear looks back, his large head rotating smoothly to the back and fore again.

"There is no one here but us, Jay."

I jump up and circumnavigate the furry beast. He is right. We are alone.

I sit back down. "But you get it, right?" I look at his face. "You understand. You're a robot. The universe isn't like you; it isn't run with precision like Disneyland. We have to make our own order."

"Disneyland?"

111

"Yes, Disneyland. All that machinery underground and people running it and making sure everything works as it should. But you know that's not real."

He is motionless.

I look closer. The glass orbs that represent his eyes stare, unblinking, at a spot over my head. There is no intelligence in them. The body is as motionless as a rock. There are no organs or muscles.

I lower my head into my hands and cover my eyes, sobbing.

A long time later, I open my eyes and found I was lying on the floor. The streetlights and trees outside made strange shadows on the curtains, shifting shadows in the wind. I climbed back onto the couch and lay down.

44

"Hey, Jay, wake up."

Reality came slowly. I was sliding through a dark tunnel to the light. I was rising through a black sea to the surface.

"Come on, bud. We gotta get going."

I opened my eyes and did not recognize anything. The ceiling, the walls, the decor, the lights. Nothing I had ever seen before. I pulled myself up and the ache in my head exploded.

"Oh." I grabbed my head with both hands.

"Yeah. Thought so."

I was sitting on an unfamiliar couch in an unfamiliar room. A smallish, narrow room. Seemed…feeble. Thin curtains over a single window across from me. A diminutive door. I looked over at the person standing nearby.

Zig.

I remembered.

I turned to put my feet on the floor. "I think…I think I owe you an apology."

"Naw, naw." He came forward and handed me a cup. It was hot. I took a sip. Coffee. "You just had a bad time of it. I've been there. Come on, we gotta get going."

He was putting some papers in a briefcase that sat on a small counter. I took another sip. "Where are we?"

"A trailer that belongs to a friend of mine. Staying here since I sold my house until I leave for good."

Ah, yes. I remembered. The hot liquid and caffeine were beginning to have an effect.

He slammed the briefcase shut and clicked the latches. "Let's go."

I turned my head from side to side, stretching my neck. "Can I take a shower first?"

"Nope, sorry, pal, I got places to be. I let you sleep as long as I could. Figured that would do you better than a shower."

I didn't even remember driving here or coming inside. I had a faint recollection of Zig handing me pills and a jug of water. Blankets. The jug now sat on the coffee table beside me. Half empty. I felt like warmed-over garbage. Like my insides had been taken out, beaten into jelly, then poured back in.

"Come on, come on." He spoke with less friendliness than last night, as if his mind betrayed his jolly salesman-like body. "I can take you back to the bus station, or, if you want, I'm going to Pomona and I can drop you at that bus station. Your choice."

I stood up. My head was swirling in circles like an unbalanced top. "Pomona. Thanks."

"Sure. Your bags are there." He pointed to the end of the couch. "The john is through that door. But hurry."

The car was an old Ford Camino, champagne colored, with vinyl seats. Clean. We pulled out of the trailer park. After a few turns, we sped up a ramp and onto the 10 freeway. Zig seemed lost in his own thoughts and did not speak. Quite different from the gregarious drunk of last night.

I was asleep before we had gone a mile.

45

It is a nice suit—quite expensive—but it means nothing, of course. It's all about the argument. Take the judge down the road of facts and lead him to the proper judgment. If done properly, the judge—any judge—will make the right decision.

I had written a new motion. This one is better, though it's true that the judge and the prosecution hold all the cards. The facts are on our side, but I need the judge to see the procedural problem first.

I look over the neatly typed pages. A "Request for Temporary Injunction" and a "Request for a Permanent Injunction." Short and to the point. Courts almost always grant one or the other if there is even a slight chance of harm to the defendant. My staff and I had labored over it for weeks, night and day. This time, we had focused more on process and justice, and less on facts of the case. I need to show the judge how unjust the process had been.

In a single brief section, it lays out the argument in three parts. The first two are arguments on behalf of fairness: "The Rule of Law Demands That the Accused Be Heard," followed by "Justice Demands That The Accused Should Know the Charges Against Him." The third and final section was a short and respectful plea for the court to estop the responsible parties from any further punishment and suffering until the case could be heard.

> Therefore, the Defendant hereby respectfully requests that the Court order all suffering, nightmares, loss, and uncertainty of future to cease until and unless:
>   (1) Prosecution brings forth, clearly and succinctly, all charges brought against the Defendant; and
>   (2) Court allows the Defendant to present his defense in full before the Court and all interested parties.

Once the judge has seen that the process itself prejudiced the system against my client, he would issue an injunction. Then, and only then, would I turn to the facts and issues of the case. A win on this first motion would be a crucial step, because a win on a preliminary matter often led to a win on the merits.

I know the counter-arguments, of course—I had read the opposing counsel's response. But his arguments are, as usual, specious and ambiguous, discussing the legal system as a whole rather than how it has been applied in this particular case.

Today, I will argue the intent of the law, public policy considerations, and other legal phrases that we all understand but do not mean much to anyone else.

I look up at the clock. It is nine-twenty-three. As I watch, wondering if the clock is functioning, the large hand clicks to nine-twenty-four. No one else is present except for the bailiff.

I call out. "Officer Rahab? A word?"

He nods, places his pen down with care, and makes his way through the dim courtroom.

"Yes, counsel?"

"Am I correct that the hearing was to begin at nine?"

"Yes, counsel."

"Once again, neither the prosecuting attorney nor the judge has arrived. Is there something I should know?"

He shrugs. "It is as I have told you. The prosecuting attorney and the judge are the same person. So, if the judge is late, then, by the laws of the universe, the prosecuting—"

"Yes, yes, no need to repeat. Tell me, will they arrive soon?"

"I have no way of knowing, counsel."

"Will they arrive at all?"

"I have no way of knowing, counsel."

I blow air out of my mouth in exasperation. "Can't you find out? Can't you make a call? Aren't you responsible for order and process in the courtroom?"

He looks shocked. "Yes, sir, that is my bailiwick."

I look at him carefully. Is he attempting a pun?

"Make a call, then, officer!"

"Oh, no, sir. I cannot disturb them."

I stare at Officer Rahab, wondering what he actually does in this courtroom.

"Is there anything you can tell me?" I pause. "Wait a minute. Did you say you could not call 'them'?"

"Him, sir."

I shake my head and avoid the temptation to argue. "Should I wait? Should I leave? Should I reschedule?"

"That's up to you, counsel. The hearing will take place when the judge decides it will. That is the law."

"You are saying that when the judge and the prosecuting attorney *feel* like holding a hearing, it will take place?"

"Oh, no, sir. Only the judge decides when hearings are held."

I sit back. "You told me that they were one and the same."

He frowns. "Well, yes, sir, they are. But the judge schedules hearings."

I throw my hands up. "Is there someone else I can talk to, another judge, a clerk, anyone? Some other motion I can file to get the case heard? I just want my client to learn the charges against him! Is that so much to ask? Can you at *least* get me a list of charges?"

"No, sir, I do not have access to those records."

"What? Aren't they public records? Can't I make a request?"

"No, sir, that is the purview of the prosecutor alone. And the judge must approve it."

I stand. "No legal system works like this! What happened to the rule of law? To due process? To innocent until proved guilty?"

Officer Rahab is abashed. "I'm sorry, counsel. I am not a lawyer, just a mere law enforcement official. Besides, every defendant is guilty."

"Excuse me?!"

"Of course. That's why we have hearings."

It is clear he lacks the most basic understanding of how the law works. How was he ever appointed as a bailiff—let alone kept the job? Maybe he is related to the judge. Or the prosecutor. (Or both, I remind myself.)

"Officer Rahab, I am quite unhappy with this court and the judge. In fact, I am furious at this entire system. How can such as system engender faith? Where is justice? Where is fairness? My client doesn't even know why he is being punished, and he can't get a simple hearing to plead his defense!"

117

"I am sorry you feel that way, sir." His unflappable deference is replaced with indignation. "This court is considered the most just and fair in the jurisdiction. The judge is well-known for his great discretion in offering stays, suspended sentences, and outright dismissals at the least sign of a valid defense. Sometimes he even dismisses cases when the defendant is merely pathetic."

"I find that quite difficult to believe. He doesn't even show up at the hearings!"

Officer Rahab stands silent.

I sit back down. "Is there nothing, nothing at all, that you can do for me, Officer?"

He thinks for a moment. "Do you have any exhibits or witness lists? I can record them and prepare copies. Might save time if the judge shows up."

"If?! Did you say *if* the judge shows up? Are you implying that he might not ever appear?"

"I did not say that, counsel. But it is entirely up to him. Do you have any exhibits or witness lists?"

I sigh and look away. My client's life is shattered, broken beyond reason through events out of his control. So be it—bad things happen. But not to be heard? Not to be told why? Was there no hope of justice—ever?

I feel quite bitter on behalf of my client.

"Fine." I reach down into my briefcase and pull out a sheet of paper.

"This is my list of witnesses."

He takes the sheet from me and begins reading.

"Ellie, Zig, a plant and a spider located at mile marker 564 of Highway 10…" He looks up. "Is this your complete list?"

"For now. As you can see, they are all hostile witnesses. In fact, I intend to name them in a cross-complaint."

"I will make sure this is filed. Exhibits?"

"Just one at the moment." I retrieve a paperback and hand it to him. It is well-worn.

He takes it and reads the cover. "*The Trial.* Never heard of it."

"I'm not surprised."

"Very well. Is there anything else I can do?"

"One more thing." I close my briefcase and stand. "When you *do* speak with the judge, tell him that I plan on filing a complaint with the Bar and begin a recall. He is not fit to be a judge. I would challenge *him* to debate me, in fact, on the merits of due process."

Rahab's eyes grow wide and he takes a step back as if I had pushed him. "Counsel! No one ever—"

"Just tell him. It's time someone stood up to this outrage. On behalf of my client and all the others who have been and will be mistreated."

He shakes his head. "You are taking your life into your own hands."

I laugh in his face. "With pleasure! It's about time!"

46

"Jay! Wake up, we're in Pomona."

I took a deep breath and sat up. The door frame I had been leaning against made the side of my face hurt, and my right arm was tingling from the elbow down. I glanced over at Zig.

"Where to, bud? Bus station is up ahead." He indicated with a tilt of his head. "Or somewhere else?"

"No, the bus station is fine."

I was sick of bus stations. Buses, people, cars, land, cities, sky, sun, moon, and everything else. I had been out just over twenty-four hours, and I was sick of it all. But I didn't know where else to go.

I've got to force myself to make those calls.

We drove a few more blocks and turned left onto a one-way street. He maneuvered the car close to the curb and pulled up to a little tram stop with a Spanish-style sloped roof.

"Station is there." He pointed past the stop to a building that looked like an old mission, set back from the street fifty or sixty yards. A sidewalk led to wooden front doors. Manicured grass spread out on either side of the walkway.

I opened the door, stepped out, pulled my bags out of the back seat, and set them on the sidewalk. I leaned back in through the passenger door.

"Thank you, Zig."

He smiled without emotion. "Sure. Best of luck to you, Jay. Remember what I said—we can all work our way back from selfishness and stupidity, just got to admit it. It's all about karma."

I nodded. I was in no shape for an argument. I shut the door and watched as he drove away.

47

The station was almost empty. It was clean, but the city leaders and the architects may have been drunk, in my opinion. Dark, rough wood ceiling beams. A faux tile floor, Spanish style. A fake old-timey crank phone on one wall, a wagon wheel beside. A hitching rail stood just inside the door (inside!). In direct contrast to the homespun elements was the modern art on the walls, computers on the desk, and a flatscreen TV. It felt disjointed, as if it had been thrown together with no thought for order. "Hey, beamed ceilings would be nice." "I like modern art." Yet another: "Let's put a big screen TV here for the customers." Behold, the Pomona bus station.

There was a bank of three pay phones on the far wall. Without giving myself time to ruminate, I went to the closest and, with notebook in hand, called the direct line to Jocelyn's office.

"Good morning, this is Ben. How may I help you?"

"Hello, this is Jay Adam. Jocelyn, please."

"I'm sorry there's no Jocelyn here."

"Is this Pemmer and Schmidt?"

"Yes, it is, but there is no Jocelyn here." He hung up.

I went to the next number in my book. I am an automaton. No thinking, no consideration, just do the task until you get a hit.

"First American Bank Anaheim, how may I direct your call?"

"Anthony Stein, please."

"May I ask who is calling?"

"Jay Adam."

"One moment, Mr. Adam."

I had not spoken or heard from Anthony since I was first arrested. No letters, no visits, nothing. But we had been friends and doing business since—

"I am sorry, sir, he is not available at the moment. May I take a message?"

"Yes, please tell him that I called. Jay Adam. I'll call back later."

Anthony was always busy. Probably in a meeting.

Okay, let's try Mayor Austin. I know he retired almost ten years ago. I had always supported him, and we served together in government. He might have some ideas or a place to stay.

No answer. Not even voice mail. I hung up and leaned my head against the phone case. I wanted to scream at someone—anyone—to stop fighting me and let me get on with life.

I went over and sat on a bench. I'm being ridiculous. There's nothing personal going on. Some puzzles are more challenging than others.

48

Stella lay in bed, a strand of damp hair stuck to her fore-head. Jay reached over and tucked it behind her ear. She looked at him with tired but happy eyes.

He smiled. "How are you feeling?"

"Tired, but wonderful. Is she really beautiful?"

"She is. So beautiful."

She raised her head and looked around. "Where is she?"

"Right there, hon. In the bassinet beside you."

Stella reached out and put her hand on the bassinet. "I am so excited to see what little Keren will become."

"She will make us proud. I know it."

✻

"Sign here, Mr. Adam."

He took the pen from the attorney and signed his name at the bottom of the page. The attorney took the docu-ment and pen from him and placed them in his briefcase.

"Congratulations, Mr. Adam. You are now the Presi-dent and CEO of Adam Enterprises."

Jay laughed. "Thanks, Stephen. Not the first time I have done this, as you know."

"But this one is going to turn out much better than those stillbirths."

"Let's not be too harsh! I got all my money out of Motor Stockades. True, Powerhouse Service did not work out so well—to put it mildly. All were part of this learning experience." He clapped Stephen on the back. "Maybe because you weren't my attorney from the beginning?"

"I am sure that was it. Now, let's celebrate." He reached into a cabinet behind his desk and pulled out a bottle, which he set between them, along with two tumblers.

Jay raised his eyebrows. "Rip Van Winkle Reserve? You *are* feeling good."

"I have high hopes for this venture, Jay." He pulled the stopper and poured two amber fingers. "I think you've really hit it out of the park this time." He pushed a glass towards Jay.

Jay picked it up tapped it against Stephen's glass. "To hitting a home run, then."

❊

"Is the doctor on his way?" Stella said as she entered the room, pulling off her jacket and scarf. She glanced over at the man lying in the hospital bed, eyes closed, tubes in his mouth and in both arms. Monitors with blinking graphs and indicators beeped softly.

Jay nodded.

"Did they give you *any* indication?"

"No. I try not to read too much into their words or facial expressions."

Stella went to the side of the bed. She took the man's hand and stroked it. He did not respond. She placed his hand down with care and went to the window. "Can I open these?"

"Sure."

Light broke into the room like a new dawn, bright and cheerful. Stella sat down beside Jay. "Isn't that better?"

He smiled and leaned over to kiss her.

"Jay, I have hope that he'll get through this one. He always has before. Your brother is so strong."

"I know. It's just that, someday, it'll catch up with him. Too much damage, too many surgeries."

"But not this time." She reached up and turned his face to hers. She fixed her eyes on his. "Not this time."

He smiled at her. "I hope you are right. The promotion—it's everything he's worked for these last fifteen years."

"He'll be able to enjoy it."

They both jumped as the door flew open and a white-smocked doctor entered, stethoscope swinging, clipboard in hand. "Good morning, " he said. He was not smiling.

49

A noise startled me awake. Someone had just come into the bus station and dropped their luggage to the floor.

I blinked my eyes. After a night like last night, I should not sit in a quiet place unless I want to sleep. My notebook had fallen on the floor. I picked it up and went back over to the phones.

"Good afternoon, Law Offices of James R. Munro. How may I help you?"

"Hi, this is Jay Adam again. I wonder if Mr. Munro might have some time to meet with me today or tomorrow?"

"His calendar is full for the rest of the week. Would you like to leave a message or call back?"

"Yes, you told me that yesterday. I hoped something might have opened up. I only need fifteen minutes."

"I am sorry, Mr. Adam."

"Okay. How about next Thursday?"

"He is will be out of town until the first."

"What? You told me he had an opening on Thursday."

"That was yesterday, Mr. Adam. Something came up since then."

"Something?" This was starting to sound like a put-off.

"Yes, Mr. Adam." A sharpness crept into her voice. "Something."

"I'll call back later."

I hung up and tried Anthony at the bank again. Still not available. I tried his cell phone, too, but it went to voice mail. A moment of paranoia came over me, but I remembered that he could not know that the number appearing on his cell phone was me.

I went over to a giant map on the wall. A red star had been stuck on "Pomona," right where I stood in this building on West First Street. Little yellow and white flags appeared all over the rest of the map. They were not in neat rows or lines. Some of the pins were different sizes, and even the yellows were different shades. One blue flag was stuck in Carson. Why was Carson blue? They were not spaced evenly. It was like someone had played darts—and wasn't very good at it.

Where to? Home? Or one of the surrounding towns? Somewhere farther away? I'll have to stay in a motel, but unless I get some work, I can't do that for long.

It doesn't matter right now. The next stop is Union Station. I'll make some more calls from there. Surely I'll be able to reach to *someone* eventually.

I bought a ticket for Union and lugged my bags over to the bench. It had only been a day and a half. Can't expect anyone to be waiting by their phones. They all have jobs, families, and responsibilities.

Of course, I had made many of these same calls in the weeks before my release. With the same results. Maybe I should have been trying to contact these people during all the years I was away. But it didn't seem necessary back then. What would I have said? "Hi, this is Jay. Just checking in. I'll be here for many more years."

I wondered how long I could just stay here, on this bench. I'd have to get up to use the restroom. Or not. I'd need to get up and eat. Or not. Maybe I could go on a hunger strike, refusing to move from this bench until things were set right. Until someone would talk to me.

I pictured myself in tattered and soiled clothes. Emaciated. Dry, cracked lips. Stiff and sore from sitting on a historical reproduction of a wooden bench. How long before someone came to help? How long could I last?

50

She picks up her coffee cup and holds it front of her face. She examines the rim. Taking a careful sip, she closes her eyes for a moment, then opens them and sets the cup down with a delicate touch. She turns her clear, blue eyes on me and shakes her head.

"That was quite a show at the bar."

I look down at the table. My plate is empty. Like a dog had licked it clean. A cup sits by the plate, filled with hot, dark coffee.

I shrug.

She lets out a small, rather unladylike guffaw. "It isn't good to have so much anger."

"I think I have an excellent reason."

"No, you don't. Look…" She reaches across and takes my hand. I look up, surprised at this intimate gesture from a someone I just met.

"You aren't better than anyone else. You aren't immune." She pulls her hand away and sits back. I notice there is a man next to her in the booth. I am pretty sure he hadn't been there before. He is quite obese. Morbidly so. Ellie is squeezed up against the wall by the window, turned almost sideways for the lack of room. The rolls of fat threaten to pop the seams of his clothes and squash her against the window.

I look at his face, but it is blank except for a vacant smile. He looks past me into the diner.

"Who is this?" I ask.

"He's quite successful. Can't you see? He is the most successful man I have ever met. Look at him."

His clothes are of the finest cloth. His shirt is a classic blue dress shirt, obviously expensive with its high thread count and hand-stitching. One arm rests on the table like a branch of an oak tree. I can read the label on his shirt cuff.

Finamore
Slim
$825.00

Part of his corpulent belly rests on the table. His trousers are pulled up so high that I can see the waistband. A plastic tag is attached to it with a string. I read the price: $1175.

127

His plump wrist is encircled by a gaudy watch, with a white face and gold band. There is no tag. I look up at his eyes. On someone else, they would have looked large. I could only think "beady."

The eyes turn to me. His smile grows larger. "Patel Philippe. Tiffany."

"What?"

He raises his chins five millimeters. "The watch."

"Oh." I look back down. He wears gold rings on each finger, each the size of the tires on Zig's Camino. Gold and silver chains encircle his other wrist, like snow chains. I begin to count, but lose my place after three hundred.

I look back at Ellie.

"See? Quite successful and wealthy. Yet he suffers. He makes terrible mistakes in relationships. He takes care of people, and he has loved women. But then he ignores, betrays, or persecutes them. He cannot find love because he cannot change his behavior. He has been to counseling; he has been to seminars; he has read a library of books. He still screws up. But he's the most brilliant financier the world has ever known."

"What's your point?"

She leans forward, placing her small hand on the table and spreading her thin fingers, painted at a salon by a woman from the Philippines who doesn't speak English. Ellie pays her $40. "You are not immune to wrongdoing, Jay."

I turn my head to look around the diner. It is just as busy as it had been when I arrived. I look for the waitress—I want apple pie.

"Jay?"

I turn back at the sound of her voice. The wealthy smart fat lonely man is gone.

"You must be brave. Patient. Everything will work out."

"I think I've been quite patient."

"But you're bitter. You're not a bad person. Not like this guy. Everyone says, 'Jay's a great guy…loving husband and father…a great boss…compassionate to those in need…gives generously.' Everyone knows that."

"Nice to hear. So what?"

"Right there!" She raises a hand to point at me. I want to break her lovely finger.

"*That* is your problem. The bitterness is worse than anything wrong you've done. And I have to say…" She sits back and scrunches her mouth sideways, as if fighting with the words inside.

I pick up my cup, take a sip, then place it back in its saucer. Into that perfectly round indentation that fit precisely into the perfect little rim on the bottom of the perfect cup.

She huffs a resigned sigh and sits forward with boldness. "I'll say it. Your actions show you are neither innocent nor wise. Innocent people are calm because they know everything will be okay. Wise people know that good people don't suffer without a reason."

I feel frustration and anger building. Like molten lava deep within a crust of stone. What she said sounded logical. But it was pure pablum. Puerile poppycock. I slid across the booth seat and stood up, banging my thighs against the side of the table and causing all the dishes to rattle as if in an earthquake. I grab an empty water glass and—

51

I came awake and raised myself from the bench. Light-headedness came over me. I thought I might fall. I sat back down heavily. Slow and deep breaths. Was I going to faint? I braced myself in the corner between the back and the arm of the bench. That helped. I closed my eyes.

I had had hangovers before; this did not feel like a hangover. My heart was racing, and I had a terrible sense of foreboding. Maybe I'm having a heart attack. I wonder how close is the nearest Urgent Care. I should…should…

It came in waves. Should I yell for help? I forced myself to slow my breathing. Deep breaths. Slow in…slow out…relax.

Since my bout with the disease, I so easily become fearful of physical problems. Almost hypochondriacal.

Calmer now. Good. Probably just frustration. People speak so easily of human difficulty. As if the answer is simple. It's not a single problem with a single solution. It has a lot of pieces to it. It is complex. But someone keeps messing with me. Hiding pieces. Removing pieces out I thought were in place. Laughing at me. I won't stand for it. Someone's going to answer for this. And I am going to win!

The panic returned. Breathe.

Breathe.

Slow. Steady. Calm.

I want Stella back. I want Keren and Ally. My company. My people.

Or maybe just someone to understand. Then I could die in peace.

I pitch the last shovelful of dirt out of the deep pit in the earth. I lean on the shovel for a moment, catching my breath.

Looking up, I see it is getting dark. I toss the shovel out and climb the wooden ladder. I knock the dirt from my shoes against the nearest tombstone.

The people are still gathered all around, watching, at a distance. A few had given up and gone home. There are still enough to make a large circle around me and my work.

They are no longer laughing and jeering as they had at first. Some are murmuring to each another. Others stand with an amused look. I catch one man's eyes; he shakes his head in derision.

I grab the handholds at one end of the coffin. It is far heavier than I expected. I tug and jerk at it, but it hardly moves. Some in the crowd laugh.

Two four-wheeled braces are sitting near the pile of dirt, shovels, and rolls of fake grass. I bring them beside the coffin and, using the shovel as a lever, I kick a brace under one end of the coffin. I do the same at the other end.

Now it is easy to move, except for a couple of bumps and dips in the grass. I line it up parallel to the pit.

Using the shovel again, I kick one brace out and push the end of the coffin until it falls in. The other end sticks up, like a car that has careened into a ditch. I brace my shoulder against the upper end and strain with all my might, pushing it towards the empty end of the pit. The crowd begins to jeer. Breathing hard, I give it a last shove. It falls with a crash into the pit. Looking inside, I see it lies in the pit, sideways at a forty-five-degree angle.

I climb down, and, using the shovel again as a lever, pry at it until it slips sideways.

It is still not level, but enough for me to open the lid.

53

The bus rolled along surface streets, stopping at bus stops along West First Street. I sat by the window with my bags on the seat beside me as a barrier against any potential seat-mates. At each stop, I fixed my stare out the window to avoid any eye contact with new passengers.

Something feels wrong. A ball of hot lava sits inside me, creeping long tentacles from my belly into my chest cavity. Fingers of heat slide through my torso into my neck, arm and hip sockets. Through the flesh of my arms and hands and into each finger; down through my thighs, shins, feet and into each toe. It reaches six or seven hot tentacles through my neck and into my brain pan. If anyone bothered to look, I wondered if they could see the tips of the fiery feelers peeking out my mouth, nose, and ears.

You're a good man no one is perfect good people suffer but not for long and then everything is okay you just have to be patient there is always a reason do you believe in prayer there is no result without a cause we reap what we sow your choices led to this wickedness has its price linguistic gymnastics logical poppycock excrement of excuses actions have consequences our destinies are aligned with our merits a bad life apologize a bad life and change your ways a bad life it caught up with you secret sin can't get away with it forever that's how the universe works—

We stopped at a traffic light, about five cars back. Ahead at the corner, I saw a woman come running out of a storefront. She was large, and wore a lovely silk blouse with brown and black print. Her slacks were black and loose. Rings sparkled on her hands, visible even from this distance. She ran in that awkward shuffle of those wearing high heels— raising the knees a little, kicking each leg forward at each step, shoes almost dragging on the cement.

She waved her hands. I listened, but even with the window open, she was too far away for me to hear. She clearly wanted someone to pay attention, but everyone ignored her, focused only on their own business. Turning down the sidewalk in the direction of the bus, she ran to a nearby man and grabbed his arm. She pleaded, but he shook her off without a thought. She turned to a young woman in jeans and a jacket walking the opposite direction. She beseeched, arms up and palms out, but the woman turned her head and kept walking.

The traffic light changed. The bus sighed and the hydraulic brakes hissed. We inched forward, jerking as the driver shifted gears. The woman had now turned back in the other direction, shuffle-running down the sidewalk, reaching out to people one after the other. She ran a gauntlet of indifference, swimming upstream in a watershed of insouciance.

As the bus drew alongside and began to pass, she turned towards the street and dropped her arms in frustration. As I came parallel with her, her eyes caught mine. I saw panic and frustration. I saw myself through her eyes: a face behind a bus window. Unlike the others, I am looking at her, but my eyes are dead and expressionless. I turned my head to watch her as we pass. She raised her head to the sky. I saw words form on her lips. A cry.

A few more blocks and the driver maneuvered the bus onto the entrance ramp to the 71 Freeway. Soon we were bouncing along at a decent clip. The schedule said it would take an hour and a half to get to Union Station with stops in between, but that depended on whether the traffic through Los Angeles was worse or better than usual.

The smoothness of the freeway and the steady humming of the tires on the tarmac was mesmerizing. I closed my eyes.

look at a woman with a leering eye the eye must come out rip it out with forceps eye roots dangling bloody do it again the other one comes out and then you'll never do it again one bad word one swear word the scalpel comes and slices it right off back just after that thing that connects the tongue to the bottom of the mouth you'll never swear again steal an apple from a street vendor out comes the hatchet and whack just behind the wrist grab it quick and bandage or there's a bleed out but you'll never take again I bet took a wrong branch finally made my way back on the right course but then there was a washout and I had to backtrack and loop around and over and then back on the path but there was a tree fallen so I had to work my way through the forest and rockslide but cut and bruised back out on the path but now it is getting too dark and the wolves are coming—

54

The angel descends from the white, fluffy cloud which sails above me in a blue-black sky. Her eyes do not look down at me; his head turns from side to side. A robe-like light envelopes her body; he is laced with a translucent rainbow of colors. White and blue and red and green and orange and yellow whirl and intertwine with a slow grace, as if a gentle wind blows the rays of light. It reminds me of a television commercial for a vacation or a sleeping medication, but better than any producer or human technology could make. It is technicolor and more; it is 3D and more; it is high-definition and beyond. It is beautiful.

I squint in the brightness and fumble at my shirt pocket for sunglasses which are not there. Oh, yes, I left them on my desk in the office. It had already been dark when I left and I didn't need them. Or maybe I forgot them. I wasn't thinking ahead.

The angel wears an expression of concern. As I gazed at the beatific face, I see her eyes are scanning back and forth, looking in all directions around him. She takes no notice of the huge black rocks that ring the carpet of green. Nor does he pay any attention to me as I sit on the grass. Looking out, I see nothing. The magnificent creature of light continues to float down until she is in front and above me about fifteen feet away, like a million fireflies coming to life as dusk falls.

I lift my gaze beyond him to the ocean. It is roiling and angry. Green, blue, black, gray, and white swirl and crash and surge and pull. The wind picks up and blows as a fierce as a gale. I feel a touch of fright, though my little island outcropping seems stable. I look at the angel; neither her station-keeping or his glowing ribbons of light are affected. She continues to search the ocean with his piercing gaze.

The wind increases. My clothes whip and buffet my body. I pull my legs up to my chest and wrap my arms around them. If I stood, the windstorm would knock me over.

The angel stops scanning and focuses on a point to the left and slightly behind her. I squint, looking out to sea.

The sky is dark gray and black. The only light comes from the angel, but even that is diminished, as if the sky, clouds, sea, and wind are sucking the light away, like a vacuum.

Far out to sea a figure rises out of the water. It keeps coming. Up, up, up, breaching the surface like a whale. Far larger than a whale. It falls back into the water, creating high waves that race away from the black body. As its head nears the surface, it dips down, diving deep under the thrashing waves. Its back raises up and follows the head. Slow, slow, slow, but with magnificent power, its tail follows the rest down into the water. With a final slap, the tail—as wide as a bus—slices into the sea. The nasty, churning waves are no match for this monstrous creature. The powerful wind is no match for its massive bulk. As soon as the tail disappears into the maelstrom, the head appears again, closer, breaching the surface like a black metal missile. The sequence repeats.

It is coming towards me.

I snap my head back to the angel and see he now has her eyes locked onto mine. I gasp in surprise, but the angel does not react, maintaining the same expression.

"What is it?" I scream into the cacophony, but the words rip away as soon as spoken, as if Ninlil herself has reached down and swiped them away. I try to shuffle back, using my arms to push, and find that I cannot move. The mighty wind pushes against me no matter which direction I try.

I look out again, but cannot spot the creature. I look right and left with increasing panic. A movement catches my attention—not fifty feet from the tiny basalt isle upon which I sit. A swirling and whirling circle of bubbles and spray and waves.

It comes up, up, up out of the dark foaming water, throwing spray away from its black body like rats escaping from a storm drain. Shiny silver rivulets stream down its sides. It pauses at the top of its leap. A pregnant pause. A calm before the storm. A fermata before the coda.

I am trapped like a hunted animal.

It holds there, a terrible and magnificent and monstrous caricature of a porpoise, waiting for someone to throw it a fish. But this creature has no playfulness in its soul. I am afraid to look away; I am afraid to keep watching. It begins to bend down toward me, and I see that a crown sits on its head—a black crown, made of rock and reef.

The cavernous mouth opens, and the creature moves its massive head back and forth, the red and black darkness inside broken only by jagged sharp teeth. Water and saliva and bits of seaweed slosh about inside its maw. Surely this is death.

The winds coalesce around the creature, like a tornado or hurricane with the monster as the eye. Wind mixes with sea foam, and as it spins around, it begins to take shape. Amongst the spinning circle of wind and water, I see fish, seaweed, bits of wood, flailing birds, and seashells. One unusually large object flies by, I cannot discern its shape. Each time it passes in front of me it is closer, spiraling outward. Each revolution gives me a glimpse of more details. It is a section of a large tree trunk. No, it is a huge, tall person! Then it is a wide, full tree, with wood and leaves and roots.

The next time it comes about, I hear it screaming.

"…rocks cannot be removed from their place…" The voice trails away as it disappears around the back side of the tornado and the sea monster. As it comes by again, it screams, "…wrong wrong wrong…"

The next time it orbits toward me it is so far out of the swirling hurricane that it breaks free. It rockets at me, but I am powerless to move. I cannot even raise my hands and arms before my face. I close my eyes and feel its mass go by, still screaming.

I turn and look back, but see nothing but churning black sea. In front of me, the angel continues to regard me without expression. With my eyes and face I plead as best I can. I feel pain in my right hand. Turning the palm up, I look down. Through the driving wind and water, I see that the skin of my palms is torn, as if I had taken a nasty slide across an asphalt parking lot.

I look back at the sea monster and its hurricane shroud. A building is caught in the tornado. As it circles and comes closer with each revolution, I see it is an office building—four or five stories tall. It spins and tumbles, it falls apart, it disintegrates. Pieces fly away and join the circling debris field that makes me think of the rings of Saturn.

I smell burning sulfur. I look down to see that I am smoldering. I feel no pain, but I know a terrible disease is coursing through me. Like a shot of Schnapps on a cold rainy day, coursing down the throat. Except this disease is flowing through my veins and arteries, through my lymphatic, endocrine, digestive, and even integumentary systems.

The angel lifts his arm and holds out a hand. I glance at the storm-whale. The angel speaks. Clear but not loud, piercing but not unpleasant, firm but not unfriendly.

"You are sick. You are dying."

I yell with all my might. No words, just a primal scream of anguish. The goddess of wind rips it from my mouth once again. I am voiceless in a sinister whirlwind.

The angel's voice comes again as clear as a loudspeaker next to my ear.

"You have no home, no work, no status."

I scream again. I don't care if she can't hear me.

"Your wife and children are dead."

I grab my knees with both arms and pull them into my torso, putting my head down to make myself into a tight ball.

"You spread death."

A powerful blast of heated air knocks onto my back, arms and legs flailing. I raise up on my elbows.

The angel is floating away, still gazing at me. Up and back, slow and steady. The monster begins to tip back, away from me, gaining speed as it falls. The maelstrom around it is gone; debris floats in the sea below. The water beneath its bulk parts and crashes outward on either side, a foamy double arc of watery chaos. The wind begins to abate.

I put my head down and sob.

55

Union Station was smaller than I remembered, though it was larger and nicer than my other stops. Its Spanish Mission/Art Deco style was interesting, if a little strange. I left the Patsaouras Bus Plaza and walked past the Metrolink gates to the main area between the two patios. There were not many people, and I was able to find an empty chair by the windows. I set my bags down and settled into the dark leather and wood seats on the end of a row. It was so comfortable that I considered taking a nap.

But it was time to make some firm plans. Before I bought a ticket, I needed to decide where to go. It was time to get serious about calling someone who could help me. I need to be more confident and firm.

Leaving my bags in the seat, I went to the phone booths. Standing with the receiver wedged between my neck and shoulder, I opened my notebook to the first page of names.

I dialed Anthony's number, listened to the recording, and typed in my code to charge the call to my bank account.

"First American Bank Anaheim. How may I direct your call?"

"Anthony Stein, please."

"May I ask who is calling?"

"Jay Adam."

"One moment, Mr. Adam."

I waited.

"I am sorry, sir, he is unavailable at the moment. May I take a message?"

"But is he in?"

"He is unavailable at the moment. May I take a message?"

"Bear with me, please. I am an old friend who has been trying to reach him for some time. Is there any way—"

"Mr. Stein is aware of your calls, sir."

I didn't know what to say.

"Sir?"

"Yes, yes. I—is he in? Can I speak with him?"

"I am sorry sir, he is unavailable at the moment. May I take a message?"

It was my turn to hang up. I stared at the phone, so large and out of place in a modern society where everyone had cell phones. Black metal sides. Shiny metal front. Big silver buttons with the black letters. It didn't belong.

I took a breath and looked to the next name. Cristy. I didn't have her new number, and she was on the other side of the country, anyway. Next on the list was John Goulden. Dead.

Joleen.

"Good afternoon, J&T Catering and Services, how may I help you?"

"I'd like to speak to Joleen, please."

"One moment, sir."

I waited, tapping the phone case with my other hand.

"Hello?"

"Joleen? This is Jay Adam."

"Oh! Jay…how are you? Are you still…?" Awkward pause.

"No, I am out. Looking for a place to stay."

Silence. "Um…glad to hear you are out…listen, I am quite busy right now—big party coming up this week—you know how it is. Could you call me back later, maybe?"

"Well, yes, I can, but I only—"

"Good. Give me a few days and give me a call. Hope you are doing well." She hung up without waiting for me to respond.

Okay. Expect some brush-offs. She was more of business contact than a friend. Next on the list is the Chief.

"I'm sorry, Mr. Adam, he says he is happy for you, but he cannot have any contact with you."

"Why not?"

"Conflict of interest, he said."

Mayor Austin was next.

"I'm sorry, Mr. Austin is not taking any calls at the moment."

"Did you tell him it was me, Jay Adam?"

"Yes, Mr. Adam. He said no calls at the moment."

The lava monster in my belly began to squirm and writhe. I felt like I was standing on the deck of a ship at sea, struggling to keep my balance. Struggling to understand.

I took another deep breath and told myself that some rejections mean nothing. Keep going until you succeed.

Next on the list was Stella's parents. Our last conversation, almost nine years ago, was a soul-wrenching disaster. They both had their say while I listened. Like standing at the business end of a fire hose with the valve on full. I figured I'd let them express their horror at losing a daughter and grandchildren. I was an easy target. But when they were finished flaying me alive, they hung up without a goodbye. There was never any answer to my calls or letters after that.

Time heals all wounds, right? I dialed the number and began rehearsing. *Hi Joan* or maybe *John this is Jay—Jay Adam.* I should say my whole name. *I know it has been a long time and perhaps you don't want to hear—*

"We are sorry, that number is no longer in service or has been—"

Munro was next. I skipped it and went to the following number: Pedro Rodriguez. An old employee who had been my right-hand man when we first started Adam Enterprises.

He hung up when I announced my name.

Peter Foucault.

His wife told me never to call again. I slammed the phone and turned around. Peter had been down-and-out himself. I co-signed a loan for him—even paid a few months when he was broke. Before I went to prison, he called and wished me good luck on the appeal. Thanked me for helping him.

I turned back to the phones, lifted the receiver, and dialed Ed Zohn's mother. I had it because I had checked up on her many times after his death. Until I left, in fact. She was no more than an acquaintance. I was not even sure she *could* help. No matter. She's next.

"Hello?"

"Hello? Ruth?"

"Yes?"

"Hi, Ruth, this is Jay Adam. I imagine this call is a surprise—"

"Who?"

"Jay Adam. Your son's boss from way back, I know it has been—"

She hung up.

Sidura was next. I couldn't even remember her last name. She was an ex-employee who had quit when she got married. I attended the wedding and gave them a beautiful gift.

"Hello?"

"Sidura, hello. This is Jay Adam. Your old boss?"

Silence.

"Sidura? Remember me? Jay Adam? I am sorry to bother you—"

"Yes, I remember, Mr. Adam."

"Oh, good, well how are you?"

"Um...I can't talk right now, I—"

"Wait, wait, wait, I just got out and I wanted—" Click.

The panic and the multi-tentacled monster inside was winning the battle. All I knew to do was to keep dialing.

"I am sorry, there is no one by that name at this number."

Next.

No answer.

Next

"...is not taking calls at this moment..."

Next.

Hung up.

Next.

"...is not available...leave a message after the tone..."

Next. Next. Next. Next. Next.

᛭

I dropped to my knees on the floor. The receiver swung from its cable, creaking as it reached its apogee, like a bandit swinging from a noose. I had no one else to call. Everyone moved, rejected me, or died.

"Maybe someone *is* out to get you."

"Like someone is out to break you."

"It's almost like a set-up."

Like a gas can touched by a spark, my self-pity and de-jection turned to anger. I climbed back to my feet and flipped the pages back to Munro's number.

"Law Offices of James R. Munro. How may I help you?"

"Hi. This is Jay Adam. I was a client of Mr. Munro's about ten years ago. We won an appeal recently. I was released yesterday, and I need to speak with him. I have tried a few times—"

"Yes, Mr. Adam, I remember. Just one moment." Monophonic music recorded in a tin can replaced the operator. Longer than my other calls. Maybe he *will* talk to me. Perhaps he *was* busy those other times. I'm sure he has a whole list of resources and options for a person in my situation—he's been practicing law for over thirty years.

"Mr. Adam?"

"Yes?"

"Mr. Munro is not available at the moment. May I take a message?"

"Not available?! I know what that *means*, miss. Please tell him I need to talk with him. Only a few minutes. Can't he spare just a few minutes?"

"I am sorry, sir. Mr. Munro is not available at the moment. May I take a message?"

"I have left message after message! He got plenty of my money ten years ago, can't he spare five minutes for me right now?!"

"I am sorry, sir, but he is not available. If you do not want to leave a message, I must end this call."

I slammed the receiver into its cradle and stormed back to my seat. My bags were where I had left them. I wished someone had stolen them. Why not? I'd *welcome* more misery. Bring it on!

I looked around the station. The few people sitting and walking paid no attention to my fury. It was a tempest to me; a teapot to them.

I slumped into the seat and closed my eyes. *I am invisible why no pity no pity steal my bags rip my clothes steal my life leave me alone no more of this retribution words judgments good suffer patience, reason prayer result cause sow choices wickedness consequences destinies merit apologize change your ways bad*

❉

With a start, I opened my eyes.

I don't need to go anywhere. I have nowhere to be. I don't belong to any place or any people.

It used to be so clear. Finish school and do well. Get a job and make money. Learn how to work. Get a promotion. Get a better job. Start a business, work hard. Take care of your spouse. Take care of your kids. Save money for emergencies. Plan for the future. Pay your taxes. Make a budget and keep to it. Be responsible. Help others. Persevere in the bad times, show gratitude for the good. It's how life works.

I believed what Ellie said in the diner. Everything had a purpose, even suffering.

I believed what Zig said at the bar. Admit your mistakes, make up for them, be better next time.

I believed everything came out in the laundry, as it should. Zig would call it karma. I called it the way the world worked. Justice.

I believed. I had believed. I had been believing. I used to believe. Once upon a time, I believed. At some point in the past, I believed. Not the perfect, not the present perfect, not the pluperfect, but the aorist, the imperfect, and the past tense.

I had believed. It was all logical, comforting, and reasonable—and dead wrong.

When the laundry comes out, sometimes it isn't even your laundry, and it can't be sorted, worn, or salvaged.

✳

I leaned forward with my head in my hands. My notebook lay on the floor, open to the last few pages. There was writing on the last page which should have been blank.

It was not my handwriting. I picked it up.

Peter McNally
Gerson and McNally Commercial Fishing Co
Fish Harbor, San Pedro

56

The courtroom is cool and quiet. The green, legal-sized folder on the table in front of me makes a nice contrast with the dark wood of the table. The table is made of hewn planks, nailed and stained. The nicks and gouges are a testimony of decades of use.

I do not have a new, carefully-written motion or brief. Instead, I have filed a one-page request to appear before the court on matters of procedure. I am asking for clarification of the case calendar, and how I had been in error by appearing twice with no judge or opposing counsel. (I decided to adopt the tactic of pretending it was my error.)

I look at the clock. It is nine-twenty-four. As I wonder if the clock is working, the large hand clicks to nine-twenty-five.

No one else is present, except for the bailiff. I call out to him.

"Officer Rahab? Any sign that the judge or the prosecutor will appear today?"

He looked up from his desk at the side of the courtroom. "It is as I have told you. The prosecuting attorney and the judge are the same person. So, if the judge is late or—"

"Will they appear today?"

He lips tightened into a thin line. "I have no way to know, counsel, as you are aware."

"Do they ever appear for scheduled hearings?"

"Of course they do! This is a court of law, after all."

I consider taking him to task on that assertion, but badgering him had not gotten me anywhere before. Filing well-researched and succinct arguments had not gotten me anywhere. So perhaps directly addressing the injustice of the system would have an effect.

"Thank you, Bailiff."

"I do believe a judge's clerk will be here today."

"Indeed? The judge's clerk?"

"One of them. He has thousands."

"Thousands?"

"Maybe tens of thousands. I don't know. But one of them is supposed to be here this morning."

I'll believe it when I see it.

I open the folder and flip through my previous motions and briefs. I had worked on them and reviewed them for so many hours, they were almost committed to memory. As I consider those painstakingly-created paragraphs, I see they are quite good. Well-structured argumentation. Sound research and citations—appropriate and on point. The text flows with enough legalese to keep it succinct without falling into the lawyer's trap of drowning in repetition and archaisms.

I stand and walk to the back of the courtroom to stretch my legs. I spin around and walk back down the middle aisle towards the Well. Then back. Officer Rahab looks up from his paperwork, sees I am not going to bother him, and returns to scribbling in a notebook.

I sit back down and flip through the documents again. I close the folder. I open it again. I close it. I am getting angry at this endless waiting and wondering. It borders on comedic absurdity.

The door to the judge's chambers opens. A young woman enters and mounts the steps to the judge's bench. Her dark hair is cropped short; a style that declares *I am a serious lawyer and on my way up in the system*. She wears a subtle application of makeup—enough to smooth out the features, but not enough to suggest glamor. She wants to portray that she is tough, no-nonsense, and smart.

She sets a stack of green legal folders on the judge's bench, off to one side. Still standing, she opens the one on top and begins to read, pen at ready.

I look at Officer Rahab and clear my throat. Twice. When he looks up, I nod towards the woman and raise my eyebrows. He looks at her, back to me, and nods.

I had hoped for an introduction. I wonder again about his job description and qualifications.

I push my chair back enough to stand and rise.

"Excuse me, miss?"

Her eyes flicker up at me and the return to folders and files. "Yes, counsel?"

"I am the defense counsel for the hearing on calendar at nine. This is the third time I have appeared, and neither the judge nor the prosecutor has shown up for any of them. I would like—"

"—As you may be aware, the prosecuting attorney and the judge are the same. So, if the judge is late, then, by the laws of the universe, the prosecuting attorney—"

"Yes, I am aware of that. But could—"

"The hearing will take place when the judge is present. That is the law. As you should know." She shoots a brief glance at me to punctuate the last sentence.

"Are you the judge's clerk?"

She stops and places her hands on the desk in front of her, on either side of the pile of files. She fixes me with a stare as if ready to do battle. "I am one of the Judge's clerks."

"I have filed several motions and requests. None of them have been heard. I have serious questions about the procedure in this court. I hope you can help me."

She does not move for ten or twelve seconds. Her eyes are on me, but I can see her mind is elsewhere. I almost hear the machinery clicking.

"Very well." She turns from the bench and descends to a small desk beside it. "Client name?" Sitting down in front of a computer, she begins to type. I tell her the name.

She utters a short chuckle. In any other circumstances, I'd ask what she found amusing. I keep it to myself. For now.

She leans in to peer at the screen and speaks to herself in a quiet voice I can barely hear. "Yes…complaint, answer…cross-complaint…MSJ…TRO…request for notice, request for adjudication, request…request…filing of exhibit—" She looks up.

"You filed *The Trial* as your only exhibit?"

"Yes, but there will be other exhibits later—there is no trial date yet, so there is no deadline for—"

"Yes, yes." She returns her attention to the screen. "And your last filing was a request for the court for clarification of…procedure and…and…"

"I am only asking the court to schedule a hearing in which the judge will make a ruling on my request to hear the charges read—we have still not heard the charges, and my client has been suffering—"

"Counsel, the rules are quite clear, and the procedures are posted online and available in the clerk's office. Can you not read?"

"Of course I can read, but my client is being mistreated and—"

"I am not the judge, counsel. It does no good to plead your case to me. Everything will be done in order and with great justice, as for every case that comes before this court. The judge's reputation for fairness and generosity is well known."

"But I haven't been *heard* even once! My client has not been charged, not been able to mount a defense, yet is already being punished! No jurisdiction that holds to the rule of law and due process—"

"Counsel."

Her voice has an almost magical power. I stop talking.

"Your case will be heard in due time. You may wait, or you may leave. You will be summoned at the appropriate time."

"But I *had* a hearing scheduled for today. Scheduled *by this court!* How can I know when—"

"I am sorry, we are quite busy."

I look around the courtroom in a show of disbelief for her benefit. It has no effect.

"Everything will be done properly and in the cause of justice." She returns to her stack of folders.

A blackness descends on the courtroom before I can yell "*Justice?!*" with appropriate sarcasm. After a few minutes, the figures depart, and a circle from a spotlight appears on a stage, illuminating a small desk, piled with papers and books. The amount of clutter keeps me from noticing, at first, that a man sits behind the desk. He is elderly with thinning gray hair. Reading glasses perch on his nose. A pipe is clamped between his teeth. Gray smoke writhes and curls about him, drifting up to join a large, thin cloud above his head. His head is bent down examining a piece of paper held in one unsteady hand.

The phone at his elbow rings. He jumps, curses, and drops the paper. He lifts the receiver to his ear. With his other hand, he takes the pipe out of his mouth.

"Hello…yes, Ilyov, how are you?…good, good…indeed I am, just reviewing a part of it…oh, quite fascinating—one moment…"

He places the pipe down on its side on top of a stack of books, taking care that none of the burning leaves spill out.

"Yes, let me find the paper…there has been so much…ah! Here it is…"

He pulls another single sheet from under a paperweight and leans back in his chair, holding it before his face. "It seems there was quite a bit of court miscon-duct...well, yes, both the judge and the prosecu-tion...sure... they are the same person, but that doesn't remove the requirement of justice, as you know...listen to this—not only was the court order made before any facts had been presented, but he never got to speak in court at all...yes...exactly...never...and there is more. The charges were never read to him or explained...quite unusual, quite...yes...mm-huh..."

He leans forward and places the paper on the pile in front of him. He looks up to the ceiling as he listens to the caller.

"I agree...I believe I can make a good case that he was treated unfairly...even if he was guilty—which, after sift-ing through all the evidence, I don't believe he was—he was denied justice twofold...indeed..." he laughs "yes, as a matter of fact, I plan on writing it up next month and publishing it. Too bad the poor sap is long dead..."

He continues talking, but the volume of his voice be-comes quieter, as if someone was turning a volume knob down. I lean forward, straining to hear. Finally, there is no sound, though his mouth is still moving. The stage goes dark and the full house lights come up in a flash.

A vast audience sits in theater seats between me and the stage. All are on their feet, applauding wildly, some shouting, "Bravo!" I jump to my feet and join in, clap-ping with such fervor that it makes my hands sting. The stage lights come up bright, and the entire cast trots out—the old man, Officer Rahab, and the law clerk. As they join hands and bow, the roar of the crowd grows...

57

I had fallen asleep almost immediately upon boarding the bus for San Pedro. I awoke, leaning against the window. It was late afternoon. We passed under an overpass sporting a green and white sign that read "Artesia Boulevard" and "Compton." We must have crossed over to the 710 freeway while I was sleeping. Not much longer now.

Assuming I could get a job with McNally—a big assumption in my mind—maybe these people would know a cheap place to stay. If not…well, homeless people find a way.

I didn't want to think about that now. I pulled a paperback book from one of my bags. It was *To Kill a Mockingbird.* I had read it when I was a kid in school. Someone had left this copy when they got out, so I grabbed it but never got around to reading it.

I opened to page one. I didn't remember that it began with a memory of a thirteen-year-old boy breaking his elbow.

The hum of the tires on the road was mesmerizing. It was warm inside the bus. Quiet and warm. Comfortable. I settled in a bit more and kept reading. Poor Jem. Poor Scout. Poor everyone. We need Boo.

❋

I stepped out of the bus onto cracked pavement. *That's one small step for man…* Railroad tracks cut through the asphalt like some giant had practiced angular geometry.

No one got out behind me. I paid no attention as the bus belched and groaned and left my life, leaving only the distinct smell of diesel fumes as a memory. Chain link fences, old industrial buildings, warehouses, and abandoned shacks made up the landscape. This was San Pedro. My destination. Not by choice, but by default.

I took a deep breath of the salty afternoon air. The driver had told me that Fish Harbor was down Barracuda Street and to the right. "Take any right," he had said. When in doubt, turn right. Someone told me that once.

I walked to the nearest street: Terminal Way. Barracuda Street should be to my right, if the driver's vague wave were accurate. I hoisted my bags and began walking. The smell of rotting fish, salt air, and bird droppings was pungent.

To my left was a vast, fenced-in storage area. Large shipping containers sat ominous and silent: green, orange, blue, and red. To the right, across the street, were large parking lots, gates open.

Barracuda Street bisected two more parking lots filled with cracks and trash. Looking both ways, I ran across the double-sided road through yet another gauntlet of parking areas. Soon I crossed Cannery Street, and the parking lots gave way to rows of warehouses and industrial buildings. Trucks were backed into gates and up against loading docks. Fenced-in areas within other fenced-in areas held plastic containers and wooden pallets. Some had small, dirty forklifts parked inside. There was not much activity. Most of the work took place in the mornings, I suspected.

The next street was Sardine. The driver said *any* right, so I turned and soon came to a narrow road that ran alongside the harbor. Wood and concrete docks sat beside the street on the water; old buildings made of wood and corrugated metal stretched out on the landward side.

Some looked abandoned, but maybe disrepair was the order of the day for an industrial harbor.

I didn't have an address, but this was the only stretch of road on Fish Harbor with docks for commercial fishing. It had to be along here somewhere. Many of the structures had no signs over the doors; all had stickers in the window declaring that the building was fitted with an alarm. The decrepit and the technological weaved together. The docks to my right creaked, keeping time with my steps. Boats, small and large, were docked, swaying as their lines tightened and slackened. There were many empty spaces. I wondered if this was an area in decline, or if those spaces were for vessels out to sea.

A small old fishing boat putted through my line of sight out on the water. I could see about four or five men standing in the back. In the distance in front of me lay the harbor, where I could see larger buildings, cranes, and other machinery.

I drew up short at a large painted sign high up on the building to my left: "Gerson and McNally Fishing Company." I had no idea of the office hours of a fishing company, but it would not surprise me if it were dawn to mid-afternoon. If no one was here, I'll be sleeping on top of a shipping container tonight.

To my relief, the old wooden door swung open to my push. Inside were four desks arranged in a square pattern: two and two. The walls were covered in fake wood panel, nailed or glued there many, many years ago. The creaky floor was covered by a gray close-nap carpet, with worn sections and discoloration in areas of high traffic. Black and white pictures in cheap frames hung on the walls without thought of spacing or height. Pictures of fishing boats, fisherman holding fish, nets of fish, and other fish-related subject matters. A few certificates and licenses were arranged along one wall.

Three of the desks were empty. Behind one sat a woman with sun-damaged skin and bleached-blonde hair with gray and brown roots. It was clear that coastal living had done quite a number on her, making it difficult to tell her age with any accuracy. Her dress and body implied that she was somewhere between her early thirties to late forties. She was attractive in a rough sort of way if you did not look too close or too long. She wore in-ear headphones that were popular now.

She did not see me until I moved into her peripheral vision. She pulled the earphones out with one hand.

"Oh, I didn't hear you come in! How may I help you?"

"No problem. My name is Jay Adam. I am looking for a Mr. McNally. Is this his place of business?"

"Yes, it is. He's not in now. Can I help you?"

"Well…I hope so. Jon referred me. He used to work here a couple of years ago?"

"Jon Ahmanson?"

"Uh, I don't know his last name." I realized how strange that sounded as soon as I said it.

"Ah. There was a Jon who worked here until a few years ago—he's worked here off and on for decades, but…" She trailed off.

It had to be him. What difference did it make, anyway? I'd either be accepted or told to get out. "I met him in prison. I was just released myself, and he told me to come here because there might be a job."

"Oh! Yes, that *is* our Jon Ahmanson! How is Jon? He was such a good worker, but he can't stay out of trouble. Too much anger."

Wow, I thought. Jon had told me the truth.

"He's doing well. As well as can be expected. I think he has a few more years. He said that Mr. McNally might have a job for me. I had a business…before…right now, I have nowhere to go, but I am a hard worker. I have no family left alive…" My turn to trail off. Too much information.

"Well, I am sorry, Mr. Adam." She *did* sound sorry, and not put off at all. "We do need some hands, even for a short time during the season. It's a good time now because we're about halfway through, and we only have a third of our quota. I can't promise anything definite, but I know Mr. McNally would be willing to talk with you."

"That would be great. Thank you."

"Mr. McNally likes Jon; he'll be glad to hear from someone who's seen him recently. He'll be in tomorrow morning, around five or five-thirty."

"Thank you. I'll come back then. Thank you very much, ma'am."

"Glad to help, Mr. Adam. I hope it works out. See you in the morning."

"One more thing, if you don't mind. Is there some motel or even a shelter nearby that you could recommend? I just got off the bus."

"I am afraid there is nothing nearby. There are some hotels down Seaside into Long Beach, but most are pretty expensive. Best is to go back up the Harbor Freeway into Carson. But…" She looked at the clock on the wall. "I don't think the buses are running any longer today. I wonder…" She stared into space for a moment, as if having an silent conversation with herself. After a moment, she appeared to have made a decision.

"Tell you what, Jay. We have a little room around the corner. It's where Jon stayed when he wasn't out on a boat. Sometimes the deck hands use it if they come in too tired or too drunk to drive. It's empty at the moment." She shrugged. "It's not much. An old converted storage room. Single room with a toilet, sink, and an old cot. It has clean sheets and blankets. It's not a hotel, but it is shelter, and it is free. I don't think Mr. McNally would mind at all if a friend of Jon's stayed there, even if it's only one night."

I'd feel right at home, sadly. "That is quite, quite kind of you ma'am, and I would be grateful."

"Good! And my name is Rikki, not ma'am. Follow me." We went out the front door and around the corner to an unpretentious door. It had a keypad instead of a lock, another example of technology amongst the antiquated. She gave me the six-digit code and had me try it. The door opened into a dark cell with no window. She flipped a switch inside, and a strip of fluorescent lights flickered to life. The room was more like a closet than a room. It had a musty smell and some other faint odors I could not place. Before she left, she told me of a few nearby places where I could get a bite to eat. Cheap seafood, of course, but I wasn't picky.

I set my bags down inside, unpacked a few items, and sat on the rickety cot. I felt some hope for the first time in a long, long time. It was not lost on me that my hope was based on a *possible* job as a deckhand on a fishing boat about which I knew *nothing*. And a closet-like cell of a room. No matter. I was here by default, not by choice, and I would bend it to my will. The beginning of some order. Certainty. Control.

Besides, I would not be here long. Work hard, make some money, make contacts, and move on to a better situation. Keep working on the puzzle until the picture begins to look like it should.

58

Zig takes a long swallow of beer from a large glass mug. He fixes me with a beery stare. "I was the perfect husband to her. Took care of her. All she cared about was showing off with money and stuff. She didn't know how to have a real relationship."

A variety of glasses, ten or fifteen, sit empty on the bar in front of us. Shot glasses, beer mugs, water glasses. How long have I been here? Glancing around, I see the bar and tables are packed with people. Talking, laughing, shouting, drinking, and eating. The lights of the bar reflect off the mirror behind it, and the brightness hurts my eyes. I've had too much. But it feels good to let go.

Wait. It hasn't been that long. Wasn't I just here?

"Hey, Jay? You still with me?" Zig laughs, and it grates on my nerves. Behind him, I see a few heads turn toward us with irritation.

"Yes, I'm here. What were we saying?"

"I was *saying* that you are humiliating me."

He stands and takes an unsteady step away from his stool. With a dramatic flair, he turns to face the room.

"Isn't that right, everyone?!" he shouts.

Those nearest stopped talking and eating and drinking to stare.

"I *said,* isn't that right, everyone?! He—" an arm stretches out and a finger points at me "—is *humiliating* me!"

A silence falls. Everyone is watching. Wondering what will come next like an audience at a stage play. The curtain opens. The audience grows quiet, ready to be entertained. The scene begins. The first character speaks.

Many are nodding their heads in agreement; others look at me, waiting.

"I—I—Zig…what are you doing?"

He turns, and I see that he has three faces. The one in the middle is Zig. The others look familiar, but I can't place them. Probably because they are grafted onto either side of his head.

"You need to be more reasonable, Jay."

I suppose he is an angry drunk, rather than a mean drunk or depressed drunk.

"Everyone in this room—" he sweeps his hand about "—knows that bad people don't succeed. Maybe for a little while, but not long. Like this—" he turns to the bar, lifts a shot glass full of some liquor and pours it on the table "—now watch."

He takes a lighter out of his pocket and holds it to the liquid. *Click.* A blue-yellow flame appears and *poof!* the blue flame expands to the edges of the little Zig-created pool, moving in a slow and sensuous dance. "Looks nice, huh? Bar flambé!" Everyone laughs. A few applaud.

The flame begins to waver. The blue fingers grow small and disappear.

"See?" Zig points with pride at the dry bar top. "See? The fuel and the fire are there, having fun and dazzling us all, and then—gone! Without a trace. Not even a burn mark."

Surely the flame and heat had burned the wax on the wood. But from where I stood, I see nothing. It *did* look undamaged.

"And that's like bad people. Doesn't matter how high they climb, or how much attention they get—they are gone. Everyone knows it. A bad life catches up to 'em. No matter if everyone knows about it or it's a secret! So—" he leans towards me, swaying a bit, "—when you tell me that someone can suffer without reason—" he stands back up "—you tell us that we're all wrong, 'cause everyone knows that good people get rewarded and bad people get punished! Am I right?!"

The crowd erupts in cheers, shouts, and applause. Many of them wear blue caps with "You Reap What You Sow" emblazoned on the front in white.

Lava gurgles and agitates in my belly. I stand and turn to the cheering crowd.

"Wait a minute! Listen to me!" They settle down. "What about that earthquake in San Francisco a few years ago? You think they all deserved that? Or kids who die of hunger in Africa? Retribution?! An innocent kid caught in the crossfire of gang violence?! *Justice?!*" I gaze around the room in triumph at my intellectual skill. Boos and hisses grow into jeers.

A woman stands. Middle-aged, she wears an old cotton dress with a sweater. She is a bit large in some places and not so much in others. She waits for the crowd to quieten. Her head bobs, like a tremor she can't control. When the room is silent, she raises a flabby arm and points at me.

"You are wrong, I *know*. I was a passenger in a terrible car accident many years ago. I was brain-damaged— now I can't always control my body. I can't eat, then I eat too much. I have had over twenty surgeries, different medications…nothing makes me better."

I shake my head with faux sympathy. She is playing into my hand. Accidents happen. Didn't mean she deserved it. "And what did you do to bring on such suffering?"

Her head bobs twice. She lowers her arm.

"My husband was driving. He wasn't paying attention. He never paid attention. He was a stupid man. I should never have married him. And so I reaped what I sowed."

I have her. "That wasn't wrongdoing—it was a mistake—at *worst*. Look around!" I turned to face another part of the room. "There are a lot of bad people who prosper! Some suffer. There are a lot of good people who suffer—some don't! Explain that!"

A murmur rises. Someone shouts "Wrong!" Others shout in agreement.

I look from table to table, seeking someone who might agree with me—or at least consider my position. I turn to Zig. He had resumed his seat and is looking at me with sadness.

"It's as I said, Jay. You don't get it. Sure, we get sick sometimes, or lose something. People die. That's not real *suffering*, just normal life. But wrongdoing always ends with consequences, sooner or later. This talk of earth-quakes and kids in Africa is a rationalization. You don't want to face the truth."

I sit down, shaking my head, trying to control my an-ger. Logic is the answer to winning this argument. "Okay, Zig, where do you draw the line between 'normal problems' and punishment?"

"It's pretty clear. You're just trying to obfu—obfusc—confuse it with petty details."

"Your philosophy doesn't match real life."

He guffaws. "You'll see I'm right. Here…" He points to some plates in front of him. There is food on each, but I cannot see well enough to tell what they are. Everything is hazy. The room wiggles then stabilizes. I think every-one has left but us.

Zig grabs a round, crusted pastry—or maybe a meat-ball—from a plate and stuffs it into his mouth. He speaks as he chews.

"Mmmm. Quite pleasant." He rolls it around his mouth, masticating, moving it with his tongue. He savors it. Swallowing, he smiles.

"What are you—"

His eyes grow large. A terrible grimace distorts his mouth. He begins to gag. The barmaid appears and hands him a metal bucket. He takes it with both hands and holds it in front of him at his knees. He bends forward in a semi-controlled flop and vomits into the bucket. Ringing metal and splattering sounds fill the room. The smell causes me to raise my hand to my mouth.

He sits up and resumes his smile. Bits of vomit hang from his chin. Without looking, he hands the bucket back to the barmaid. He wipes his face with his sleeve.

"See? Eat bad stuff, suffer the consequences."

I start to respond, but he raises a finger in front of my face. With his other hand, he grabs at another plate. He lifts a battered, oval-shaped *something*, with sauce dripping from it. He begins sucking and licking it.

"Mmm...quite delicious."

He takes small a bite, nods to himself, and pops the rest into his mouth. He chews and swallows. His face shows great delight.

"Bad acts always catch up with us. It might seem good—but it isn't good *for* us."

I look at the barmaid, wanting to share my incredulity at his meaningless antics.

"He's right," she says, still holding the bucket of his sick.

Turning back, I see Zig's face is bright red. Beads of sweat appear on his forehead. He takes a few short, quick breaths. His eyes roll back. In slow motion, his body slumps. He slides off the stool and onto the floor below.

I jump up and move toward him but lose my balance. Someone shoves me aside and a stumble to my knees.

"Excuse me, sir. Please stand back." A paramedic in uniform.

Two more EMTs join him and began a choreographed dance around Zig's body. They take vitals, insert needles into his veins, and place an oxygen mask over his mouth. They pass hand-held medical machines to each and take them back again. Each medic has a precise function, performed with the well-practiced actions of professionals.

After a few moments, the one nearest me reaches up and clicks a microphone clipped to his shoulder.

"We need the stretcher."

Two other medics appear with a stretcher, as if they had been waiting just off-stage. With a "one-two-three" they lift Zig onto the thin white mattress. His body flops. Arranging his arms and legs, they buckle straps across him. One of the medics inserts a tube into Zig's mouth and makes adjustments to a device which sits beside Zig's shoulder.

Zig's eyes fly open and fix on me. "Sseee? Tastes gud 'ut its koison."

The medic at the head of the stretcher glances up at me. "He said, 'See? Tastes good but it is poison.' He's right, you know."

"Okay, everyone," says the medic who had called for the stretcher. "Let's move!"

As they roll past, he turns to watch me, grinning around the plastic tube in his mouth. Then he is gone, out the door.

I turn to the barmaid, who has not moved. "What—what is going on?"

She dimples at me and sets the bucket down on the bar top. Crossing her arms, she leans on the bucket. I like her smile. Friendly. Open.

"He eats everything in sight, but he is starving. He'll die soon." She laughs. "Kinda proves his point, huh?"

An imminent explosion boils inside me. It comes fast. I have no time to think. The gasses and molten rock had been down there too long under extreme pressure. Magma shoots upward through the fissures. I grab a glass from the bar top—

59

I sit in the open door of the helicopter, white-knuckled on the grab bars. Despite the tether clipped to my harness, I'm afraid I'll fall. The pilot circles, keeping us about fifty feet over the same area of the battlefield. Every ten or fifteen seconds, he jerks in a different direction to make it harder for the AA weapons to track us. I am deafened by the noise of the rotors, the whistling of the wind, the *rat-a-tat-tat* of guns, and the explosions.

"What do you see?" The pilot yells over the intercom. It is loud but tinny inside my headphones.

I see Zig on the ground below, fighting against two enemy combatants. Despite his girth, I am impressed at his skill. He parries and lunges and deflects with skill and grace. One opponent's head is separated from his body. I watch as it rolls away. Blood sprays out of the neck of the body, which hesitates a moment before collapsing, as if surprised by this turn of events. Nice touch of drama.

Zig pivots with ease, parries, sidesteps, and lunges. The second opponent's head snaps back as Zig runs him through.

"He got 'em both!" I scream into my microphone.

Zig looks up at me and waves. I start to wave back, but don't want to let go of the bars.

A military vehicle careens over the ridge behind Zig. It slams to the ground in a spray of dirt, rocking and bouncing. Mounted on the back is a Gatling gun. A dark figure clings to it for dear life.

As the vehicle stabilizes, I realize it is headed right at Zig. I scream to him, but my voice is whipped away by the wind. The helicopter banks and I lose sight of him. When we turn back, I see fire spraying from the nozzle of the gun. Zig has seen it, too; he dives and rolls behind a small hillock. He raises up and makes a throwing motion then ducks down and curls himself into a fetal position.

The vehicle explodes in a mass of fire, smoke, and flying metal. The gunner flies off the back, a black scarecrow defying gravity.

Burning debris lands around Zig. He jumps up and waves.

"He's ready! We gotta get him out of there now!"

I hear a whoosh from my right and see a flash of green. A terrific blast of fire and smoke erupts where Zig had been standing. The explosion is so great I fall back, losing my grip with one hand. I slide back into the fuselage, my hold on the single grab bar acting as a pivot point.

The helicopter cants and then dips down and back up. We are climbing at an impossible angle. I scrabble with my free hand to grab a tiedown, holding so tight my hand hurts. Darkness closes in. I shut my eyes. The battle noises diminish. The rotor chatter fades.

Silence.

The helicopter levels out, but I still cannot hear anything. Did the explosion make me deaf? I pull myself up and scoot to the door.

I see a faint, round glow far below. A glob of light. My eyes adjust. It's a blue-white sphere. A small crystal marble in a black expanse. Billions of tiny twinkling lights appear as a stunning backdrop. A white-gray disk floats off to one side. There are other, smaller discs, each a different color.

BOOM! I jump at the sound, feeling it more than hearing it. *BOOM! BOOM!* Everything goes dark. I lean back into the fuselage.

A voice sounds, clear and firm. "All rise!"

"What's going on?" I say into my microphone. "Are we dead?" No answer.

I twist around to peer into the cockpit. The pilot stands in the cockpit door, holding on to the bulkhead. He pulls off his oxygen mask and soft helmet.

It is Officer Rahab. I gape.

He removes his gloves.

"Rahab? What are you doing here? You're supposed to be in court."

He throws the gloves to the deck and begins to unzip his flight suit.

"I *am* in court, Mr. Adam. The hearing is about to begin. I am sure the sentence will be death."

60

I awoke during the night with severe stomach cramps and a fever. Hurrying to the toilet bowl, I vomited a concoction of partially digested fish, breading, and fries, all churned together with beer and stomach secretions. I heaved a few more times, convulsing like a fish on the deck of a ship.

167

After a few dry heaves, calm was restored, replaced by a deep and broad exhaustion. I lay on the cool floor for twenty or thirty minutes, then got to my feet, trembling, and flopped onto the cot.

It seemed like no time passed before it was five-thirty. I sat up and rested for a moment. *I have to get up.*

I shuffled to the sink to rinse my face and armpits. I rinsed my mouth again and got dressed. The movement and increased blood flow cleared my mind, but I needed rest.

The remains of last night's dinner sat on the floor where I'd left it. I could scarcely look at it. I stepped out the door into a chilly, humid morning. The door closed and locked behind me.

Rikki greeted me and buzzed Mr. McNally and said it would be a few minutes. I asked and received aspirin and a glass of water. If she noticed anything amiss about me, she refrained from mentioning it.

I had just sat down in a chair and took the pills when a man came through the interior door in a hurry.

"Jay?" He strode over with his hand out. I did my best to offer a firm and confident handshake.

"You're a friend of Jon?"

"Yes, of sorts. We were inside together for a couple of years."

He shook his large head. "Poor Jon. A good worker, nice guy, but can't stop doing stupid things. Mostly alcohol and anger. Guess he can't help it."

I thought of Zohn and felt a pang of guilt.

"So you need a job?" Jon's character flaws and his pre-destined life were forgotten.

"Yes, sir. I'll take anything, and I'll work hard and learn."

He nodded. "Glad to help out a guy getting back on his feet. Some of my best workers have been down-and-out—at least the ones who want to change their ways. Had some bad ones, too." He took off his cap and scratched his head.

"In fact, quite a lot, actually." He frowned for a moment, then smiled. "Ah, but the good ones make up for it!"

I doubted they did, but I appreciated his attempt to find meaning amidst chaos.

"So, Jay, I need a deck hand. No prior experience, though if the crew tells me you can't handle the work I'll have to let you go. Got a business to run. Fishing is our business, day and night, good and bad weather. Lots of hard, nasty work—but on the other hand, you're out on God's blue ocean enjoying the sun. Hard work'll make a real man out of you. Are you interested?"

My head swirled at this high-speed interview. At least he didn't need references and already knew my past.

"Yes, I am. I've never been out to sea—was in an office all my life. But I can work as hard as anyone."

He slapped his cap back on his head and pulled it down. "Excellent! You'll know soon enough if you are a seaman or a landlubber!" He laughed and clapped me on the back, then turned serious with scrunched eyes.

"Come on back to my office and let's talk a few others things."

I followed him through the doorway, down a hallway, and into an office. While the rest of the place showed signs of age, his office was a pleasant surprise. It was clean. The paneling on the walls looked real. There were leather chairs and large desk— the desk of a man who wanted to appear larger than life. An ornate bookcase dominated one wall. It had some books, but was mostly decorated with mementos and pictures. Everything was of a marine nature: pictures, knick-knacks, wall maps, and books.

McNally indicated a high-backed leather chair that sat in front of the desk.

"Have a seat."

He took the throne behind the desk. It was clear he relished the role of boss. But graciously, I thought.

"I understand that Rikki allowed you to sleep in our little guest room last night—glad she did that. That's what it's for."

"Yes, sir. I appreciate it." No reason to give him the details of my culinary disaster.

He leaned forward and held his hands together in front of his mouth.

"First, I gotta ask you about your crime. Don't care about the details, but, for example, I don't want a violent man at sea—though there are always extending circumstances." He looked at me with a studied eye. I tried not to show any reaction to the malipropism '*extending* circumstances.'

"No, it wasn't violent."

"Good, good. I sometimes make exceptions. Had a good guy on the crew years ago. Assault with a weapon. He was defending his brother from a gang. So I hired him! I like a guy who stands up for family. We're family here. Still…glad we don't have to worry about it. I'm sure you are a fine man if Jon recommended you."

The next fifteen minutes were filled with questions about my past. I had anticipated such grilling, and had been running through scenarios in my head for many months. I described the accident, the financial accusations, the health problems, and the court proceedings. I tried not to sound too angry or indignant. It seems people don't like to hear others speak of injustice. I had heard 'Where there's smoke, there's fire' too many times. I also played down my business acumen, experience, successes. I didn't want to not be hired because I was "overqualified." I needed a job now.

He asked a few questions about the specifics of the accident and the financial problems and seemed satisfied. A few inquiries into my experience soon demonstrated that it had little to offer commercial fishing at sea. He waved his hand and dismissed the entire discussion.

He gave me a brief description of the business and what I would be doing. It brought to mind old movies which took place aboard wooden ships. There was always a young kid who did those things that required no skill and that no one else wanted to do. I was not a young kid, but I was a "greenhorn." I would be tying hooks, cutting up bait, cleaning the deck and the equipment, making coffee for the crew (but not cooking, I was glad to hear—they had a cook on board or made do themselves). I'd learn on the job—crew members would teach me as we headed out to the first fishing grounds.

Pay was non-negotiable and a deal-breaker if I didn't like it. It was not much, but it would do for now, especially since he offered the room to me for five dollars a night. He'd do it for free, but he believed "ya got to have skin in the game." This led to a brief sermon about personal responsibility and the failure of the modern welfare system.

I nodded until he came back to the subject at hand. A boat is usually at sea for three days to a couple of weeks, depending on where the fish were biting. I hadn't known that it meant sleeping, eating, and living on board. I felt a bit queasy at the thought. Perhaps it was only the bad fish from last night.

"Well, Jay, I am satisfied. One last thing: any problem from you—*any* problem—and you'll be fired on the spot! A recommendation from Jon is a good start, but it ain't the end-all-be-all. Can you handle that?" His eyes bored a hole through the spot between my eyes.

"Yes, sir. I have no problem with that. I ran my own business the same way. I am grateful to have a chance to get back to real life, do some hard work, and learn something new." Those seemed like the things he would want to hear. Despite my weakened state, I felt I had done well.

"Good!" He slapped the desk and jumped up with a grin. "Come on, let's fill out your papers and make you an official crew member aboard the *Sea Bull*!"

The *Sea Bull*. I pictured a manatee—slow, ponderous, and not particularly smart. Though I know nothing about manatees. Perhaps they are the royalty of the sea, fat and slow because other sea creatures bow to their superior intellect and bring them succulent delicacies.

The *Sea Bull*. My place of employment. For now.

※

I sat at one of the empty desks in the office and filled out forms provided by Rikki (who seemed more excited about my job than I did). As I was scribbling answers with a dodgy pen, the front door exploded open as a man burst in. I jumped as Rikki vaulted away from her desk. She rushed over to him, wringing her hands.

"Mr. Gerson, Mr. Gerson, so good to see you this morning!" Her effusiveness had transformed into groveling sycophancy.

The man before her was large—not fat, just big. Big torso, big head, big arms, and meat mittens for hands.

He wore a dark suit that fit him with perfection. Its creases could be used as a straightedge. His white shirt glowed with cleanness and whiteness; a lighthouse in the dingy room. If I wanted to make an impression, I would've worn a tie like his: quality fabric, power colors, and a classic design. A gold watch adorned one wrist. His dark sunglasses had gold rims and looked expensive. I noted some wrinkles and age spots on his hands and face, but he stood straight and healthy. He exuded power and intimidation.

He whipped off his sunglasses as if he were the star of a B movie. Ignoring Rikki's genuflecting, he scanned the room like a king surveying his kingdom. His mouth curled a bit in distaste, as if his own business offended him.

His eyes landed on me. I had seen such eyes before. I saw no fear or care. Only a singular desire to do as he wished. Obstacles are to be ignored or thrown aside—including people. A bit of narcissism here, a bit of sociopathy there. Not enough to keep him from being successful; enough to make everyone around him miserable.

"Who are you?" Gruff and toneless.

"A new employee, sir." I was intimidated, and it angered me. I had always tried not to be that kind of owner.

"Where is McNally?"

I started to answer but realized he was speaking to Rikki without looking at her.

She ducked her head. "In his office, sir. Waiting for you. I will let him know you are here." She scurried back to her desk. Mr. Gerson was already headed to the hallway door.

"Shall I get coffee…?" she called out as the door banged shut behind him.

Rikki stood beside her desk. I think she was trembling. She turned to me with a pained expression.

"I'm sorry, Mr. Adam. It's always a bit of an event when Mr. Gerson shows up." She went behind her desk and sat down. "A bit like an inspection." She giggled without whimsy, as if a storm had ended and she was giddy with relief. "Actually, worse than any inspection I can imagine."

"Is he always that abrupt?" I was being nice: as long as I didn't have to deal with him, I didn't care.

"It's more than that. He is *such* a mean, mean man. Just terrible." She glanced over at the door. I followed her eyes and then back. She waved a hand. "Oh, don't worry. We'll hear him in the hall long before he comes through the door. Yelling at poor Pete."

"I'm sorry." I didn't know what to say. Her raw openness with a relative stranger surprised me.

She pursed her lips. "Last summer, we had a woman working here in the office. She got pregnant and was really sick. We have employee insurance, of course, and the law says that she was allowed time off—paid—and maternity leave. He fired her because she missed days. She brought a complaint against him, but nothing ever happened. I tried to call her a few times, but she would not talk to me. I don't know why."

"I've known people like that." Money and connections affect the path of justice—intentionally or as a side-effect.

"I think he threatened her. And he berates poor Pete. Pete's a good man. He lost his wife a while back, and Mr. Gerson refused to allow him *any* time off. Mr. Gerson didn't even go to the funeral!"

Yeah, the guy was a jerk. I get the picture. They exist. I've met them.

She wasn't finished.

"We had an old fisherman, Sal. Worked for us for *decades*. He'd never known anything *but* the sea. Was the sweetest old man—tough, but a good heart. And a great fisherman, one of the best. He fell during a storm at sea and broke his leg. Of course, he was laid up a while, being older. Mr. Gerson paid him while he was in the hospital recovering, but when he came back he fired him. Said he couldn't do the job anymore."

She shook her head, but I knew this was not unusual. Mean bosses, nice bosses, terrible co-workers, good ones. Injustice sits side-by-side with kindness. Unfairness alongside undeserved boons.

Her eyes glistened with tears. "He died a few weeks later. Fishing was his *life*."

"I'm sorry."

She lowered her voice. "And everyone knows that Mr. Gerson has been in trouble with the IRS, the Labor Board, everybody. Nothing ever happens. McNally started the business and Mr. Gerson agreed to back him. But after a few years, he tricked Pete out of his part of the ownership. I don't know how. At first, Peter got a lawyer, then just dropped it. Wouldn't talk to anyone about it. Meanwhile, Mr. Gerson owns hotels and rental buildings and office buildings all over the Southwest. What does a rich old man need with a small fishing business?"

I wished she would stop, let me finish my forms so I could go back to my closet and sleep.

"Oh, Mr. Adam, I am sorry. I'm speaking out of turn, with you so new here. Guess I kind of think of you like Jon—we used to talk all the time. This is a great place to work, and Mr. Gerson doesn't come by too often."

"It's okay."

Despite her apology, she forged ahead. "Mr. Gerson used to have a wonderful family. His first wife was *so* nice.

He treated her something terrible, but she just *doted* on him. He'd come here with young women—gold diggers, you know—and she'd just smile and dismiss it as nothing. Maybe she loved the money and the lifestyle, but I don't know. She seemed like she *really* loved him, you know?"

I did know. I'd seen it. I didn't care.

"Then he up and divorced her! Married this young twenty-something. Yet his ex-wife *dotes* and never says a bad word about him. Five kids the same thing. One's a doctor; one's a lawyer; daughter married some big financial guy—I don't know what he does. Another owns cattle or horses or something. We see them at company parties. They all have the most filthy mouths."

I thought I might faint. "I've known people like that."

She nodded. "I'll let you get back to the forms." She looked down at her desk.

I turned back, but she had one last comment.

"You know what I think? In the end, it doesn't matter. He'll be dead and in the ground, just like the rest of us. Sure, his funeral will be super nice. But he'll be dead. And no one will be sorry."

She raised her chin in triumph at the philosophical insight which gave her hope that, at least, Mr. Gerson's death would result in his comeuppance.

61

The sun burns my hair. A dry, brown, stiff plant stands before us. It is utterly still. Dead. Desiccated.

"See?!"

Ellie is beside me, staring at the plant. There are tears in her eyes.

"You see?!" She turns to me, and I see that they are tears of anger. She trembles with rage.

I step back. Behind her, a man sits on the ground. He is quite thin, and wears only a worn pair of cotton shorts that are much too large. His hair hangs in dirty strands. His skin is dry and sunburned; his lips are parched and white.

"Do you *see*?!" She spins around to point at the man, then whips back to look at me. Her hair follows, slaps at her face, then falls back into place. Tears fly from her face. I watch as they fall, in slow motion, to the sand. Each landing spot smokes and sizzles.

"You did this!" The sun makes her blonde hair so bright I squint. Her eyes are red, and her mouth is ugly with displeasure. She advances toward me and raises a fist.

I step back, hands up. "Ellie, I don't even know this man."

I am surprised at how calm and emotionless I sound.

She flings her arms in exasperation and casts her eyes to the blue, clear sky. A growl of frustration is followed by a steel gaze which pierces me.

"Exactly, you horrible, horrible man! You don't even know his *name*! He needed little, but you ignored him. You took his clothing; you refused him food and water."

"I did not. I have never seen him." I am still calm, but anger grows. She continues staring at me. I see hateful contempt in those baby-blues.

I take a breath, and the hot air expands my anger. "Even if I *did* know him, I don't treat people like that. I help anyone."

Her anger focuses, like a mighty river flowing down into a deep box canyon. More controlled, but more powerful.

"You heard his wife screaming for help and you ignored her. You heard his children sobbing, and you ignored them."

Has she lost her mind? I look back at the man. Do I know him? I see nothing familiar. He sways back and forth, looking as if he might topple at any moment.

"Ellie, listen to me." I try to remain calm and rational. "I *do not* know this man. I am a good person. I help people. I'm a man of integrity. What you are saying is not true."

She is unmoved. "I keep telling you, Jay—it's what you *didn't* do. You *failed*."

The plant's withered leaves begin to rustle. Though the air is heavy and still, the leaves stir as if a breeze blows. My eyes re-focus, like a pair of binoculars changing magnification. I see tiny details that were not visible before. There is some green on the central stalk, close to the ground.

Near the trunk of the plant is a spider, lying on its back, legs curl inward toward its desiccated body like a gnarled, arthritic old hand grasping at something.

Ellie spoke. "You have nothing to say?"

I laughed without mirth. "Since you can't find anything I *did* wrong, it must be something I did *not* do?"

She shrugged. "Makes sense, doesn't it?"

I spluttered. "No! Why does the problem lie with me? Maybe the problem is other people. Maybe the problem is *life*!"

She flung her arm back towards the man on the ground. He had fallen over on his side, knees pulled up towards his chest, skin burning in the sun.

"Look at him!"

"This isn't real, Ellie! This is a dream! If it were real, I'd help him!"

She dropped her hands. "You don't get it. It's not *him*. It's *all* the actions you should have taken and didn't."

"No one can be held responsible for every time they *didn't* do something! That's like—like—ludicrous—"

"—That's not what I am saying. You're a good man, but stuff like this doesn't happen for no reason!"

"Maybe it does!"

She approaches and places a thin hand on my arm. Her eyes are no longer laser cannons but soft disks of blue and white. "Jay, you have to face it. Maybe you don't know what it is, but *life* knows. And you are paying the price."

An idea dawned on me. "I know what's going on, Ellie. This isn't about me. It's about *you*. You're desperately trying to salvage the meaning *you've* given *your* life. In the face of evidence that shows it to be utterly false."

She gives me a tight smile. "Typical. Deflect."

I turn away enough to cause her hand to drop. I face the open desert. The plant's leaves rustle once more. Maybe if I just said the words she wants to hear, she would go away.

A familiar voice speaks. "She's right, Jay. No one is innocent of anything. And it catches up with us."

※

A gust of wind blows sand and dirt into my eyes. I blink and rub them. When I look again, I am standing in a hospital room.

"Is the doctor on his way?" It is a woman—a young mother, entering the room as she pulls off a jacket and scarf. She goes to the infant lying in the bed, with tubes stuck in the little veins and a ventilator down the small

179

throat. Sensors are taped all over the frail body. Monitors blink with graphs and numbers, emitting soft beeps.

"I…I don't know…"

She wipes away tears and strokes the child's hand. There is no response. She places the hand down with care and goes to the window. Sheets of rain pour down from a dark sky. "Can I close these? It is so dark and depressing out there."

"Uh, sure."

The curtains muffle the sound and cut some of the cold. The antiseptic glow of fluorescent light makes the child look dead. She returns to the the bedside "That's better, isn't it, my love?"

She leans over and kisses the baby's forehead.

"I knew this day would come. They told us it would. Right on schedule. I just didn't want to believe. I hoped…"

I don't know what to say. I don't know this woman or the child.

The woman shakes her head. "The cancer has caused too much damage. Too many surgeries."

She fixes her eyes on mine. "Is it my fault? Something I did? Didn't feed her right? Didn't get her to the doctor on time?"

"I…I wouldn't think so." How would I know?

"Maybe it's the doctors' fault. Tried the wrong things. Wrong treatment. Misread diagnoses."

"Well, doctors are usually pretty—"

"Maybe it is just her fault." She looks down at the still body. "Maybe she would have grown up to be a serial killer. Maybe she needs to die now to save others later."

She looks back at me. "It's so hard to know who is at fault."

We both jump as the door flies open and the white-smocked doctor enters, stethoscope swinging, clutching a clipboard. "Good morning." He does not look like he has good news.

✳

The wind whips and howls. It seems to come from every direction. I cower inside a small structure—a café stand that serves the guests on the beach. It is made of reinforced concrete. Open where the customer counter is located. The winds have made a mess of the little place. Broken bottles, pieces of wood, palm fronds, and the heavy sweet smell of spilled liquor fill the little shelter. The tables and chairs just beyond the counter are long gone. Even here, I am soaked from the torrent of rain blowing in all directions.

The hurricane hit with no warning. At first, people were amused as their drinks toppled over and their wraps did somersaults onto neighboring sun chairs. When the rain began bombarding them like small BB pellets, they began gathering their things. When the chairs and tables begin to lift and fly, they screamed and ran for the hotel, flip-flops, towels, books, and phones all betrayed.

A man falls and the wind rolls him towards the sea. A hotel worker—probably the man who was behind the counter before I jumped inside—helps an elderly couple away from the beach. A flying table catches them all broadside and they go down in a tangle of arms and legs.

A woman clutches a tree—one arm around its trunk, the other stretched out, holding the hand of a thin, elderly woman. The younger woman screams as the wind lifts the old woman. They cannot hold against the power of nature. The old lady is whisked away like a newspaper in a gust of wind. I watch the thin body flail like a rag doll. I lower myself behind the counter before the body slams to the sand near the violent sea. I squeeze my eyes shut.

❋

It is quiet. I open my eyes. The plant. The spider. I take a deep breath; it is like inhaling a furnace. I cough and look at Ellie. She is still fuming.

A sound to our right causes us to look. Paramedics are pushing an emergency stretcher. Zig is strapped to it, wearing an oxygen mask and needles in his arms. The medics push the stretcher, bouncing and jerking among the sand and rocks. Zig raises up on one elbow, winks at me and gives me a thumbs-up.

One of the paramedics sees me staring. "It'll all be fine, buddy. Nothing to worry about. Just a rough patch!"

62

Rikki said the *Sea Bull* was due back mid-afternoon, and McNally wanted me to meet the crew. I went back to my little room—grateful for it—and slept for a few hours. After a quick lunch at a nearby place, I headed back to the office.

I considered that, at least for a while, this was "home." Yet I was a stranger here, and everything was new. I couldn't recall if I had ever been to San Pedro before, though there was a faint memory of sightseeing at the Queen Mary when I was young.

When I entered the office, Rikki was speaking to a stocky middle-aged man. He had a blond and gray mustache with a matching bowl cut. His jeans and a gray sweatshirt were covered with dirt and oil.

"Jay! This is Brian, the ship's mechanic."

We shook hands. "Welcome aboard, Jay." He turned back to the desk and Rikki. "So that's all I need to sign?"

"Yes. I'll let you know when the change is made."

"Ok, thanks." He nodded to me and left.

"He's a nice man. You'll get along with him. Let's go see if we can find Eli. He's the First Mate."

We headed down the causeway to a set of docks. A few boats were moored there, but only one showed signs of activity. "Sea Bull" was emblazoned on its bow. It was larger than I expected.

About seventy-five feet long, it had a high fore-deck/bow area. A superstructure sat forward of amidships, topped by a bridge with windows on three sides, from which a bristle of antenna and radar stretched to the sky. On either side were big long booms—I was not sure of their function. Behind the superstructure was a long cockpit with metal tables, large bins and buckets, and lines and fishing gear. At starboard, near the superstructure, was a heavy-duty winch and crane, with a chain loaded upon a spool. An arch, stretching from one side to the other over the stern, had a spool of nets at the top. Below that was a small metal boat, which looked like someone had merely welded together sheets of metal and mounted a large outboard engine on the stern. But it was big enough to hold eight to ten people, I guessed.

The entire boat looked like it had a long history. The hull had a number of weld repairs and repainted patches that did not match. The booms looked like they had been

added later, too. I learned later that the boat had origi-
nally been a stern trawler, but some equipment was
added later to make the vessel more versatile.

Three men were working in the aft cockpit. When
Rikki called out "Eli!" one of the men straightened and
came to the side. He was the epitome of a fisherman: wiz-
ened, dark wrinkled, sun-damaged face, a wiry black and
gray beard. I would have guessed he was seventy-five
years of age, but I later learned he was 61.

After Rikki introduced us, he invited me to come
aboard. Rikki took her leave. I climbed the creaking
steps, took a stretching step across the gap between the
platform and the gunwale, and came aboard the *Sea Bull*.

Eli was much shorter than I, but made up for it in character and presence. "Forgive me fer not shaking yer
hand, got fish guts on 'em. I'm Eli, First Mate. We been
needin' a hand. Got any experience?"

"No, I'm afraid not."

"No matter. Easy stuff, long as you got the stomach for
it."

I nodded. "I'm game. Ready to learn and work hard."
I didn't want to be a fisherman or a deck hand. I wanted
to sit in my office, lead my team, and engage in business.
And while I'm at it, I wanted my family back. But for
now, the *Sea Bull* offered some order, stability, and the
means to make my own plans. Besides, I didn't have
much choice. For now.

"We'll see. Reason we need you is 'cause we had a
greenhorn who got so tired of the work and weather he
wouldn't come out of his bunk. Said we were mistreatin'
him. When we got back to dock, Captain fired him on
the spot. McNally backed him up."

I nodded again. What could I say?

He turned to the two other men. "Robert! Mike! Meet our new deckhand!" The two others turned away from what they were doing and came over. I told them my name, but did not offer to shake hands. Neither did they.

The larger one spoke first. "What's your experience?" His experience appeared to be with lots of hamburgers and beer. He wore a blue baseball cap over longish brown hair, and a short beard shot through with gray.

"None, but I'm a hard worker and ready to learn."

He snorted. "That's what the last guy said."

The other man spoke up. "Hi, Jay, I'm Mike. Glad to have you aboard. Don't mind Robert. He's been too long without a beer."

Eli laughed and said, "Ya, true, but he's always like that! Knows his marine electrical and mechanics, though."

I could not read the blank stare on Robert's face as he continued looking at me.

"Come on, Jay," Eli said, "I'll show you around."

The others returned to their work, and Eli took me to the bow, showed me the windlasses, the double anchors with their thick ropes and various other stored gear. He gave me brief descriptions of most of it. We returned aft and mounted the ladder to the bridge, a large, single-room cabin with windows on three sides. Eli told me that the Captain, J.B. Holland, spent most of his time here, but had already left for the day. The helm was a dizzying array of instruments and another example of haphazard additions and deletions of equipment over time. I recognized the wheel, throttles, and radios, but nothing else. At the back was a padded bench. Tables along the side, with lips on the edges, were filled with papers, books, and charts. Bottles of beer and liquor dotted the landscape, some full, some empty, and many at some place in between.

"You'll have no reason to come up here. Unless we are all dead and you're all that's left!" He cackled at the macabre joke.

"Well, let's hope that never happens."

"I'm just joking with ya. Accidents do happen, of course. The sea is nasty, and she'll find out every mistake you make. Long as you respect her, you'll be fine." He walked to one of the instruments and tapped it. "This is the VHF radio and…" he tapped one next to it "…this is the SSB. The two instruments everyone should know how to use. Pick up the mic, push the button, and talk. Say the name of the ship and 'over' when you are done. Change the channel with this knob and this knob. Sixteen is for hailing and emergency."

He took me down belowdecks and showed me the galley, which boasted a beaten-up oven, stove, sink, and refrigerator. A new-looking microwave sat on a counter, strapped in place with flat cables bolted to the wall and top of the counter. A booth held enough for six to sit at one time.

Beyond the galley (forward), were a series of tiny cabins on either side of a narrow passageway, each with two bunks and two storage bins. He pointed to one of the upper bunks.

"That's you. Don't bring any more than you need. Maybe a couple of books or music player or whatever."

Back out on the aft cockpit, Eli came alive. It was evident he loved commercial fishing.

"Here's where the real work happens. See those nets? We lower those as we move into place. You'll help make sure they deploy and spool properly. Over here…" he pointed at a large davit with a motor attached "…is the davit we use to bring in larger fish, haul in traps if we are fishing for lobster or crab. And up above…" now pointed up on either side and the back of the bridge superstructure "…are our trolling outriggers. We use downriggers and spreaders with 'em. When we're trolling, you'll be connecting lures and baiting, changing 'em out. Most of the time, though, you'll be cleaning equipment, cutting bait, handling and storing fish, shoveling ice, and helping do whatever needs to be done. How's that sound?"

"Sounds great." Sounds terrible. "I'm interested in learning." I couldn't care less. "And I appreciate the opportunity." That, at least, was true.

"Well , we'll see day after tomorrow. Be here at 0430 before that to get settled and be ready. We set off at 0530."

"Will I get some more training before then?"

"On the job, my boy, on the job! It's sink or swim—so to speak!"

✳

My first trip out was a short one—only two nights on board. The fifty-hour maiden voyage was a blur. It consisted of little sleep and a lot of fish, blood, and guts, with some sea salt air. Most of the time I was either trying to stay warm or sweating. I did avoid any problems with seasickness, but they told me it was pretty calm this trip. I'd find out later if I could handle it.

The crew consisted of eight men, including me. I had already met Eli, Robert, Mike, and Brian. I was assigned the cabin with Raimundo, a quiet, small man, born in Mexico City. He worked hard, kept his head down, and rarely talked—the only social interaction I saw him interested in was playing cards. He did have a quick smile, though. He smoked little brown cigarettes constantly.

I met Captain Holland that first day, too, but had not seen him since except as a shadowy figure behind the windows of the bridge. The other crewmember was a long-time deckhand that everyone called "Fishbait." He seemed to be Robert's right-hand man; the guy who laughed at his jokes, joined in with Robert's jeering, and was as shallow a person as I'd ever met.

There was only one mishap. We were preparing to drop some traps near a small island, and Eli was showing me the anchoring equipment. We went out to the forward deck, beside the large anchor and mooring gear. He checked with the Skipper for the depth of the water, then showed me how it works: motor controls, chain stoppers, dog clutch, and more. Since the swells and winds were up, we were going to lower both anchors. Once he explained the system and procedure, he had me operate the starboard. I had released the anchor properly, but I left the dog clutch and chain stopper in the wrong positions. When I put the motor in neutral to wait for his order to drop, the anchor fell in a free-fall from the side into the water and all the way to the bottom. The noise of the huge chain made a cacophony of metal on metal as the chain slid free through the hawsehole. He cursed and ran over to me. The anchor had already hit bottom, but the chain was still streaming overboard. He engaged the clutch part way, eased the windlass into reverse. With the motor and cloth squealing, he brought the chain to a stop. He showed me the right way, then flipped the dog clutch and had me operate the motor to bring the chain back up to the proper scope.

He let out a sigh. "Well, that could'a been a disaster if we weren't in only sixty feet of water. Could'a lost the anchor or burned up the motor."

"Sorry."

"Ever brought up anchor manually? No, 'course you haven't. Worse still is running the chain all the way out. We call the end of the anchor line the 'bitter end' for good reason. Reach it at speed and all hell breaks loose! Bust off its weld and it whips around the deck like an angry serpent! Kill you with one swipe!"

I wanted to tell him that a five-minute survey was not enough training for something so important. I had a feeling he wouldn't care. "I'll do better next time, Eli."

"Yeah, you will. Or it'll be the bitter end of you."

63

Light appears. Dim. I look up. Little suns, spaced in four neat rows. The light grows. Ceiling lights. A courtroom. Blue carpet. Paneled walls. Brown wood tables and railings. I am at the defense table. I am alone.

The lights continue to wax, so slow as to make me wonder if my eyes are playing tricks. The judge's bench is massive and solemn. It is empty of both judge and justice.

Along the right wall, at the front, is an L-shaped desk: the bailiff's station. It is empty of both Officer Rahab and assistance.

The prosecution's table is to my right. A mirror image of the defense table. A long brown table with three chairs, high-backed with blue upholstery. The kind of upholstery that has little tiny bumps on it. Black plastic arms. Five wheels each. The chairs are empty of both the prosecutor and the rule of law.

I spin in my chair. Just behind me is a dark wood partition, lower than waist-height. Beyond are six rows of theater-style chairs, divided down the middle by an aisle. The same blue upholstery as the other chairs. They are all empty of the public and transparency.

The back wall rises twenty feet in deep-paneled solemnness. As I watch, the double doors open and a man strides in.

"Mr. Adam! Glad you are here early." His tailored suit is expensive—I would guess a million dollars at least. He wears a crisp white shirt—I would bet he took it out new this morning. His tie is striped power red, matched with the red pocket square at his left breast. Italian-made shoes reflect the recessed lights in the ceiling, now at full brightness. Cufflinks, a watch, and a ring shine with a light that bespeaks rare metals and genuine diamonds. It is extravagant yet understated; it fits this room with intentional accuracy. A briefcase swings in his right hand. He sets it on my table and takes the chair next to me.

"Now, Mr. Adam—" he taps on a phone as he talks "—I am hoping that the hearing today will shed some light on your case, and the judge will see the strength of our argument. I have prepared—"

"Who are you?"

He looks up from his phone. "I am your attorney, of course." Back to the phone. "Now, I did not have time to go over this with you, but I have prepared a—"

"I didn't hire an attorney. I am representing—"

"Everyone has a defense attorney. Now, as I was saying—"

A door at the front side of the courtroom opens, and Officer Rahab enters. The attorney stands and tucks the phone inside his suit jacket.

"Bailiff, good morning! Are we ready?"

Officer Rahab takes a seat at his desk. "Good morning, Counsel. Almost. Waiting only for the court reporter."

I lean over. "What about the judge and the prosecution?"

He ignores me and fumbles with the latches on his briefcase.

"Will they be here today? They have not made *one* appearance, in spite of—"

He stops me with a raised finger. The briefcase is empty except for a black, rectangular device with three buttons. He removes the device and sets it on the table as if it is fragile. He closes the case and sets it on the floor, folds his hands before him, and stares at the judge's bench.

Did the court appoint an attorney for me? Did all my appearances and requests and pleadings make a difference? Maybe *now* the prosecutor will show, I will hear my charges, and the judge will see how unjust it has all been. My spirits rise. It has been a long time since I felt any hope.

The back door opens again and a woman enters, carrying a laptop and a bag. Paying no attention to us, she strides to the bailiff's desk and speaks to him in whispers. She takes a seat at a small, one-person desk in front of the clerk's station, sets up the laptop, types for a moment, then nods at Officer Rahab. He stands and faces the courtroom.

"All rise!"

I stand with my attorney, heart pounding. *Finally!* I am intimidated at the thought of seeing this judge—this officer of the court who has failed to show for any hearing. This emblem of justice who has violated the rule of law and all standards of fairness, yet seems to have complete control over every element of the system. Which seems to bother no one but me.

I fix my eyes on the door behind the judge's bench. What will he look like? What will his demeanor reveal?

Officer Rahab speaks again. "Be seated." He takes his seat at his desk and looks our way.

"Counsel? You may begin when ready."

I remain standing.

"Thank you, Bailiff." My attorney picks up the device from the table and leans over to me. "Sit."

"Where is the judge?"

He clenches his jaw and hisses, "Don't screw this up. *Sit.*"

I sit, flummoxed. I want to scream. My attorney should be objecting to this farce of a courtroom—you can't hold a hearing without the judge!

Instead, he walks down into the Well. He gestures and, on the left side of the room, a projection screen lowers from the ceiling. The lights dim.

"If it pleases the court, I have prepared a short, two-part visual display to highlight my client's defense and cross-complaint. If you will attend to the screen."

The screen now shows a picture of an outdoor ranch or farm. A few people stand in the foreground, dressed in simple, threadbare clothes. Their hands and faces are dirty. Their expressions are hollow.

"First, I emphasize what this court already knows: that it and its processes are the *only* path for a defendant to seek vindication, should he or she be innocent. No other person, place, or organization can make that declaration but this court."

He touches a button and the picture changes. It is still a farm, but the people are gone; the focus is on a wooden fence in disrepair. He clicks to the next picture: a well that has been filled with dirt. Then, a roadside sign. The posts remain, but the sign itself is so battered and torn that the original wording or symbols cannot be discerned.

"You see," he says, "these people have had the landmarks of their life destroyed or stolen. They beg for vindication, but the court has refused to act."

What did this have to do with me? Maybe he's showing a pattern—the court has treated others like they have treated me? He's setting up my cross-complaint by showing the court's unjust precedents!

The next picture is a herd of sheep and cattle being driven into a loading ramp and onto a truck. A line of trucks stretches behind the one at the ramp, each waiting its turn. I can almost hear the hoofbeats on the wooden slats, the groaning and lowing.

"Their livelihood was taken from them. When they complained, they were insulted and told they were worthless and useless."

I await an objection from the prosecutor for relevance—but there is no prosecution! At last, this court's bizarre procedures might work in my favor! I feel a pang of hypocrisy, but I don't care. The tables have turned!

The judge may not be here, but it is an official hearing with a court reporter and called to order by the Bailiff.

Now my attorney presents pictures of the poor people picking meager amounts of corn from a sparse field. They pull up a few potatoes from a sad little plot near their shabby home. The lawyer keeps speaking, though it is chiefly repetition now.

His cadence indicates the slideshow is near its end. The last slide shows people sleeping out in the open with only a few moth-eaten blankets to cover them; then the first picture reappears: a group of poor, forlorn farmers huddled in front of their pathetic land.

"Would anyone deny these people justice? They have done nothing to deserve such terrible treatment. Of course," he adds with haste, "we know that no one is perfect in the eyes of the court—but this is a punishment beyond any minor code violations. These are good, decent, hardworking people who deserve to be heard and restored. Yet this court, known for its justice, has turned a blind eye and *allows* it. It must end!"

The lights come back up and the screen fades. The attorney returns to the Well and faces the empty bench.

"This court has not listened. It has remained silent in the face of suffering."

This is it. He'll pivot to show that my case is the same as theirs. He has placed my case in a larger context. Excellent.

"This court prides itself on justice. Yet not only have these poor people been mistreated, but the one body that could relieve their suffering has *ignored them*." He draws out the last two words, letting them roll out of his mouth like cold molasses. "This court has purported to administer justice, but has administered *injustice* through *inaction!*"

I feel the urge to stand and applaud! Some might recoil at such a harsh critique of a court and its judge in his own courtroom. But sometimes justice requires harsh words!

"And if the court does not hear this complaint, then hear my second point! Lights!"

My attorney is a confident actor in a play. Sensing the audience is with him, he engages in righteous indignation! I feel my face splitting in a grin of delight. Perhaps it is not fitting, but fairness and the rule of law have departed—why not employ tactics of acting and the stage? It does work: the Scopes and the O.J. trial come to mind.

The lights dim and the screen lights up again. It is another farm, but it is green and prosperous. The people in front are dressed in the finest clothes I have ever seen. They are all well-fed and plump; their faces show happiness and contentment. The ranch house behind them is a mansion, bristling with balconies, columns, bay windows, and chimney stacks. Perhaps this is the former farmers restored? To show that justice *has* been done before? That's even better. There is precedent!

"Behold! Look at the prosperity of *these* people!"

The following pictures show cars in the driveway: Bentleys and Mercedes, trucks and sports cars and SUVs and convertibles; an Olympic-sized swimming pool in the back yard, and four tennis courts.

"These people are well-off, well-fed, and comfortable. They have none of the sufferings of the previous group."

Previous group? Are these not the same people? Did the poor farmers not received justice?

More pictures reveal the lavish interior of the home: plush furniture, finely-appointed decorations, thick carpets, warm fireplaces, and fine art. Then, outside, pen after pen of large, healthy sheep and cattle. Cadres of workers toil in the full and plentiful fields.

"Do we criticize these good people? Of course not. But their prosperity is marred by their guilt. These are the ones who *caused* the suffering, who stole the crops, who destroyed the property, who took food from the mouths of the children. *Yet they prosper, and the court does nothing!*"

I see. That's not as strong an argument as precedent. Surely a prosecutor would object, if present. The pattern of injustice applies to my case, but the prosperity of others—even if they committed wrongs—does not. It's irrelevant to my case.

What is he doing?

The lights come back up, and the attorney takes a deep breath.

"*This* is the second part of our complaint, built on the first. The innocent suffer, and the court does nothing. The guilty prosper, and the court does nothing!"

He pauses and takes a look around the empty courtroom. It might have been a dramatic pause, but in this courtroom, it seems wasted.

"This is no court of justice—it is a court of *in*justice! This court is on the side of anarchy and suffering!"

That may be too far. While judges are supposed to be fair and impartial, to attack the court might border on contempt—even if true. I hold my breath.

My attorney stands motionless as his words die in the cold room. Both arms are held high; his hands balled into fists. He stands as if waiting for applause.

My heart sinks. This is no legal argument, though it reveals injustice. But it lacks reference to case or statute law. It is merely an appeal to fairness and a blistering critique of the court.

He dropped his arms and resumed his seat beside me. The court reporter types; the bailiff concentrates on some piece of paper on his desk.

I turn to the attorney. "You understand my case."

He smiles and shrugs with false humility. "Of course."

"But I thought you might ask about the charges and offer some legal—"

The typing stops. Officer Rahab stands. "Is that all, Counselor?"

"Yes, Bailiff. Thank you."

Rahab nods to the court reporter. She closes her laptop, packs up, and, without a glance at us, leaves the room. My attorney lifts his briefcase onto the desk, places the device inside, and closes it with a snap.

"But…? That's it? You have nothing further?"

He stands and grasps the handle of the briefcase. It drags across the table and swings to his side.

"It's up to the judge now."

"But the judge wasn't here! Will he read the transcript? This is highly irregular!" My stomach begins to boil.

Shrugging, he steps into the aisle. "I filed the papers and the exhibit list."

"What exhibit list?"

He huffs in irritation and raises his head without looking back. "Bailiff, would you ask the clerk to give a copy of my exhibit list to my client."

"Certainly, Counselor."

He nods at me, then tromps up the aisle and out the door.

I turn to Officer Rahab. "Bailiff! Where can I find the judge? Do you have a personal number for him or an address? This is the most corrupt court I have ever seen!"

Officer Rahab is typing on his computer. "Please be respectful, Mr. Adam, or I will have you removed. I am printing your exhibit list."

I sit, fuming that I may be worse off now *because* I have an attorney.

Officer Rahab stands, lifts a piece of paper from a printer and approaches. He thrusts a single sheet of paper at me.

It is a list of four items.

1. Heidegger. *Being and Time*, 15:98.

2. Wiesel. *Le procès de Shamgorod tel qu'il se déroula le 25 février 1649*.

3. de Lassus. *Sacramento Lectiones Novem ex Propheta Iob*.

4. McLeish. *J.B.*

"Heidegger" only name that I recognized—a philosopher, I believe. Where is the evidence of my suffering? My mistreatment? The injustice I have experienced?

"Officer Rahab! What *is* this?"

"Your exhibit list."

"I know *that*. Books?"

He sighed. "They are *your* exhibits, Mr. Adam, prepared by *your* attorney. If you have questions, I suggest you ask him."

"Have I fallen into one of Dante's levels? I demand to speak to the judge! There must be *some* way to communicate with him!

I scream and slam my fists on the table. The room sways back and forth. My feet slip out from under me. The floor is slick; I scramble to get a purchase. The table has turned a whitish-gray. I grab its sides, which feel like wet steel. In the dim light, I see that it is covered with blood and gore.

I gasp as a cold spray of water washes over me.

64

"That was a close one, eh, Jay?!" Edwards stood not far away, hanging on to the bulkhead which led below. He was wearing yellow rain gear.

The ship rolled and jerked. A gray day. The ocean is choppy. The wind whipped. The swells were much higher than my first trip, as the crew had promised. Tall enough to slosh the deck—and me—on occasion.

"Grab them chum buckets and let's get them secured before they spill all over the deck."

We had already hauled in the nets and were now on our way back to the harbor with the trolling lines out. We made quick work of it, albeit stumbling and almost falling at times. I had learned, from this second trip at sea: always have one hand on a handhold.

As we finished storing equipment below, someone yelled on deck. We ran up to find that Raimundo and Brian had a large fish—perhaps eight feet long—flopping about on the deck. I thought "tuna," but it was a kind I had not seen. The men were dancing about the writhing creature; Raimundo with a gaff and Brian with an aluminum club. Eventually, Raimundo got his gaff into the fish just behind the head, deep in the flesh. Edwards, grabbing another gaff, gigged it on the opposite side. They held the beast steady enough for Brian to whack it behind the brain pan, rendering it still.

"Wow," Edwards yelled over the noise of the sea and the engines. "Shark!"

"Yeah," Brian growled, wiping his face with a forearm. "Got caught in one of the lines, was upon us before we knew it. I swear he jumped right up on the deck over the gunwale—almost took Raimundo out!"

The shark was no longer moving, but it still looked dangerous to me. Wet and glistening, the open mouth was filled with jagged teeth. It was a far more fearsome-looking creature lying on the deck than in any picture, film, or aquarium I had seen. I was glad I had not been on deck when it leaped.

"We hate sharks," Edwards said to me. "Some people fish for 'em, because there is a market, though not for this species. To us, they are demons that steal our bait and eat our prey. And they are *mean*."

Brian and Edwards dragged the shark over to the transom. I felt helpless, not knowing if I should do something or stay out of the way.

"Mako shark?!" It was Eli, who had appeared at my side. "Good for nothin'! Nothing but a monster—toss him over!"

Raimundo opened the transom hatch. With great effort, the other two maneuvered the creature to the opening, while I stood by. Once they got the bulk of it through, they gave it a good shove. It fell overboard, spun and flipped a couple of times in the double rooster-trail of our propeller wash before disappearing.

Eli cackled. "Now he's just foam on the water!" I was surprised at the glee in his voice.

"No one'll ever fear him agin!" He clapped me on the back. "But they never give up until they are dead! Come on, Jay. Let's go have a beer. Good fishing, good day!"

✳

My third trip was a four-nighter. Leaving the dock before dawn was like sailing aboard a ghost ship. No one spoke unless necessary, as we stumbled around in the dark like zombies.

As the *Sea Bull* cut a quiet path through the glassy sea on this morning, I stood at the transom, watching the expanding "V" behind us. The geometry of the wake mesmerized me, perhaps all the more so because it was 5:40 am.

"Jay." I turned. It was Raimundo. "Help me with the bait table, *por favor*."

We shuffled over to the bulkhead where the stainless-steel bait table was secured. It was on that surface that I learned to cut bait, dress fish, and bait the hooks when we were trolling. Raimundo wanted my help to unlatch the table from the bulkhead and secure it to the middle of the deck for working.

Once we had wrestled its legs into divots set in the deck and secured it with clasps, we made sure that tools, knives, and buckets were in place and clean. He sent me to the cooler to load a couple of buckets with frozen bait fish. I set them in their racks along the gunwales, making sure the lids were tight so the gulls wouldn't steal them.

"Cut bait?" I said.

"Not yet. Couple hours." He shuffled off belowdecks. I stood for a moment, looking out to port. Early in the morning, the sea was like a sheet of glass. As the day progressed and the winds picked up, it began to dimple and move. Then the swells begin to roll; sometimes large, sometimes small; sometimes far apart, at times close together.

By late afternoon it would be rough, and the *Sea Bull* would roll and jerk when we hit a swell head on. It rocked with the chop and winds. I imagined that there was some mathematical process that could predict it all.

I was stirred out of my reverie by Eli coming down the ladder from the bridge.

"Morning, Jay. Nothin' to do 'til we reach our numbers. Go grab some shut-eye." Taking his own advice, he ducked his head and disappeared through the bulkhead.

I followed. Raimundo was already snoring on the lower bunk.

This was the best part of my Job. Trying to sleep

65

"Hey! Wake up! Want another shot?"

I blink and open my eyes. The light from behind the bar is blinding.

"Jay? You okay, buddy?"

Ellie sits next to me, though she looks more like Zig. She is large and wears a rumpled suit. She is obviously drunk. An extensive collection of empty glasses—pints, shots, and tumblers—sit before us.

"Yeah…yeah."

She nods and almost slips off the stool. "Good. Got another shot of that French vodka coming for us! Nothing like celebrating a divorce, yeah?"

"Divorce?"

"My divorce! Heading off for a new life! Leaving San Berdoo forever!"

The bartender appears and sits two shots down before us. He is dark—not ethnically, but because of prolonged exposure to the sun. Wrinkled, dry skin. Ugly spots and bumps cover his face and hands. His lips look parched even now.

"Hey, barkeep!" shouts Ellie, far louder than necessary, "tell my friend here—no one is good, right? We're all screw-ups!"

"Yup," the man croaked, his voice as dry as his skin. "Everything in the world is tainted. Getting worse all the time. So ya might as well get used to paying the price."

"See, Jay? Told ya."

"I don't know what we're talking about," I said, unsure of how I got here. "Yeah, life is complicated and bad stuff happens. But we can make good choices. Isn't that what our moms teach us? Make sound choices, so things go well for us." The barkeep shook his head. I hear a rattling and rustling sound.

"Jay, Jay," Ellie says, "we can't even figure out the best way to live! It's all too vast and complicated. We're talking the *whole universe* here. You're arrogant and stupid if you think you know the answers!"

I am surprisingly clear-minded despite all the alcohol. "Not true! Religions, philosophers, great thinkers—they have all given us some insights into the best way to live. Work hard, treat others well, be thankful, and things will go well for you. And so on."

The desiccated vocal cords of the barkeep sound out. "No, my naïve friend. Those words seem logical but cannot be more wrong. The test? None of it works in real life."

"Yeah," Ellie agrees. "It's all ivory-tower stuff. Look at me! I had a great life, working hard to be the best salesperson, nice to people, did no wrong. Yet here I am, a drunk in a bar with no wife and no prospects."

I shake my head, confused. "That's not your story—"

"—and me," the barkeep says. "I landed in this little town. Seemed like the perfect place to set up work. Spent time and money helping others. Didn't need a fancy house—I just wanted to serve others. Then all hell broke loose, and now, nothing. Everyone left, the department shut down, the economic crash—I have nothing."

"Come on," I say, "You're talking about bad luck—it happens—take me, for instance—"

I lose my train of thought. Take me. For instance. What was I going to say?

I look up. They are both gone. The bar is white and bare. The shelves are white and void of bottles. I spin around and see the room is empty. No tables, no chairs.

The carpet is torn up, the curtains are torn down. Someone had whitewashed everything—floors, walls, ceilings, bar, and stools.

The light coming through the bare windows is blinding. As if someone had set up gigantic mirrors that redirect the noon sunlight inside. I cover my eyes and stumble to the door.

Outside is a scene from an apocalyptic movie. The restaurant, the gas station, the bus station—collapsed and derelict. Sand covers most of the parking lot and roads. Signs—those which have not fallen—are rusted and time-damaged.

A gust of wind blows grit in my face. I cover my eyes and spit. I turn my back to the wind and reach for the door, but it is no longer there. Only sand, stretching as far as the horizon.

Keeping my hands around my eyes like horse blinders, I turn back. The bus station is gone. The gas station is gone.

Everything is gone.

66

The ship rolled both sideways as well as forward and back—at the same time—which seemed mathematically unsound to me. I lost my footing more than once to the enjoyment of the crew. Robert and Fishbait would hoot and shout, "This is nothing, greenhorn! Just wait!"

I begged to differ. "Nothing" wouldn't have raised the boat five or six feet. The bow went go up, up, up, the ship would level out at the crest, tilt forward ominously, then slid down the back of the swell, throwing spray as the ship crashed into the bottom of the trough.

Most of my time on board was spent working or trying to sleep. The stainless-steel table was my desk. The fish locker was my office. I entered through a two-sided hatch in the deck. Filled with ice and containers, this is where our catches went, and I went with them—shoveling ice, arranging and covering the fish.

The crew either tolerated me or were waiting for me to fail badly enough to be fired. At least that how it seemed. Edwards treated me with decency; so did Raimundo, but there was no interaction beyond business or necessity. I didn't talk to Brian much—he was usually in the engine room or working the controls for the nets and lines. I rarely saw Captain Holland. When I did—in passing to or from the head, or in the galley getting some coffee or food—he spoke only of fishing, marine safety, or business. Beyond those rare occurrences, he was a shadowy figure above, and a disembodied voice over the loudspeakers giving orders.

Robert and Fishbait, however, took every chance to ridicule or harass me, as if we were in junior high and I was up against the school bullies. I had never experienced such problems as an adult or child. What was it? Because I was a greenhorn? Because I wasn't like them? I had always known how to deal with people and get along, but I was at a loss. Maybe I had never been around people like them. Maybe I had changed.

It didn't matter. Once I had enough money, I'd be out of here—to their delight and mine.

If I had anything resembling a personal relationship, it was with Eli. He was responsible for overseeing my work and taught me a good deal. "Stay alert!" he'd say. "You never know when something might go wrong. And believe me—something *will* go wrong if you go to sea enough."

That seemed melodramatic. GPS electronics, automatic pilot, three different communication systems, radar with automatic warnings, automatically deployed emergency systems, computer-assisted plotting, monitoring systems for the engines and pumps and more. Even if something did go wrong, we could fix it or get help within hours, I was sure.

Still, he insisted. So one afternoon, when the skipper was sleeping and Eli had the helm, he called me up to the bridge.

"You need to know the basics of navigation. We got three things going on here that affect us. First, we got tides. Everyone knows what they are. The moon and gravity. Somewhat predictable—but don't let anyone tell you it's all plotted. No one ever knows exactly."

I nodded, more concerned at how the rocking of the ship seemed more pronounced up on the bridge than belowdecks.

"Then there's the swells—measured by the height and distance between 'em. There's lots more measurements about 'em, too, but we'll leave that for later, if you are ever more than a greenhorn. Right now—" he leaned over and gazed at a computer screen "—the swells are five point five feet at twelve seconds, north-northwest."

I could see the long, slow swells from up here, moving like a snake rolling sideways underneath a blue, glistening blanket. But there was a lot more activity than that on the surface.

"There's secondary swells, too, from other directions. Smaller. It gets crazy when they are at cross-purposes— like today."

I couldn't see anything, but he said they were there: two point three at eighteen seconds, west.

"Don't ever let anyone tell you it can be figured out and plotted. It's too complex. There are always surprises."

I didn't say anything, but that seemed contrary to my understanding of science and technology. I was pretty sure we have everything figured out about natural forces and weather.

"Then we got our local weather. Wind, rain, cloud cover, water temperature, and so on. No one can predict it with great accuracy—don't let anyone else you otherwise."

I sensed a theme. At first, I thought he didn't like technology. But he found it useful—he just didn't trust it to tell the whole story. Usually, he admitted, all the equipment and logs were right. But sometimes they were quite wrong. And that could mean the difference between life and death.

❋

As we slid between the finger piers, I held a 3/4-inch line as they had shown me: a few coils held loosely in my left hand, the monkey ball in my right. I heard Eli yell "make her fast!" and I threw the line down to a waiting dockhand. It was a bit short of its mark, but he grabbed it before it slid off the dock.

Edwards called me over. We made five trips back and forth from the bait table to the stern, hauling almost-empty buckets of chum and tossing the remaining contents overboard. By the time we dumped the last one, the number of birds wheeling around us had quadrupled from the flock that had followed us in from sea.

The engines shut down, and the silence felt strange after a full day of their noise. We secured the lines and gear as others scurried about the decks securing hatches and doorways. Brian was down below, in the engine room, shutting down valves and switches and whatever else he did once we were docked.

Glancing up to the bridge, I saw the skipper moving about, performing his mysterious tasks.

Our last task was to haul the huge plastic ice containers, filled with our haul of fish, to the dock. We used the ship's davit, then a crane on the dock was used to lift them onto a waiting forklift, which trundled off to store them before shipping.

We worked about an hour. Once we finished, we waited for the skipper. We could not leave until he gave permission. Fishbait, Robert, and Raimundo leaned against the gunwales, smoking. Eli was up with the captain. The rest of us stood the deck with arms crossed, huddled in our jackets. I was leaning against the ship's dingy, as tired as I could ever remember. I still felt like a greenhorn, but I had learned a lot in the last few weeks.

The door above swung open, and the Captain stuck his head out. I could hardly see him from the light of the sulfur lamps behind him on the docks. "That was a good day, men! Five o'clock sharp tomorrow—we head out at six!" He disappeared into the darkness, as Eli passed him and climbed down the ladder.

Everyone walked to the gangway. I brought up the rear as Eli joined me.

"Well, Jay, four trips behind you! Good work! No major mishaps. Ready for a *real* voyage next week?" Our next trip was only three days, but he was referring to the one after that: nine days at sea.

"Sure." I didn't like the work or the people, and I had never been so unsure of myself. The lack of community bothered me, though I wondered if it was just me. They *were* a team, but had no sense of brotherhood. As if they depended on each other for safety, but nothing beyond that.

"Good, good." We stepped onto the dock. "Remember—respect the sea. She's gonna find out everything you ever did wrong!" He laughed.

Before heading to my little cell—which I appreciated more and more—I had planned to find somewhere for a nice dinner. Some good, solid food, well-prepared. But I was too tired.

I made my way to the same fish place I had bought dinner the first night. No fish and chips this time. I stood by the bar and ordered a chicken sandwich and two beers (one to go). As I waited, I drank one.

I spotted Robert and Fishbait sitting at the other end of the bar, drinking and laughing. I did not think they noticed me, and I avoided eye contact.

Back in my room, I folded a blanket on the floor and set out my food before me. It was excellent—because of my own hunger or the chef's skill I did not know. Once the sandwich was gone, I licked my fingers, propped my back against the cot, and picked up the plastic cup of beer. Sixteen ounces. I sighed and drank it down. The only thing I knew for sure in life was that food and drink made me feel better. And that sleep brought escape.

Usually.

67

I stood on the deck, looking back at land. Or rather, where land should be. The horizon disappeared into vapor. Turning in the other direction, I looked to open sea—but it didn't look any different.

"Move it, Lobster." Fishbait nudged me with his shoulder as he fiddled with something under the gunwale. I had learned that he was from Canada, which explained his accent. He was outgoing and loud, crude and rough, and could switch from friendly to angry at a moment's notice. He'd been working on board the *Sea Bull* for five years. In that time, he had fallen overboard once each season, except for his first, when he fell overboard three times: thus his nickname.

I went below to the galley. Edwards was sitting with Robert and Raimundo. Raimundo had a Catholic cross in front of him, saying prayers, it seemed.

Unlike Raimundo and Edwards, Robert talked a lot, most often to hold forth on all he knew about fishing and boats. While it was possible he enjoyed what he did and wanted to share it with others—me included—more often it sounded like he just wanted to show off. He thought it stunning—so he said—that a man my age did not understand the basics of fishing or boats. He swore constantly, weaving offensive words into parts of speech where they did not fit grammatically, syntactically, or logically.

I dealt with him, and the others, by reminding myself that I wouldn't be here long. But sometimes, lying in my bunk at night, I wondered what difference it made. What if I kept doing this until the end of my days? Who would care? As my lifeless body lay in its coffin, what would be said? He fished. He was a good deck hand. He was dependable. Would it be all that different on another path? He worked. He was a good businessman. He was dependable.

At moments like that, in the dark of night, swaying gently aboard the boat, I realized I was angry. Furious.

"Coffee?" Edwards had the pot in his hand, raised. Edwards and Eli were the only ones who treated me like a regular member. I gathered that the others saw me as an outsider who wouldn't last long.

"No, thanks."

"You feeling the swells a bit?" Edwards said, replacing the coffee pot. Robert and Fishbait had their eyes on me, expressionless.

"No," I lied. "I'm just not sure what to do with myself during the lulls in work."

Robert spoke. "You just gotta know how to plan your time. That's the life of the fisherman."

He always had advice, even when no one asked for it. He always knew the answer, no matter the topic. Everything was black and white in his world.

"Get your tasks done efficiently and perfectly. No more, no less. Rest when you can, because a time is coming when you will want to rest, and can't."

He raised his cup to me, a self-toast to his voice of experience. He had been working at sea for over twenty years.

"You see," he continued, "the sea doesn't let you determine what you will do, and when you will do it. It's all-powerful, and it's all wise. It's gonna be calm when it wants, stormy when it wants, let fish gather when it wants, or make them run to sea when it wants. Your engine blows a gasket, your bilge pump dies, or you have the best fishing day you ever had in a spot you never caught nothing before. It's all up to the sea, and she don't care what you want."

Edwards and Fishbait nodded in agreement. Raimundo, his lips moving, continued his prayers.

"You gotta just go with the flow, greenhorn. That's all you can do. That—and practice and plan for *everything*—

then, when it happens, there's no panic, no worry. Do what's required and go with the flow."

All well and good, I suppose. But what do I practice? What do I plan for? *They* haven't trained me, except as things come up. They keep *saying* things can go wrong. How about some specifics? Otherwise, it's just cheap philosophy without practical application. Useless advice.

I took a sip and set my cup down. "Very zen, I suppose."

He looked a bit uncomfortable. "I don't know anything about crazy new age stuff. Just know the sea and what it takes to be a man out here."

At another time in life, I would have responded to the implied insult.

※

The moon had just gone down over the horizon. The sea was calm and quiet. It was cold, but there was no breeze out on the foredeck near the bow. Eli, Edwards, and I sat watching and listening.

"I don't think deeply too often, but night at sea brings out the poet in me. I look at this—" he swipes an arm across the firmament "—and wonder how the earth can just sit here in space, a big old ball, with water stuck to it. How does it stay?"

"Well—"

"I know it's gravity. But—why? *Why* does gravity work like it does—not the science stuff, I've read that. Look at that horizon where the dark water meets the dark sky. Such a perfect arc. Why doesn't it all just fall apart? When the clouds gather, and there is water down here, and water up there, why doesn't everything just explode in chaos?"

A seabird cried out somewhere, as if offended by the questions.

"All the stuff that goes on—wars, murders, people dying or just fading away—they don't matter. Time goes on. But this—" a finger traces the Milky Way "— *this* matter. We gotta live the best we can and just enjoy it."

"Sounds like some crazy spiritual talk. Mother earth stuff. Or my Aunt O'Reilly."

"I don't know. I think it's all random. Explosions in space. Collisions. Just how it goes. People do bad things; others work hard. What difference does it make? Pays off for some, not for others. Look at Mr. Gerson—terrible guy. Took advantage of good old Peter, but doing great. Meanwhile, some fine person is out there with no family, no friends, no prospects. How about us? Who's to say we shouldn't be doing more than just fishing?"

"We got our health, a job, opportunity. That's good. Can't go around feeling sorry for ourselves."

"Okay, but did we do something to deserve health, job, opportunity? Gerson doesn't deserve all he has, yet he has it. Peter deserves more, doesn't have it? The sweet old lady that gets brain cancer. Crime boss lives a life of luxury. It's all random."

"Nah, I disagree. It all comes out in the wash. Like fishing—some skippers fish on someone else's numbers, treat their crews bad, cheat their owners—but eventually, they lose out. They have a bad year, lose their license. Something. But the ones like our Captain—always does right, always helping other crews and captains—cares about his crew. Might have some bad years, might get taken advantage of, but in the long run, he'll come out okay."

"You say that only because you want it to be true. Ask the Jews in the Holocaust. Ask the little girl that got beat up for stealing food when she was hungry. Ask the mother who lost her child to some disease."

The swishing of the swells against the hull, the drone of the engines was mesmerizing. The breeze picked up as if wanting to caress the pathetic beings sitting on the bow. A whistle sounded as the breeze passed through the lines and stanchions.

Eli began to sing, surprisingly melodious for such a gravelly voice.

> *We mine the sea for* pesca *and* ichthys,
> *We stab and cut and freeze*
> *We end the dark wet night*
> *Seeking far out on the sea*
> *Under the gloom and dark*
> *We feed the shaft of white and black*
> *And no one knows our broken backs*
> *And no one sees our misery*
> *We think and build and master it all*
> *We make fire from the dead*
>
> *No whale or shark can match our take*
> *No squid can see as well*
> *No animal land or sea can pride*
> *The paths we cut ourselves*
>
> *We put our hands to wave and wind*
> *We cut the path we choose*
> *Our eyes to see wonders others do not*
> *The source of all that breathes*
>
> *Where do we find our rest?*
> *Men do not know, despite our achieve*
> *Neither land nor sea grants behest*
> *The deep says 'not here'*
> *The rich cannot buy*
> *The price of it cannot be fixed*

No pearl or gold or silver or gem
Discloses the wisdom of life

The star-filled sky looks down on us all
It knows our every move
Under and over and through the sea
And all land between and above
The wind touches all, the rain falls on all
The thunder and lightning as well
It is all a great big mystery,
So we fear it and love it and live it out here
Upon the sea of our lives.

68

The helicopter flies in low over the neighborhood. It is no typical tract housing, but a high-end market. Large houses, each with a different floorplan, sit on significant amounts of land. Pools, tennis courts, and lavish landscaping. Luxury cars and SUVs. The people who live here work hard, persevere, and reap the rewards.

As we approach a cul-de-sac, the pilot hands me a pair of high power binoculars. The radio crackles in my headphones. "Thought you might want to take a look, boss."

He points down to the left. I don't remember getting on this flight. Where am I?

We are close enough to the ground that I see he is pointing at a house at the end of the cul-de-sac. I put the large, awkward device to my eyes and train them on the home.

Big. *Really* big. New. Some of the landscaping isn't even finished yet. There's a large pool in the backyard; beyond that, a circular built-in fire pit, with seating for at least twenty people. Nice.

I scan back to the front door. Huge, arched, made of dark wood and iron. A couple stands in front of the door, facing each other. A man and a woman, I think. He holds something up and she hugs him, then he opens the door and they enter.

Shifting the binoculars, I see splashes in the pool. Two kids are swimming and jumping and running. The fire pit is filled with people drinking, laughing, and talking.

The pilot banks left and climbs. I lower the binoculars to my lap and click my microphone.

"Who's house was that?"

"Hang on!" We bank right and descend. A city lay below. Office buildings reach into the sky. Industrial parks, restaurants, and shops radiate in all directions. Vehicles crawl through the streets, like lines of ants along pre-determined paths, each with purpose.

The pilot maneuvers us beside a tall tower, a few floors down from the roof. I lift the binoculars and spot a meeting room filled with well-dressed men and women, sitting around a table. One man stands, addressing the group. A screen displays a presentation behind as he gestures. He is quite animated, and the listeners appear enraptured. Something quite important, I am sure. A door opens, and a woman comes in carrying a stack of folders.

We bank again, tilting left towards the building as we pass around one corner. I lower the binoculars and see, far below, entrances to the tower. Each walkway is bordered by a trough, like a human-made waterway. Both are filled with a viscous liquid that billows in soft waves down each channel. One is milky-white, like heavy cream; the other is translucent gold-green. like oil. Beside each trough was a line of olive trees—each one old, thick, and heavy with fruit.

I click my mike again. "Where are we?"

Again the pilot does not answer as we climb high above the city, bank, and then down again. Ahead, I see a building with a dome that must surely be the city hall. It looks familiar, but I cannot place it.

We hover over the dome. Looking down, I see it is translucent; inside, a large group of people are gathered. A man stands at a podium giving a speech. Every few moments, the crowd erupts in cheers and applause. I wish I could hear what he is saying.

We move away and descend. The pilot sets us down on the street beside the building. People are crowded all around it—a huge crowd.

"Okay," the pilots shouts. "Here we are! Hold for a moment."

"Where?" This is so confusing. Had I called for this 'copter? What was I doing?

The people seem to be waiting for something. Many of their clothes are in tatters, and most are thin and frail— even sickly. Some hold papers and envelopes, and have worried looks on their faces.

"Who are these people?"

As I speak, a doorway opens and people pour out of the building. Their faces are happy; they laugh and smile. As they spread out, each seeks someone in the waiting throng. Finding them, they join hands and talk excitedly. I see disbelief, hope, and relief, in many of the faces.

I pull on the latch to unlock the door. I want to hear.

"No!" the pilot yells. "It isn't safe!"

A cheer goes up from the crowd. A man has appeared at a balcony a few floors up from the ground. He waves to the crowd, and everyone cheers and applauds. It is such a scene of joy that it hurts my heart. It has been so long since I felt joy.

Yet my cynicism, developed and honed over the years into fine, sharp realism, tells me that these people are deceived. If he is a politician, he's promising them something he can not or will not deliver—but it will get him votes. If he is a businessman, he started some foundation or pledged to build something that would make their lives better—but would only make his life better. If he is a citizen organizer, then he, as "one of them," is plying fear—but his solution would only result in an increase of power and status for him.

The crowd falls silent. In unison, they turn to me, as if they hear my thoughts. The mass moves as towards the 'copter. Soon, the people in front break into a run.

"Okay, that's our cue!" The engines growl in fury, the rotors whip up to speed, and we jump into the air. I am pushed into my seat. The g-forces continue to increase. I am surprised that the machine can reach such speed. I turn my head as if someone piles bags of sand on top of me, more and more and more binoculars on lap dig into my thigh cannot move my hand to reach vision iris blackness

❋

The helicopter is flying low over a fancy neighborhood. I can see it is fancy because the houses are huge, and no two are alike. They all have four or five acres, with pools, tennis courts, trees, paths, and beautiful landscape. Expensive cars sit in every driveway. These people have power, money, and influence.

We approach the end of a cul-de-sac and the radio crackles in my headphones. "Get your binocs, boss; I think you might want to see this."

I frown as he points. Hadn't we already done this? What was I doing here?

…

"Okay, that's our signal to get out of here," the pilot yelled as he went full throttle and we lept into the sky. The g-forces—

…

❃

We flew in low over the neighborhood of mansions. No two alike, each with expertly manicured yards, pools, tennis courts, and—

"Hey, take these binocs, boss, you want to see this!"

I'm confused. What are we doing? Didn't we already—

…

"Woah, time to get out of here!" the g-forces crushed my chest as we—

…

❃

The neighborhood came up fast as we…

69

I awoke to Robert banging on the bulkhead.

"Get up, greenhorn! I know your previous life was cushy, but you're doing *real* work now. On deck!"

I resented him being the one sent to get me. As I struggled to awake and prepare a response, he left. Muttering to myself, I pulled on my clothes and boots and clomped up on deck. Robert and Fishbait were by the nets, having already unreeled about half. It sloshed about in the sea as it spun out, floating briefly on the surface before the bottom weights took it down, leaving the top edge floating with its buoys. The Captain (or Eli, I couldn't tell from here), was maneuvering the boat in a large circle at low speed. We were about halfway around the circumference already; I could see the first buoy at a ninety-degree angle to starboard.

"Come on!" Robert shouted. "Don't stand around!"

I was confused because until now we had not worked in the early morning since leaving the dock. Why had they started now? And why didn't someone tell me yesterday?

Mike was at the stern, to starboard, hooking bait to the traps attached to the net at ten-foot intervals. Two large bait buckets sat by his feet. Raimundo was at the table, preparing the bait fish.

"What should I do?" I yelled over the wind, engines, and motor noise.

"Help Mike with baiting the traps!"

"No!" Mike shouted back. "I can do that. I need more bait. Help Raimundo get more ready!"

I went, with some unsteadiness, to the bait table. Raimundo looked up. "Nice of you to join us." Uncharacteristic.

"Sorry."

I pulled on my gloves and began. Once a bucket was full, I'd haul it over to Mike and bring back an empty. I'd jump down into the fish locker and pull another container of bait fish whenever we needed it. I felt like I needed to make up for my lateness, but was still irritated that no one told me. Was it on purpose to make me look bad? Despite all the talk of the "camaraderie of the sea"

220

and how "we all depend on each other out here," I didn't see it. It was more like "every man for himself."

After another hour or so, the circle was complete. Robert climbed out onto the transom platform to connect the ends of the nets. Then, the Captain (it *was* him on the bridge) took us about a mile away, close to the southernmost island in the chain, and we dropped anchor. Raimundo and I cleaned the bait station and buckets, put everything away, and then went down to the galley.

I arrived last because I stayed to scrub down the table, even though Raimundo had said it could wait. Everyone was there except the Captain and Eli. All the seats were taken, though if Robert had not spread out with a leg up on the table, there would have been room. I didn't ask him to move; he didn't offer.

As I finished loading a bowl with fish stew, Eli came in. He beckoned me to follow him, and we went back up on deck. He motioned to a bench along the gunwale. "Sit. Go ahead and eat."

I sat. He'd probably tell me to ignore Robert's insults again.

"Jay, I know you want to do well, and you mean well. But you gotta be up on deck with everyone else when its time. We let it go before 'cause you was new. Best is to get up for breakfast with the rest of 'em."

I was taken aback. How was I supposed to manage that when I didn't know?

"Uh, sorry, Eli. I had no idea when breakfast was. As for work, I thought there'd be an announcement or something. There are no clocks down there."

He laughed without humor. "Announcement? This is no cruise ship, boy." I was no "boy," even taking into account our ages. "Everyone else manages to be on time.

You get a break this time, being a greenhorn and all, but don't let it happen again."

I had never worked on a boat. "Eli, again, sorry, but how can I know when things are supposed to happen when I have not been told? I'm happy to do anything, I just—"

"Part of the job. Figure it out. You're supposed to be a smart guy, aren't you?"

I bit my tongue. Better to buckle under for now. "Yes, sir. My apologies. It won't happen again."

I'll be out of this chaotically-run business as soon as possible.

Eli sat down. "Look, Jay, I get it. It's tough out here, much different than anything you've done. McNally's like that—willing to take people on to help 'em out. You've never worked hard like this, might take some adjustment."

I kept my thoughts to myself and tried to look penitent.

"Okay, you know the score? Know what you have to do?"

"Yes, sir."

He slapped my thigh, nearly upending my bowl of cooling stew. "Good! You'll work out fine, I'm sure."

He left. I stayed.

I'm out of my element. I know that. But it's not rocket science—or even as complex as business or securities law. It's just a matter of gaining the knowledge and experience. I can learn fast, and I am smarter than any of them. It shouldn't matter, since I'm not staying, but I refuse to give them the satisfaction.

I took a few bites of the stew, then tossed the rest overboard.

❋

The next day, after setting more nets and trolling, I had not been late for any meal, meeting, or work. In fact, I was early and did more than asked. But the mocking didn't stop. Raimundo, who partook in some of it, though with a bit more lightheartedness, told me that it was normal for greenhorns. The newest crew member got blamed for everything. I guess it was like boot camp for privates.

Still, Robert and Fishbait's attitude seemed less like hazing and more like persecution. They didn't think I belonged and were trying to force me out. Each night, after all the chores were done, they gathered on deck to drink and talk and laugh. I joined them the first couple of times, but they ignored me except to haze. When they started a card game, I was not asked to join. I suppose I could have invited myself, but I was not inclined or interested.

On our last day, well before dawn, we hauled in the last of the nets and stored the fish in the ice locker. It was by far the most difficult work so far. Not only was I wet, sticky, and exhausted, I had to wait until last to take a shower (greenhorn). When my turn came, there was no hot water left in the tank. Shivering, I dried off, pulled on multiple layers of clothes and went out on the bow to lay down. The day was supposed to grow bright and warm. Since we were heading back home, there would be nothing to do for about five hours.

❋

A change in the sound of the engines woke me. My eyes felt sticky and swollen. The sun was halfway down to the horizon.

I sat up and saw we were close to shore. I opened my mouth wide to stretch my numb lips and cried out in pain.

Though I did not remember, at some point I had taken off the layers of clothing, leaving only a tank top and trousers. My arms were bright red and felt like a thousand needles were stabbing them over and over. I lifted a hand to my face and felt the blisters.

I stood up and groped my way along the gunwale to the aft cockpit. As I stepped down onto the deck, I saw that three or four of the guys were sitting near the stern. I could barely make out their identities.

"Greenhorn!" It was Robert. "What have you *done?!*"

"Oh, no, Jay." This was Eli. "I saw you on the foredeck, but you were covered, so I didn't bother you."

He rose and came to peer at my face. "That's a bad one. Out here the sun and wind can crisp you up pretty bad. And it did!"

I heard whooping from the group. "He looks like a lobster!" That was Fishbait. The others joined in the merriment.

"Come on, my boy. I got some stuff we can put on it and some other remedies, but yer gonna be in a bad way for days. Real bad. Don't think I ever seen such a sunburn."

That meant a lot, coming from a guy who's face looked like old leather.

❄

A knock sounded at the door of my tiny room. I got up, with much pain, and opened it to Rikki.

"How are you, dear? Better?"

I nod. It *was* better. But that was relative. Eli had taken me to the emergency room after we docked. Neither of us said anything as we drove through the dark in his 1960's Chevy Sedan which smelled of cigarettes and medication. I'd had to stay overnight, then spent the next two days in this cell. Rikki had stocked my room with some cans of soup, bread, meats and cheese, and bottles of water. For the first thirty-six hours, it was nausea, headache, and chills. I was supposed to drink a *lot* of water, apply various lotions and unguents, and take antibiotics and silver sulfadiazine. Of course, I had to stay out of the sun. Fortunately, there were five days before our nine-day trip began.

"Oh, good. You look better. I brought you a few things. And…and sorry to ask, but did the doctors given you any idea when you could return? Peter wants to know." She seemed genuinely put out for having to ask.

"They said whenever I felt strong enough after tomorrow. Three to five days is typical. I can make the next trip. Is that okay? Am I in trouble?"

"Oh, no, dear, no." Yet I knew it was one thing to get sick or have an accident; quite another to have done something irresponsible. I probably would have already fired me if I were in charge. Offered a nice severance with a kind admonishment to be more responsible in the next job—for which I'd be happy to write a positive recommendation.

After Rikki had left, I realized that I would welcome being fired. It would be a relief.

I had ended up in commercial fishing by default, without planning or brainstorming. I had panicked at the prospect of not having work. That's not how I used to do things. Think. Plan. Strategize. That's how things work out. This was no way to work. Communities—and businesses—show their value by how they treat newcomers and who they exclude. This was a shallow group—just a bunch of individuals who happen to practice the same craft. I needed a better community than this. One that would—

A cold wash of despair washed over me. I felt woozy, as if there were birds and stars whirling around my head like a cartoon character.

My former community had been no better. They were a false group, with a disingenuous sense of loyalty and a desire to avoid the uncomfortable. The connections turned out to be thin and weak when called upon. They gave it lip service, but it meant nothing when it really mattered.

Every person listed in my little notebook had rejected me. They were no different than the *Sea Bull* crew.

I stood and, with all the volume I could muster, screamed "I hate you!" It was deafening in the cement cubicle. It felt good.

"I hate this place!" If I wasn't so weak, I'd go outside and bellow my condemnation at the whole universe. And *include* the universe! A universe where humans are an *infestation*, lucky to get through life long enough to enjoy a few pleasantries before their wounds bring death.

A lonely death.

70

"Now, I need to review this list with you. My paralegal will use your answers to draft a declaration for you to sign and notarize."

"What is it?" The courtroom is empty at the moment, except for my attorney and I. The room is dim, but a lone spotlight shines on the defense table. It's like being in a stage play. One which doesn't make a lot of sense to the audience, but they applaud anyway, because they do not want to seem gauche. "Ah, the characterization! The sublime plot elements. Bravo!"

"We'll use it as an attempt to get a more specific response from the court as to your charges."

"How?"

"By filing a declaration of all the things you have *not* done wrong. If they disagree, they will have to say so. Then we'll know!" He appears proud of this tactic, and looks at me as if expecting a reward.

"What? Are we going to work through the entire criminal and civil codes?"

"It's the only way."

"Okay. I guess I should be happy you are doing *something.*" He appears hurt, which I find unbecoming an attorney.

He consults the paper before him. "Have you ever had sexual relations with another woman who was not your wife, or, before you were married, sexual relations with another man's wife."

"No!"

He looks up. "You must be honest with me. I mean, in this day and age…"

"Yes, I'm telling the truth, as hard as it might be for you to believe. Besides, that isn't illegal."

227

"Actually, it is, Mr. Adam. Just because no one is ever charged doesn't mean it isn't illegal. There are many laws on the books which are no longer charged. They've not gotten around to repealing them."

I was dubious. "Like what?"

"Aside from adultery? Well, for example, it is illegal to wear a zoot suit in Los Angeles."

"It is not."

"I tell you it is. I can look up the statute if you like. While I am at it, I'll give you the Federal Code that makes it a crime to skydive while under the influence, criminalizes the selling of anti-flatulence drugs without making clear that flatulence means 'gas,' makes it illegal to sell wine with the word 'zombie' as part of the name—"

"Okay, okay! I think we're off track."

"Indeed." He returns to his paper. "Have you ever participated, directed, or sanctioned a deceitful business practice?"

"No, those charges were found to be the practice of prosecutorial misconduct. As you should know, if you—"

"Yes, yes. I refer to *other* acts you have not been charged with as far as you know."

"No, I have *not*."

"Have you ever violated state or federal employment laws in the hiring, firing, or dealings with any employee?"

"No. As a matter of fact, I went beyond what is required."

"Irrelevant. We are looking for crimes or violations. Have you ever mistreated a child, a mentally-challenged person, or an elderly person—'elderly' defined as over 65."

"No."

228

He arches his eyebrows. "Please, Mr. Adam, surely in your forty-plus years, you have done so. Even in an understandable moment of passion or frustration?"

"No. Maybe when I was a child or a teen. But nothing that would rise to the level of a crime."

He sighs. "Very well." He continues, asking whether I had laundered money to avoid taxes or fees (no), engaged in lewd public acts or disturbing the peace (no), or practiced frivolous financial or legal retribution on anyone. "That's a crime?"—"Indeed: misuse of funds for frivolous legal action"—"Well, I haven't!"

We continue working out way through every criminal and civil crime on the books, State and Federal. Hours pass, then days, and finally, after months of questions, he sits back with a sigh.

"Mr. Adam, I am at a loss. We need to find *something*—even a minor infraction—it will give us a line of investigation. Then I can mount a defense. With your exemplary life, we might get an acquittal—even a dismissal! Maybe we should work through all the administrative codes?"

"The answer will still be no, no, *no*!"

"Very well. No need to get all exercised…Ah, how about charity work? Have you—"

"I have done all *kinds* of charity work. I gave to reputable organizations, but I also donated my time and gave cash—"

"—Mr. Adam—"

"—because I didn't want to be doing it for tax write-offs! Ask my accountants—they tried to—"

"Mr. *Adam*, please! I am asking if there could have been anything untoward in your donations. A quid pro quo? Anything—even if you didn't intend it, that could be construed as questionable?"

"No. Absolutely not. I would have refused to help. People with means must guard against ulterior motives, they must—"

"I don't care about your philosophy of philanthropy. I care about finding something—even the tiniest thing—that the prosecution might have on you. There *has* to be something."

"There is *nothing!* Nothing I tell you!" I stand and my chair bashes into the partition behind us. "That's the reason for all my anger and frustration! I have not done anything, *anything*, to warrant this outrageous—"

He grabs my arm. "I understand," he hisses. "But if you keep up these outbursts, you'll give them a reason to charge you with contempt of court or even disorderly conduct. *Please* sit down and be calm."

I want to rip his head off. Yet, I reminded myself, he is trying, and maybe he'll be able to get me before the unjust judge. Eventually.

I sit down.

"Thank you. Now, my paralegal has typed up all your answers and—"

"Already?"

"Of course. She's quite good at her job. And the NP—" he gestures at a woman now standing beside him "—is here to notarize your signature. If you are confident that your answers are truthful and correct, and that no one can impugn them—"

"Gladly, sir, *gladly*. I'll take this paper—this declaration—and have it framed! I'll have it gilded and wear it as a *hat* for the rest of my days!" I reach over, snatch the pen out of his hand, and sign with a great flourish. The woman takes my fingerprint, then places her stamp on the document.

"And if anyone *can* find anything," I tell them both, "*I'll* demand that I be punished to the fullest extent—no, *beyond* the fullest extent of the law!"

71

The seas were as calm as I had seen them. Out on the distant horizon, however, there was a dark black border, as if someone had drawn a line with a thick black marker. Our wake stretched behind us like a mile-long serpent's tail.

"Well, here's the real test, greenhorn. Nine days at sea. Weather's been easy so far. Now we'll find out what you're made of." Robert stood on the opposite side of the deck, leaning against the gunwale. I could smell the smoke from his cigarette. There was no breeze, except the fourteen-knot wind we created with our passage. Back here, we were protected from it by the superstructure.

"I suppose so." I did not turn around.

The storm we had come through on our way back from San Diego waters had seemed pretty bad to me. I had vomited twice. Eli said it seemed worse than it was, because we were heading into the swells and the wind.

"Farthest from shore, too. *Way* out there, nothin' but sea." He laughed. "We'll hit that storm in three days. Thirty to forty knot winds, swells at twelve feet."

It was obvious that he was trying to rattle me. But I figured that if it was bad enough, we wouldn't go out. Gerson might send us out when it would make us miserable, but not if there danger of damage or loss to his boats.

"Scared?"

I turned to face him and leaned against the gunwale. Somewhere in that tiny brain was a fear that he might not be as smart or as brave as he wanted others to think. So he dealt with it by claiming stupidity, cowardice, or inexperience of others.

In the past, I would have bristled, though my better nature would have led me to find a way to help him boost his confidence. Yet what difference had it made? I thought of John. People don't want to change; they want others to change.

I shrugged. "Not scared. Some anxiety about the unknown. But I'm on a boat full experienced sailors. I think we'll be fine."

Robert stared at me for a moment. He couldn't argue with that without insulting himself. And I took some wind out of his sails by admitting that I was a little anxious.

He took a drag from his cigarette, tilted his head back and blew a stream of smoke. It swirled around his head, protected, until it drifted far enough to be whipped away into oblivion.

"Yeah. Well, you aren't experienced. But I guess you don't have much to lose. I know about your background."

Ah. He'd done some research. His attitude made even more sense now. I refused to bite. "Yeah, I went through some rough stuff. It is what it is." A stupid tautological phrase, but it suited the discussion and my adversary.

He nodded and took another puff. "I'd like to hear what happened." He looked at the stub in his hand, then back up at me. "I like to know what kind of people my life depends on."

We're on a commercial fishing boat, not fighting a war. You just want me to supply you more ammunition.

"Not much to tell. You've heard it."

"Yeah, but I'd like to hear it from you. See how you spin it."

I was having a hard time maintaining my blasé attitude after that, but a noise up from the bridge caused us both to turn and look. Edwards and Brian had come out of the bridge and were climbing down the ladder.

"Good, both of you are here." Edwards talked as he descended. "We need your help to reattach the motor on the starboard davit."

It had stopped working during the last trip, so four of the crew—not me—had unbolted it and taken it below for Brian to repair. He had assured the Captain that it would be ready as we headed out on this trip, and had made good on that promise.

"We'll have to haul it up from the work bench in the engine room," Brian said. "That's the easy part. Once it's on deck, you three will hold it up in place while I re-seat the bolts and tighten them." He looked astern and to port. "Need to do it now—wind and swells are gonna kick up later."

We all made our way down through a narrow passage-way to the engine room. The engines—huge diesel pow-erhouses—chugged and clacked so loud it was hard to hear. On the floor near the workbench was the motor, about the size of a large oven. It must weigh over 500 pounds. We'd have to maneuver it through a narrow bulkhead, down the passageway, and up the stairs on deck. In spite of Brian's words, that seemed harder than holding it up to the platform while he attached it.

As we gathered around the machine, Robert held forth, explaining the physics and the strategy, along with each person's task. I had found that the crew let him drone on, even when it was unnecessary.

After much swearing, smashed fingers, and scratched arms, we got it up onto the deck. We set it down, with some effort, just outside the bulkhead. It was as difficult as I had feared.

"Alright," Robert snarled. "That was worse than I thought. You guys aren't very strong. Especially Lobster. Probably never lifted anything that heavy in his life."

I ignored him. Brian walked over to the davit and motor platform. He pointed to a place about chest-high, where shiny metal betrayed where the motor had been attached.

"This is where it goes—see the bolt holes here, here, here, here, and here?" He pointed at the motor on the deck. "That side goes against *here.*" Along the circular pattern of bolt holes, between each, were metal posts upon which the motor would sit as the bolts were inserted and tightened. Holding up a five-hundred-pound chunk of metal might be a challenge.

"Alright, let's do it," Robert said, moving to one side of the motor casing. "Lobster should do the bolts while the rest of us hold it up, since he's the weakest."

Brian handed me a small bucket. "Here are the bolts, washers, and nuts. Once it's on the posts, attach the bolts and the nuts a few turns. I'll make sure the gears and cable guides are lined up. Once it's aligned, you tighten 'em."

The four of us lifted the motor, shuffling and lurching our way to the davit. At Robert's command, we lifted it up to the platform, straining, while he yelled "more this way!" "No no no—to starboard!" and "Lobster, up, up!" until we were lined up with the post holes.

"Now! Shift it in!"

After a few more shouts, the motor was flush against the plate, with the posts through the holes.

Robert yelled, "We'd don't have all day, Lobster!"

I slid out front under the machinery and, moving around and between the men, inserted the first three bolts with no problem. The fourth wouldn't go through.

"You wasting time on purpose?!" Robert grunted.

"This one's binding. Shift it up."

"No, idiot," grunted Robert. "Get the nuts on the others first; then we can move it without worrying about it sliding it off the others."

That made sense, much to my irritation. I ducked back out, grabbed three nuts from the bucket, then slid between Brian and Edwards, up underneath the motor, to thread the first nut. It was awkward, but I got the first and second one in, all the while with Robert grunting insults.

Once the washers and nuts were on and tightened a few turns, I went back to the fourth bolt.

"I can't tell which direction it needs to go."

Robert swore. "Alright, guys, let's lift up just a bit and to starboard."

After a bit of juggling, it went through.

"It's in!"

"Shut up and finish."

I'd had it. "*You* shut up!"

Robert exploded with a stream of profanity focused on my birth, my genitals, and my mother's character until Brian interrupted.

"Hey, guys, *focus*! Safety first, then rip each other apart for all I care." I was surprised at the calm but forceful authority of his tone.

I inserted the remaining bolts and put the nuts on.

"Okay, done."

Edwards dropped his hands and stepped back.

Robert and Brian both shouted at him, but it was too late. With the nuts only loosely attached, the weight of the top-heavy motor cause it to fall forward. It caught on the washers attached to the end, but all that weight could snap them off. I leaped in and pushed at the top to try to take some of the weight off. Brian jumped next to me, adding his strength. Robert kept holding the side and Edwards returned to his spot.

"We got it for now…tighten the bolts," Brian grunted.

I ducked down and began tightening the nut.

"No, idiot!" Robert again. "The top bolts first!" I didn't understand what difference it made.

Robert saw that Brian was having trouble. "Edwards, slide over and help Brian."

Soon I had the bolts tightened as much as I could without a wrench. The motor was stable, but still askew.

Brian spoke. "Robert, come over here and push with Edwards. I'll check the gears and guides before we tighten with the wrench. You hold the bottom, Jay." He slid around behind me and reached into the gap between the motor housing and the mounting plate. He grunted with effort as he twisted himself into an awkward-looking position.

I moved my legs aside, to give him more room, bracing myself against the starboard gunwale. I couldn't get much leverage on the motor housing at that angle though, so I slid back.

"Was better the other way, Jay," Brian said.

"Couldn't get a good foothold."

"We can hold it," Robert said. I slid sideways and back, trying to brace myself against the gunwale.

At that moment, the ship lurched and tilted to starboard. My feet slipped and I lost my hold on the motor. As I scrambled, the ship lurched again and listed even more. I heard yelling as I lost my balance and crashed into the side of the boat pain yelling flipping falling panic water cold spinning cold pain dark can't breath cold wet cold dark

Part Three

CODA

72

"How big is the crowd?" the D.A. asked.

"Hundreds. They may reach a thousand before the end of the day."

"Ugh. I wish there was a way to make them go home."

"I knew this would happen. When a community leader is discovered to be corrupt, the hard-working people come out. It's worse if he's a rich guy who lorded it over everyone."

"Come on, Adam never acted that way."

"You just can't see it because he contributed to your campaign and invited you to parties. Now we know why—he wanted you on his side."

The D.A. shook his head. "No. He's a good guy that just got caught up in stuff."

"Come on, chief. You saw all the evidence."

The D.A did not respond.

"I'm gonna open the window. I want to hear it."

With the window was open they could hear the buzz of the crowd outside city hall. *It does sound like a lot of protesters,* the D.A. thought. They sat without speaking until a microphone squealed and the crowd grew quiet.

"Thank you to all of you who came out today!" The voice was muffled and tinny from this distance. "We demand *justice*. We are the workers who keep this town running. We are the people who live from paycheck to paycheck! And all we ask is that our leaders serve with integrity and not for personal gain!"

Cheers erupted.

"Maybe some do," the speaker continued. "But not Jay Adam. He said he was for *us*. He said he'd serve *our* community. He said he'd be a generous employer."

Boos.

"But we found out, didn't we?! Like all rich people, he was taking advantage of us of the whole time! He stole from us! He kept food from the mouths of our children! It was not enough to have great wealth or a successful business. He wanted more, more, *more*! So he broke the laws made to protect us. He even murdered two of his fellow citizens!"

Screams and cries from the crowd.

"Poor Betty was just riding her bike and minding her own business. Coming home from cleaning other peoples' homes. Did you know her little boy had just been diagnosed with leukemia? Did Jay Adam care?"

"No!" yelled the crowd with one voice.

"And poor Ed Zohn! A kind, good man, struggling with life and the hardships of those who actually *work* for a living. Did Jay Adam care?"

"No!"

"No, he did *not*! Do you know why? Because we're *nothing* to people like him. The rich don't care about us!"

The crowd screamed, yelled, and stomped. It was some time before the speaker could continue.

"They tell us the economy has been bad. But *we* are the only ones who suffer—not Adam and his cronies! They tell us they'll keep us safe from crime and disease—but the only ones who are safe are Adam and his friends!"

More shouts and screaming.

"We *demand* justice! We've been patient! No more! We *demand* justice! We want justice! We want justice!"

The crowd took up the cry. It grew louder.

The D.A. looked over at the detective. "What are you smiling about?"

"It's nice to hear people standing up for what's right."

His colleague said nothing.

"Come on, boss. It's not a gray area. Right or wrong. Someone has to pay. It's only just."

The D.A. grunted. "Justice," he whispered to himself.

73

Voices. Pain. Headache. "—I don't think so—" "—not the motor, it was the davit arm—" "—quick thinking—" "—can you hear me—" "—was my fault—" "—it happens—."

It used to be so good. Such a fine life. Wasn't that a song? Something about stealing a sailor from sea?

❋

Stella sits beside the bed, holding my hand. Tears are in her eyes. "Jay, can you hear me?"

I try to speak, but my throat and tongue feel like sandpaper. All I can do is croak.

"Oh, oh, Jay, I love you so much." She puts her head down on my shoulder, shaking with quiet sobs. I look around. A hospital. I remember. I just had surgery.

Stella. Such a wonderful woman. So perfect. And our kids…

She raises her head. "Do you remember anything? Remember why you are here?"

I nod and try to clear my throat. It hurts.

"The doctors said it went well, though recovery could be six weeks—as they told us before, if you remember. We can handle that, right?"

I love her blue, pleading eyes. Such love. I'm able to squeak, "Of course."

She smiles and gives a little laugh as she wipes an eye with the back of a hand.

"Everything will be fine, Jay. Soon we'll be back home, with the kids, having friends over for dinner. You'll be back at work, stronger than ever, making deals and succeeding at everything."

The door crashes open and a police officer storms in. Stella jumps up.

"Mr. Jay Adam?"

I nod.

"I hereby place you under arrest for manslaughter, driving under the influence, criminal fraud, domestic terrorism, money laundering, wearing a zoot suit in the city, sedition, tax evasion, assault with intent to do grievous bodily harm, skydiving under the influence, and second-degree murder."

The room lit up like someone had tossed flares inside a foxhole. My head spins. Gravity fails, and I float above the bed until the tubes in my arms stop me.

A SWAT team storms the room. Some were dressed as marines, others like Star Wars storm troopers. One wears an ancient Trojan soldier's helmet; another swings a Roman *gladus*.

As one grabs Stella by the arms and holds her back, the others surround my bed. I grab the railings and try to pull my feet to the floor, but four of the goons hold me down. "Let me go!" I scream. They have faces like Anthony, Zohn, Zig, and Robert.

As they pull me down, a doctor appears.

"Mr. Adam, this is for your own good." I see he's not a doctor, but Officer Rahab wearing a lab coat. He stabs a syringe into my arm.

The nurse to his left looks remarkably like Ellie.

74

"—Normal now—" "—he'll be okay?—" "—no need—" "—stay a little longer—" "—Jay? Can you hear me?—"

✻

Stella. Keren and Ally. Friends and employees. House and home. Little closet on the docks. Sickness. Injury. Outcast.

✻

Eli sat beside my bed, with a face full of concern. "Jay? Can you hear me?"

I tried to speak, but my body ached and my head throbbed like I was beaten up. All I can do is nod.

"Ah, good. You're awake." He patted my shoulder. I looked around. Ship's cabin. I remember. I was knocked overboard.

Brian. Robert. An accident. Such a dysfunctional crew.

✻

Eli leaned over and fixed his eyes on mine. "Do you remember anything? Remember why you are here?"

245

I nod and try to clear my throat. It hurts. The room was rocking gently. I could hear the wind outside.

"I went overboard?"

"Right."

Davit. Motor. Bashing. Yelling. Falling. Cold. Blackness.

I tried to raise my head the result forced a groan from me.

"Yeah, you're gonna hurt for a while." He grimaced. "I had the helm, and three whales breached right in front of us. Never seen that before, in front of a boat under power. I went hard to starboard. The bolts on the motor broke and it fell. The davit swung around and knocked you right over."

"I don't remember that."

"You took a pretty good hit. Brian and Edwards got scraped up bad. Robert climbed the ladder and yelled at me to pull down the throttle and come about. Edwards went right over the side after you. Held on without a PFD until we circled back. You blacked out."

"How…how long?"

"That was this morning. It's 1800 now. Robert fixed you all up, nothing broken. Scrapes, bruises. Drank a lot of seawater. Maybe a mild concussion. You'll be fine."

"I think I'm hungry."

"I'll send someone down with some soup and water. We'll be at our spot tomorrow afternoon, so we can make do without you until then. Just rest."

75

Someone had put glue in my eyes while I slept. I try to pull them open with my fingers without any luck. I hear someone talking, but in such low tones I can not make out the words. Chairs scrape on the floor.

I reach down to find I'm sitting on a chair. A cushioned seat. With plastic arms.

"Hello?"

"Ah, good! You are awake."

"I can't see."

"We're about to begin."

"Begin what?"

"The hearing."

I recognize the voice: it's my attorney. "The hearing?"

"Yes, indeed."

"I can't see. I can't open—"

"Shhh! It's starting."

"All rise!" I hear Officer Rahab's voice. Am I finally getting a hearing? I stand, holding the table in front of me.

"May it please the court—" That's not my attorney. To the right. The prosecutor? Finally!

My attorney's hand on my shoulder pushes me back into my seat. The other voice resumes.

"I wish to read a statement to be entered into the record."

A woman's voice speaks from the front of the room. "Begin."

That's the judge's clerk, I think. Why doesn't the judge speak? I lean over and whisper.

"Hey, if the judge and the prosecutor are the same person, then the judge *is* here!"

"Quiet!" he hisses. "It's only an assistant."

Of course it is.

"—Placed on this isthmus of a middle state, a Being darkly wise, and rudely great: with too much knowledge for the Sceptic side, with too much weakness for the Stoic's pride—"

I can't contain myself. "What—"

A strong hand squeezes my arm and I fall silent.

"—to deem himself a God, or Beast; indoubt his mind or body to prefer; born but to die, and reas'ning but to err; alike in ignorance, his reason such, whether he thinks too little, or too much."

Silence.

"We thank the court."

"Thank you, counsel." The woman again.

Chair legs scraping.

"Does the defense have a statement?"

"No, ma'am. Not at this moment."

The boiling creature who lives in my stomach begins to stir. "*What* is going on?! What *was* that? Why aren't you—"

"Keep your voice down."

"Isn't he going to read the charges? Did the declaration—"

"Very well," the voice from the front says. "Counsel, do you have anything further?"

The prosecutor speaks again.

"Yes, and if it may please the court, I wish to enter the following into the record: 'If only it were all so simple! If only there were evil people somewhere insidiously committing evil deeds, and it were necessary only to separate them from the rest of us and destroy them. But the line dividing good and evil cuts through the heart of every human being. And who is willing to destroy a piece of his own heart? ' That is all."

"Very well. Defense?"

"Our only response at the moment is the declaration we filed last week."

"Okay, gentleman, thank you for your time." Rustling of papers and chair legs scraping.

"Wait!" The shout was out before I could think about it. "I demand to hear the charges against me! It's my *right!*"

Silence. No sounds, no voices, no movement. I cannot even hear my attorney breathing.

"Do you *hear me*?!" I want to offend them with my fury. "Those words mean nothing! No one is perfect, but that doesn't mean you can punish me without impunity! I have committed no crimes! If you think I have, *tell me!*"

I pant with the effort.

Silence.

"Hello?!"

Silence.

I reach out to my left and right, but there is nothing. Without warning, the blackness is overwhelmed by blazing whiteness.

✳

The desert burns my feet as I walk. Walking faster does not help. I try walking on the outer edges of my shoes, which helps until my ankles begin to hurt.

I look ahead, shielding my eyes from the blinding sun. The mountains in the distance are a hazy mix of grays and whites. Just before the foothills sits a shimmering black lake. Parallel lines of white and blue float above it, shifting and fading. There is no water. It's a mirage.

The bright blue sky is cloudless. The sun, directly overhead, assaults my head like a god holding a blowtorch.

The sand and dry brush extend in every direction, like a sea of yellow and brown. Ahead, closer than the mirage, I see what appear to be sailing ships in a parallel line, perpendicular to my path. They look about three inches tall from here, all the same height, stretching from right to left. At random times, flashes appear. Sunlight momentarily reflecting from a porthole or mast, perhaps.

How did I get here?

I begin singing. "Where's my beautiful wife…my beautiful house?!" What was that song? Something about being held down under water—

A tall plant blocks my path. It is at least ten feet tall.

"Well," says the plant, "are you going to keep shouting like that?"

"I was singing."

"Didn't sound like any singing I've heard. In any case, you are late."

"Late for what?"

"The meeting. Everyone else is here."

Ellie sits on a nearby rock. She is wrinkled and sad. She looks old. Her hair is a mess. She stares at the ground. Zig is beside her, about two feet away, sitting on another rock. He also stares at the ground. His clothes are disheveled; he looks gaunt and sickly. Between the two rocks stretches a shimmering web, in tatters. A large brown spider clings to it.

"Ellie! Zig! What are you doing here?"

"Silence," the plant says. Neither Zig or Ellie acknowledge me.

"Okay, we can begin. Robert?"

Startled, I turn to see Robert standing beside the plant. He wears a long black robe.

"I am angry! Do you hear? *Angry*!" His face becomes red and he stamps his feet.

250

No one moves or speaks. Am I supposed to answer?

The spider speaks. "You're an arrogant ass. Why have you called us here?"

I think he is speaking to me, but Robert responds. "I may well be, but that does not mean I am wrong! Who says you have to be old or educated to be wise? I know things!"

"I agree," a new voice says. It is Eli, standing on the other side of the plant. "Someone needs to say something. This is outrageous!"

I am confused. They look like themselves, but they do not sound right. The patterns of speech are all wrong. How did we get here?

It must be delirium. From the anesthetic. Did I have the surgery already? No, that was before. I had an accident. I fell in the ocean. Am I dead? No, they rescued me. Didn't they?

"You! Woman!" Robert points at Ellie. "What are you doing with your life? *Nothing!*"

It was my turn to be angry, but when I open my mouth, no sound comes out. I shake an indignant fist at Robert and go to Ellie. She looks up, and I place my hand on her shoulder, but she shrugs it off. Robert appears at my side and shoves her. Falling backward, her head snaps as she lands, slamming into the dirt beneath. She rubs the back of her head.

"I may not know much," Robert says, "but I know that you want to be liked so badly that you will lie about anything. You talk about how hard you work, but inside, you know you don't really work that hard. You're afraid everyone will find out. Right?"

Ellie does not respond as she sits up with her mouth open. I don't know if she is stunned by the fall, by his words, or both.

"You tell people that you're not married because you love your job and you love helping others. But that's a lie. Truth is, no one wants you."

I grab at Robert's arm, but he shrugs me off. "More than that, no one *ever will*. You are a shallow, self-absorbed, worthless, *woman*!"

Ellie looks up at Robert. "You know *nothing* about me."

"Your sister never answers your calls, does she? You pretend you're normal that your life has meaning, but you are a basketful of psychoses that *no one cares about!*"

Ellie's eyes brim with tears. "You…you…" She falls silent.

"Yeah, that's what I *thought*, loser." He dismisses her with a wave and walks to Zig, who sits with his head in his hands.

"And *you*. You, fat, self-centered blowhard. Your constant berating of your wife is what made her hate you! She was a beautiful and compassionate woman until you wore her down. And your affairs—yes, of *course* she knew!—and your smug condescension made her retreat into herself. You *destroyed* her, you pig!"

Zig does not move.

"But underneath all that arrogance and apparent self-confidence lies a sad sack of pain. You have no idea how to sell, no idea how to be a friend, and no idea how to love someone. You'd like to, but instead you turn to drinking—the weakest of *all* responses! Not even enough of a man to admit it and get help—you laugh it off in public and cry to yourself when alone! Good ol' gregarious Zig. A worthless façade!"

Zig shoots up from his seat with anger and draws back a fist. But Robert was prepared and landed a roundhouse on Zig that sent him sprawling. He lay in the sand, still.

I turn on Robert. "Ro...Ro..." The words would not form.

"Shut up, Lobster. I'm not done."

"No!" Eli shouts. "I have something to say."

Finally. Someone with sense. Robert, with a short bow, waves to Eli.

"You!" shouts Eli, as he passes between Robert and I to bend down before the spider. "You make me sick with your false honesty about yourself and your self-deprecating attitude! It's just more deception!"

I'd never seen Eli this angry. This was not his usual firm and steady demeanor. This sounds more like Robert—but Robert doesn't sound like Robert, either.

"You use this ruse of honesty about yourself to gain sympathy, and then you strike with the vilest of words! 'Actions have consequences' and 'we reap what we sow'—what a load of excrement you spew! You *know* that's not always true. Yet you keep clutching at it. 'Poor me, I was made this way'—it's all garbage!"

With that, Eli raises up a booted foot and brings it down, crushing the spider to the ground. He whirls and addresses the plant.

"You don't escape either, you bundle of firewood! Your faux intellectualism is old and tired—you sound like a British house-servant in a B movie!" He moves closer. "In fact, you're the worst of all! You have the fake self-deprecation and false humility of the spider, the façade of Zig, and the uselessness of Ellie. You spout the same tired old sayings: 'oh, it's not Fate, but a cause and effect' and your stupid, sorry story about Enlil and—" Eli stops, choking with anger.

Robert comes to his side as the old man coughs, "He's right, you bundle of dry sticks! What do you have to offer—old, dry, and nearly dead! Yet you hold forth like you are the sage of the universe. Everything is clean and logical. I have *had* it with you, too!"

Robert swings about, searching the ground. With a cry of delight, he bends down and picks up a thick branch. He wields it like a bat as he rushes the plant. It shudders at the blow, as pieces of dry leaves and sticks fly off. Robert swings again, "It's your time, firewood! Is this an effect or a cause?!"

Eli recovers and approaches the plant. Picking up a large stone, he falls to his knees and begins to pound at the main shaft near the ground. Robert continues to bash away at the upper stalks. Both scream profanities with each blow.

I spin, looking for help. Ellie lies on the ground, sobbing. Zig lies still on the ground, his mouth leaking a trickle of blood. The spider is crushed collection of a thorax and broken legs.

I raise my face to the sky. My voice freed, I wail and cry and scream.

76

"It isn't that complicated, my boy."

I sat on the lower bunk, my back against the hull. Raimundo had switched bunks with me while I recover. I sipped some soup that Eli had brought.

"Accidents happen," he continued. "I seen 'em over and over again in my time. Nobody did nothin' wrong. Just a bad collection of events. You heard the phrase 'perfect storm'?"

"Yes, of course. When everything comes together to make the worst possible situation."

"Well, yeah, that's how landlubbers use it, but out here, it's real. Wind direction, force, position of the moon, tide, swells, all come together *just so* to make the worst storm imaginable."

"Yeah. I saw some movie about that."

"I don't speak of no movie. This is real life, boy. And it's no one's fault. Just random events coming together. But it does have a *purpose.*"

I was better. I was pretty sure I didn't have a concussion—though my head did still hurt. But the physical toll of the cold water and the salty ingestion of seawater was dissipating.

"If it's random, then it has no purpose."

"Not true."

"Please don't say the purpose is to make us stronger."

"No. Well—maybe sometimes. I'm saying it's a warning."

"A warning?"

"Yeah. When I was a young teen, I wanted to run a business. Got a job, through my dad, as an apprentice at a bank. The boss liked me and he gave me a lot to do. One day I screwed up so bad—well, no reason to go into it. The bank was robbed, my boss was killed, and I was badly injured. I was devastated. But I was determined. After I got out of the hospital, I got a job right there at that same hospital—working in the records department. Not long after I was there, there was a huge scandal where my boss had been selling patient records. Fired the entire department, even though I had nothing to do with it. And you know what?"

"What?"

"It was a warning that I was not cut out for business. I couldn't tell good from bad; the sensible from the questionable. I didn't have the mind for it. Ended up being a fisherman—and will be until I die. It suits me. I was being warned, and I listened."

"Maybe the next job would have been perfect for your skills. A vehicle service center? A retail business? Who knows?"

"Ah, but that's my point! Maybe it would have been—but how could I know? Everything is more complicated than just this or that! Maybe it was a warning. Maybe I was to learn from it and do better in the next!"

"So it wasn't a warning?"

"No, it *was*! That's what I'm getting at. When things go bad, you gotta fight it out. Wrestle an answer out of that sucker!"

"So you wrestled and discovered it was a warning."

He sat back against the bulkhead. "Yep. Exactly. *That's* what I'm telling you. Maybe this accident happened to teach you to be better. Maybe to warn you to get out. Maybe something else. You gotta figure it out!"

I finished the soup. It gave me a warm, comfortable feeling in my belly. My brain still hurt.

77

"You think you are *innocent?* No one is innocent, you arrogant—"

"Objection, Your Honor!"

"Sustained. Counsel, please refrain from insulting the defendant."

"Very well, but he is an arrogant bastard, Your Honor."

"The Court agrees, but please refrain."

"As the Court pleases. I continue with further—"

I lean over to my attorney. "Is that the judge?!"

"No, he's a *pro tem*."

"But a pro tem *is* a judge. He can make a ruling!"

"No, he can't."

"Yes, he can. He's just sitting in place of the regular judge and—"

"Doesn't work that way here. This is just a dress rehearsal."

"A *what?* There is no such thing—"

"Quiet," he hisses. "He'll hold us in contempt."

"He already does," I say under my breath. The prosecutor is still speaking.

"Only a guilty person runs away. After all, as Shakespeare wrote, 'Suspicion always haunts the guilty mind.' Furthermore, the person who profits from the crime is always the one who committed it."

My head is reeling. These aren't even legal arguments, aside from being demonstrably false.

"We also know that guilty persons always answer a question with a question. As some famous writer said, whose name I cannot recall at the moment, 'Guilt is never to be doubted.'"

I decide to risk the wrath of my counsel again. "These aren't legal arguments. They don't even apply here. Can't you object?!"

He looks at me over his spectacles. "I *could*."

I raise my eyebrows. "So…?"

"Objection, Your Honor?"

"Grounds?"

"Relevance. These arguments have no bearing on the case at hand."

"They are wise sayings. Everyone knows them to be true. Overruled."

My attorney looks at me as if to say, "See?"

"Thank you, Your Honor," the prosecutor says. "Moreover, this arrogant defendant has impugned this very Court on more than one occasion. As Disraeli said, 'Justice is truth in action.' This defendant has ridiculed this court for taking its time, but, to quote Shakespeare again, 'Time is the justice that examines all offenders.' Moreover, that venerated philosopher, Paul Valéry wrote, 'our judgments judge us, and nothing reveals us, exposes our weaknesses, more ingeniously than the attitude of pronouncing upon our fellows.' It is as if he wrote that for the defendant here today."

"Objection."

Finally.

"Valéry was a poet, not a philosopher."

That's his objection?! I am apoplectic.

The judge glances at the prosecutor. "Counsel?"

"I beg to differ. While he *wrote* poetry, he held forth on many subjects, including guilt and innocent. Just read his *Mauvaises pensées et autres*!"

"Overruled."

"Is that true?" I ask my attorney, having no idea who Valéry might be.

He shrugs. "I suppose."

"Even if the defendant was not guilty of the crimes arrayed against him, his continual rebelliousness against the rule of law is a crime in and of itself! He is a rebel without a cause. 'Disobedience to conscience makes conscience blind' and 'The secret of all failure is disobedience.' Therefore, your honor, I submit that the Court should also add charges of contempt of court, domestic terrorism, rape, sodomy, high treason, and sedition."

"What?!" I am on my feet before I could think. "I have done none of those things! This is—"

The judge shouts "Silence!" as my attorney grabs my arm. Officer Rahab jumps up, hand on sidearm, ready to act.

I sit.

"Counsel," the judge says, "I suggest you control your client. His actions merely support the honored prosecutor's claims, and if I had any power in this court of law, I would order these charges added to the others. This court will take a ten-minute recess."

My attorney sits back and sighs. "You are going to lose this case for us. I had a good argument for a temporary injunction, perhaps even a dismissal, but your continual pronouncements that the *court* has committed a crime…well…I don't know what you are thinking."

"But…I never committed any crimes! I never drank a drop of alcohol. I was working to solve a financial problem and did not violate any laws. The prosecutor was found to have violated the rules! The woman rode her bike right out in front me!" I am so exasperated I don't know what to say. "The court *is* wrong. In fact—" I stood up, pointing my finger at the now-empty bench "—I don't think there *is* a real judge here. I think this is a kangaroo court. A collection of thugs attempting to ruin me! I will not stand here and take it in silence."

My attorney stands, tosses his papers into his briefcase and slams it shut. "That's fine, you go right ahead, Mr. Adam. But you will do it without me. I no longer represent you."

"You can't do that! You were appointed by the court, and I have a right to representation!"

"Watch me." He turns and walks out.

78

A night's rest and a hot breakfast were a fine elixir. After I had finished eating, Eli suggested I get out of the cabin if I was up to it. We sat out on the foredeck, near the bow.

"How long until we reach our numbers?" I asked.

"About four or five more hours. You never been out this far, huh?"

"No."

The morning was clear and bright. Around us, a blue, calm sea spread out in all directions. No distant mainland mountains or islands. No fog banks. No other vessels. It was a strange sight.

"I love it out here," Eli said. "So big, so complex. Rhythms and cycles. Regular swells. Calm in the morning, more pronounced and rough as the day progresses."

"What about sudden storms and tidal waves?"

"They aren't sudden. When you hear about accidents at sea, it's the captain thinking he can handle the conditions or outrun 'em. Arrogance. As for today—we can't predict earthquakes yet, but we know when a tidal wave's coming."

"Okay. What about rogue waves?"

He cocked a pirate eye at me. "You been readin' up. There are stories. Disasters brought on by massive waves outta nowhere. If you believe them—and I do—it's more of the same. There's science behind it, we just haven't figured it out yet."

That's convenient, I thought.

A slight breeze wafted across us. Though it was light, it had a crisp bite.

"You feel that, Jay? Seems a nice day, but the breeze is cool, coming from the west. That wind's gonna pick up and in a few hours and the temperature will drop. We'll have so much chop we can't stand up. See those, high, flattish clouds off the bow?"

I looked and saw them, far ahead. High. Blue-gray and thin.

"Altostratus. Earlier, they were cirrostratus. Soon they'll become stratus clouds. Then the storm."

"How do I know you didn't check the forecast this morning?"

He laughed. "Well, I *did*, as any proper seaman would! Often! But I would've known anyway. I haven't checked the barometer yet, but I can guarantee it's dropping."

"How bad will it be? Robert said—"

"High winds, lots of rain, combined with high swells. Nothing we can't handle. But it's strong. You'll be gettin' a trial by fire, no doubt! As for Robert, well, don't take it personal. He puts greenhorns through hell. To see if they match up."

"Seems personal."

"Nah. We're out here, depending on each other. It ain't like on land. One guy's wrong action and we can all die. So we gotta be sure you can handle it. If you don't, you don't belong. That's all."

The breeze picked up again, stronger this time. I shivered. The clouds were already closer and darker.

❋

The thunder sounded like it was just outside my cabin. The rain began pattering on the deck above. It would be relaxing except that we had also been rocking and rolling dramatically for about an hour. The ship is bashing ahead against the swells and wind. I kept thinking I might rather be on deck.

261

After Eli and I had come back from the bow, I worked with Raimundo and Edward preparing some lines and bait. I was still pretty weak, so Edwards told me to go rest—they'd need me for net retrieval.

I couldn't read because it was so rough. So I lay there, feeling useless and a bit guilty.

Some time later, Brian went past the bulkhead, then came back and stuck his head in. "You alright? It's pretty crazy out there."

"I'm fine. Wish I was out there helping."

"We're okay now. We'll need you later, though." He left.

Everyone was being kind, but it can't sit well with them. Since the accident, Robert and Fishbait had stopped talking to me (or *at* me), as if I don't exist. It infuriated me because know I am smart and capable. Give me time—and proper training—I could outmatch them. Could even be a Captain eventually.

But that's not my goal. I had been neglecting the puzzle of my path. It won't assemble itself. I need to start working on a plan. On my own. A strategy. Bring some order to my life.

It's time to take action.

79

I came awake with a start and grabbed the rail at the side of the bunk. A particularly violent fore-and-aft motion ended with a jarring lurch and bounced me into the air. The ship shuddered.

Edwards appeared in the doorway, holding the sides, swaying back and forth at the motion of the ship.

"Can you come on deck? We're about reel in the nets and having a lot of trouble in this weather."

"Yeah, I'll be right up."

"Hurry. Full rain gear and life jacket."

I hoisted myself over the rail. Holding with one hand, I leaned down and peered out the small porthole. Violent seas. Slashing rain.

I was still weak. I pulled on my rain-slicks, then sat on the lower bunk to yank on my boots. My stomach began to protest. I told myself it would be better out on deck than in this claustrophobic cabin.

I lurched down the passageway and into the galley, ate a granola bar while swaying and shifting on my feet. The wrapper fell to the deck. I made my way out.

The scene was a drastic change from the last time I was out. Cold—even for this time of year. The wind whipped around stronger than I had ever seen on land. The deck rocked and swayed, and the occasional jolts made everything and everyone jump.

Robert, Raimundo, and Edwards were struggling to get the nets reeled in. I wondered why they had even let them out in this weather. Raimundo was at the console, both hands on the metal box, operating the buttons of the winch motor. Robert and Edwards were at the stern, on either side, trying to keep the nets straight as they fed into the wheels up above—no easy task as the ship pitched and rolled and turned. Like trying to pull a single shirt out of a running washing machine full of clothes while riding on the back of a flatbed truck over rough terrain at high speed. Only worse.

I made my way toward the stern. The winch motor and net reel squealed and moaned as Raimundo shifted from forward, to stop, to reverse and back. I looked up at the pilothouse and saw two figures through the wet glass: the Captain and Eli. Brian was probably in the engine room, but it made me wonder about Fishbait.

"Jay! Come help us!" It was Robert, wedged in the aft starboard corner. I made my way over like a toddler learning to walk, then grabbed for the transom. I gazed at the churning chaos below. To my right, Edwards was leaning out over the stern, his belly pressed against it, feet splayed out to brace himself. His hands were stretched out, pulling on the edge of the nets.

Beside me, Robert was in the same stance, except the boat was leaning to starboard. The water and wind were pushing the nets against the boat. I saw the problem. If the nets went underneath the boat, they could get caught in the propellers, which would leave us dead in the water. Sending someone down to free them in this weather was not possible.

I moved to the other side of Robert and grabbed as much of the netting as I could, helping him pull it out of the water and away from the sides. We made some headway until a violent shift of the boat yanked the nets out of our hands. We stumbled back. I caught myself and jumped forward to grab another handful. The stern fishtailed, the boat came up level, then tilted to port. Now we were pulling in the wrong direction. We scrambled to reorient and brace our feet anew. As we pulled on the net, Raimundo engaged the winch, spooling it up and out of our hands. We'd grab another section lower down and repeat the cycle. The work became a timeless blur of motion, sound, water, and wind. We were making progress, but it was two forward and one back. I slipped twice and fell to the deck.

Without warning, the ship's engines went into neutral, and the vessel lurched rearward. A wall of water fell on us like a truckload of wet blankets. The force and cold took my breath away.

Robert yelled. I could not hear the words but could guess the content. The boat's backward motion had forced the net flush against the stern and it was being pushed up over the transom. Raimundo put the winch in neutral, hoping it would allow the weights on the nets to pull them down away from the hull and the propellors. It worked, and the nets began to fall away. As we relaxed in relief, the engines powered back up in gear. The sudden acceleration threw all three of us to the deck and we rolled up against the transom. The nets unreeled forty or fifty feet before Raimundo could get back to the console and engage the clutch.

All of our work had been for nothing.

As Edwards let out a frustrated curse, Fishbait appeared on deck. "…need someone to come help raise anchor!"

"It's already raised!" Robert yelled back.

"Not all the way—the motor burned out—thought it would be okay while we got the nets in but it's causing problems with holding the boat steady—we need to hand crank it!"

"We're having enough trouble here—"

"Hey, come on guys!" Edwards yelled. We looked back. The boat's forward motion and the waves had unreeled the freed nets a good distance out—stretched taut from the reel high above to the surface of the water far behind. The drag on the ship was pulling the stern down into the water, causing more fishtailing. And even more difficulty for the Captain: he had the anchor dragging the bow and a net dragging the stern.

Robert saw things would only get worse if we didn't act. "Jay, go with him—but get back fast!"

I followed Fishbait to the foredeck. We moved as quickly as we could along the gunwale, beside the super-structure, hand-over-handing it. With my back to the sea, I tried to ignore how close I was to the water when we rocked to our side. I looked up at the gray, black, and white sky, a swirling menace matching the green, black, and white swirling water. I had a vision of myself—a tiny human stick figure, standing on a piece of balsa wood in a maelstrom. Birds and fish and whales and creatures swam all about, leaping and twisting in the storm, paying no attention to the little piece of wood or the frail figure clinging to it.

On the foredeck, Brian and Eli were crouched down beside one of the two windlasses bolted to the deck. So here is where they'd been. We crab-crawled forward, grasping stanchions and tie-downs along the way.

They had the cover off of the motor and Brian was fiddling inside it. The movement at the bow was worse than aft, especially up and down. My breath caught as we topped a huge swell and then dropped down the other side, speeding towards the roiling trough.

Fishbait motioned to me to grab the anchor line and help him haul. I wondered why we weren't using the hand winch, but surely they had a reason. At first, it seemed almost impossible. The anchor weighed seventy-five pounds, but the motion of the water and the boat put an ever-changing drag on it.

"I can't fix this in these conditions!" Brian yelled. "We either gotta pull it up or cut it!"

"Maybe if all four of us—" began Eli, as the bow pulpit buried itself in the water at the bottom of a trough. We all grabbed handholds to keep from falling and sliding into the water. The ship's bow rose up, throwing water over the deck and us.

"Never mind!" Eli again. "Cut it!"

Brian turned to me. "Jay, go to the engine room and get the cutting torch you and I used last week!"

I nodded and made my way back, doing the tight-rope shuffle along the gunwale. A panic began to rise in me as I made my way down on the side, alone, where I could not see any crew members. I took a deep breath, put my head down, and kept going.

The engine room was a mess. Tools and containers were strewn all over the deck, rolling this way and that. Brian kept a neat place; this was the result of violent motion. I made my way to the tool locker and grabbed the cutting torch and a bottle of propane.

As I turned to leave, the ship lurched far to starboard with a massive jerk. My feet slid out from under me, and, with my hands full and no time to grab anything, I slammed to the deck.

80

I had no idea how long I was out, only that now I lay on the wet and oily deck. The lights were off, but cloudy daylight came through the doorway and the small port-hole. I sat up.

My head was pounding. I touched it, and it came away bloody.

The ship was listing heavily to starboard and still rocking. As I struggled to regain my equilibrium, the torch and propane tank rolled by. I scrambled on hands and knees to retrieve them and staggered to my feet. The motion of the ship seems more pronounced but less violent.

I made my way up the stairs and onto the deck. The tilt was extreme enough that the starboard aft corner was only a foot above the waterline. Water sloshed over it with every wave, flowed across the deck, then drained out the scuppers. The wind was still whipping, and the swells seemed higher than before.

To my horror, I saw that the nets had come completely unreeled to starboard, leaving only the last part of the net attached to the reel high above the deck. The weight of all the netting in the water pulled on the reel, causing the ship to tilt to starboard.

Robert and Edwards were no longer on the deck.

I slid over to the port side. I could hear the engines running steady. I pulled myself along the walkway, easier because the ship was leaning to starboard.

There was no one on the forward deck either. I called out for Eli, Brian, and Fishbait, before I realized they wouldn't hear me in the cacophony of wind, waves, and engine noise. I scrambled upon onto the foredeck and crawled to the bow. The anchor was still deployed. The windlass motor was still exposed, its cover gone.

Hanging on to the bow railing, I maneuvered into a half-crouch, half-standing stance and scanned the water. I saw nothing but swells, chop, and whitecaps in every direction. Maybe Brian went to get the torch himself. But we'd have passed each other—unless he went down the starboard side while I was coming up the port. And where were the others?

I made my way over to the starboard side and looked down the length of the ship. There was no sign of the crew, but now the aft corner of the boat was at the waterline, and water was pouring in. More than the scuppers could handle.

We're taking on water.

An alarm sounded. That must be the Captain! I have to get to the bridge—he'd tell me what to do. Maybe the crew was up there. Though they could be down below—maybe the bilge pumps failed.

I was reluctant to head down the starboard side with it so low to the water, but I didn't want to go back to the bow and then aft. So I forced myself to crawl, staring at the deck as I went. I tried not to think about how close I was to the churning water, even as waves washed over me.

The ship jerked sideways and slammed me against the side of the superstructure. One hand came loose and I fell, crying out as my left side slammed into the deck.

I half-crawled and half-dragged myself the rest of the way. Reaching steps, I grabbed an inside handrail just as the ship tossed again. I lost my grip and my feet slid out from under me as I fell back.

I was underwater, ice cold and heavy. Again. I was in a monstrous washing machine. I did not know which way was up. My life jacket should take me to the surface, so I thrashed and kicked and held my breath. I opened my eyes, but it was if someone had poured fire into them.

I was fighting a mighty monster, with more power and strength than anything on earth. I was going nowhere.

I stopped kicking. I relaxed my eyes, my arms, my legs. It was peaceful, being tugged gently to and fro. Like being rocked to sleep. I curled into a fetal position. I started to warm up.

This isn't so bad.

81

Water swirled all around as I was dragged by my armpits. I couldn't take a breath without some salt water. I came up against a hard surface. Cold, cold, cold. Like frozen metal.

I was yanked up and out of the water and over the gunnel to fall onto the deck. Breathe. *Breathe*.

A voice called my name. I couldn't open my eyes.

"Jay, Jay! Can you hear me?"

I nodded.

Someone fiddled with my life jacket. Stealing it? Do they think I am dead? I tried to fight back, but had no strength.

※

I opened my eyes to angry gray clouds above me. The ship was still rocking a good bit. My head lay up against the bottom of a metal panel two or three feet high. Rain pelted my face. Large drops. I could hear the wind howling, but could not feel it.

There was no engine noise.

"Hello?!" My voice sounded foreign.

"Jay?"

I turned to the voice and saw Eli's face a few feet away, also lying down. "You okay, Jay?"

"I think so. Ship's ok?"

He didn't answer for a few moments. "We're on the lifeboat…I think the ship's lost." His voice was weak and thin.

"What happened?"

"Don't know…storm worse than…we thought." He was having trouble breathing. "Engines failed."

"I fell in the engine room and must have passed out…"

"…yeah…nets must've gotten fouled in props as Captain went throttle up…weight of full nets jerked the ship over…"

270

The metal lifeboat was being tossed about by the storm. Up one side of a swell and down the other. Spun by the wind and the chop. If I focused on the motion, I got dizzy.

"...I went to the bridge, Captain was...dead, I think...must've gotten tossed around...bridge was a mess...windows shattered—." He took a painful breath. "Blood everywhere...wheel and throttles didn't respond...I shut 'em down..."

"What about the others?"

He shook his head. "...I didn't see anyone from the bridge...listing almost forty-five degrees...no one below...I sounded the abandon alarm...released lifeboat...saw you fall in..."

I waited. He seemed so tired.

"Started up motor and went to you...in these conditions...thought you were dead at first."

Me, too.

"...pulled you up...outboard died and won't start."

"We're floating free?"

He nodded.

"Radio? EPIRB? Flares?"

He shook his head.

How can there be no emergency equipment? "Supplies?"

He closed his eyes and didn't answer. My head was pounding. I closed my eyes, too.

✻

Something felt urgent. Our little boat was rocking and spinning. The storm was still raging. Was I supposed to do something?

I looked over at Eli. Still asleep. I turned to my side and reached up to grab the gunwale. My body protested, like a heavyweight champ had pummeled me. I pulled myself up and peered over the side.

It is one thing to see a devastating storm from aboard a seventy-five-foot vessel; it is quite another from a twelve-foot lifeboat. In every direction, the ocean roiled without ship or land in sight. I slid back down. It didn't seem so bad when I couldn't see.

Eli must be wrong—there has to be some signaling device on board. I was pretty sure I remembered being told it was required by law.

I dragged myself over to Eli and tried to wake him. No response. I pulled him up to a sitting position against the hull. His hood fell back.

The left side of his head was a thick, sticky mass of blood and hair.

"Eli!" I pulled him closer and unclasped his jacket. Inside it was sticky, congealed, and thick. I slipped my hand down inside his shirt and placed my palm over his heart, touching my ear to his mouth.

He was dead.

82

It is dark. I hear explosions. I am inside a huge egg. A hammer pounds on the outside. No, wait—not an egg. Not a hammer. The lifeboat. The storm. Thunder explodes all around. The waves hammer my little vessel. I roll left and right like a rag doll. It is cold and wet. I try to raise my pounding head, but cannot.

Eli.

Every move causes water to slosh about the bottom of little boat. The rain pounds my exposed face. Are we sinking?

As if in answer, everything goes quiet and black. My eyes began to adjust. A tiny pinpoint of light appears above. A star?

The light grows. I wonder if it is my eyes playing tricks, but it keeps growing. Coming right at me. At high speed.

I push my arms down in an effort to raise myself up and find that I am already seated. I touch the surface— rough cloth. I'm sitting on a chair.

The light is not one light, but a collection of them. Brilliant, bright, like high-power halogens. They are spread out, illuminating a work site with a partially-built structure. A frame. Millions of ants crawl around its base. As I watch, I realize the ants are humans. The building is huge. More than huge. Massive. Gargantuan.

The scene zooms in, and I see that some of the workers are using sophisticated laser instruments to take exact measurements. Others consult computers and hand-held devices. Drones fly around the structure, in a dance that seems random. Somehow, I know it is not.

Motion to the right catches my eye: a monstrous crane swinging a palette into place. The palette is at least the size of a city block. A woman occupies the operator's cab. She reminds me of my mother. She's even dressed like her. As I watch, she sees me and waves.

With great skill, she moves the load beside the structure and begins to lower it. Workers wait below. As it touches down, a cloud of steam erupts, enveloping the crate. Some of the workers open large grates which are set into the worksite floor. The white cloud—steam?—pours down through the grates. The mist and smoke begin to solidify into a liquid. Roiling, boiling water, a mini-ocean, with its own little swells and whitecaps, dancing in a perfect rhythm, like precise dancers perfectly choreographed.

The water keeps flowing, far beyond what the crate could have held. As I squint through the fog, one light begins to grow brighter than the others. It rises, and is so bright I look away. It is the sun, creating a new day. The worksite was bright before; now it is blinding. Everything turns white, even the workers. They run for cover. Some stumble, fall, and do not get up. As I watch, the bodies begin to smoke and turn to ash.

Bang bang bang. I jump at the sound which reverberates around the world. Like a hammer on wood. Like a gavel.

A dark robed figure appears above the scene. I cannot make out any details; his face is shrouded in shadows. He holds something in his right hand.

He stares at me without moving.

"Who are you?" I squint, trying to make out a face.

"I think you know who I am," his voice boomed, sounding a bit like the hammer. "Why are you here?"

"Here?" I see we are in a courtroom. Dim and empty. The only light comes from emergency flares set in each wall. Now the figure sits at the judge's bench. In front of him is a live model of the worksite.

"You're the judge? Or just another clerk?"

"Do you know where the water goes?"

I hate it when people ignore my questions. "Water?"

A robed arm indicted the scene below that I had been watching.

"No. I don't."

"There's a massive aquifer underneath, with all manner of gates and tunnels and control doors. Have you been to Disney World?"

He seems to enjoy *non sequiters*. "Disney World? Yes."

"Underneath it is a vast city four times as large as the park. All the controls, machinery, electricity, pipes—everything! That's what it's like in the aquifer, but a thousand times more. It's like a maze that defies mapping. But it all works perfectly, just like it should. *That's* where the water goes."

Surely this is not the judge. "Why am I here? Is there a hearing scheduled?"

"There is always a hearing scheduled."

I look down at the image of the worksite and see that it is dark and still. The sun is gone. No one is working. As I watch, the moon rises behind the spidery latticework, and the workers begin to reappear. The enormous worksite lights ignite, and work begins once more.

After a time, the sun rises once more. Some workers die, but most make it to shelter.

"I don't understand what's going—" The robed figure is gone.

I turn back to see the sun setting. This time, no moon rises. The emergency lights in the room began to dim. A muffled hum sounds at the outer limits of my hearing. As it grows in volume, the room began to shake.

As it rises to a level that alarms me, a splash of water cold water hits me in the face.

83

I floundered for a handhold as the boat jolts and rolls. Regaining some stability, I hauled myself up on the middle bench seat. The wind hit me like a thousand needles. Icy rain? This far south?

As I sat, gripping the cold seat on either side, the cold rain turned to hail. Tiny marbles of ice pelted me with a fury. I leaned forward into crash position and covered my head with my arms. Every few moments I yell as an icy bullet hits me soundly on the head. As I began to wonder how long it might last, the frequency of the falling pellets began to wane. A few more moments pass and the hail stopped. It became quiet. I raised my head.

It was snowing.

Not a heavy snow. A light, beautiful snow. How it could fall so gently in a raging maelstrom was beyond me. And how can it snow off the southern coast? I cannot have been on board so long that I drifted into another climate! As I marveled, I see a dark figure at the bow.

Eli's body.

Shock and disgust flowed inside my belly. I wanted to retch. A dead body is in the boat with me. I didn't want to see it. Didn't want to think about it.

I should get rid of it. Throw it overboard.

You can't do that.

Why not? He's dead.

It's not right.

None of this is right. I am going to die, too.

Well, maybe you need him so that you can live, then.

A darkness grew in my chest. What do you mean?

You know what I mean.

That's disgusting. It's human flesh.

Not if you get desperate enough. Everyone has a limit. The Donner party ate their own family members.

I slipped back down into the bottom of the boat. As I slid off the seat, my jacket caught on something. Turning, I saw clasps. The seat had hinges. Storage. Buoyed with hope, I turned the key latch and opened the seat lid. It was dark, so I felt around in the bottom. Rope. Some plastic containers.

An EPIRB. I can signal for help! I pulled it out, flipped up the little red cover, and punched the button.

Nothing. No light, no sound. I stood up, hoping for a bit more illumination to read the control labels. The boat rocked, and a wave came over the side, knocking me down. The EPIRB flew out of my hands. I scrambled and searched, flinging my hands all about, splashing the water that had collected in the bottom of the boat. Where was it? Did it go overboard? Maybe it flew forward.

I was *not* going up to the bow.

The water sloshing around inside the boat was growing. If the rain didn't stop, I would not be able to lay in the bottom much longer. There should be a pump on board—a hand pump, at least. The forward bench might contain storage, too. But I refuse to go up there. I don't want to see…it.

I am submerged. There is a dim light. Diffused. A green glow. I look up and see a mottled white-green ceiling. It appears to be receding. I am sinking.

A panicked cry rises up in my throat, but I make no sound. I am not taking in air (or water), yet I can *feel* the exchange of CO_2 in my lungs.

A creature appears, swimming in front of me. In the sameness of this watery world, I cannot tell if it is far or near. If far, it was huge. It looks like an eight-legged bear with pinkish fur. It has no head—the body stops at the neck. As I watch it swimming—using its legs as if it was walking in the water—a tube of flesh telescopes out of the neck and then retracts. I recoil in disgust.

"That's a *tardigrade*. Ever seen one?"

Floating beside me, in uniform, is Officer Rahab.

"Did you hear me, Mr. Adam? A *tardigrade*. Or *kleiner Wasserbär*, if you prefer the original name."

"What does it do?"

He shrugged, an amusing gesture in these conditions. "No idea. It's quite small—less than half a millimeter. But he can live anywhere—ocean, mountains—even in space! Can go without water and food for almost thirty years, then rehydrate and reproduce. Amazing, no? Ah, look coming here—"

He points to the right at three other creatures. The closest looks like the ghost of a horse. I can see its backbone through the translucent body. But its two front legs are claws, like a crab, and the back two are tentacles, like an octopus. A yellowish glow takes the place of the horse's jaw.

Two other creatures follow. One looks like some kind of jellyfish, though it has no tentacles dragging below. It is elongated, as if someone ripped out a human colon and let it soak in seawater until it became ragged and waterlogged.

The third creature is more like a fish, but without a tail. It has a large mouth, the size of the whole body, and it is open. The entire fish glows dull red, with stripes of multicolored lights running down each side. A couple of antennae stick up here and there. It looks like an animated spaceship.

"Beautiful, aren't they?"

"What are they? Do we fish for them?"

"Oh, no, these creatures live way too deep and are of no use to humans. The first is a *phronima sedentaria*; the red one is a *torquaratorid hemichordate*. Pretty big, huh? That's feces trailing behind it—always a constant stream of it because it eats and digests without pause. That bubble on top? A balloon made of mucus so that it can float from one place on the sea floor to another. Nice, huh?"

"I—"

"But the last one is the most interesting! No one knows what it is. Only one has been seen, before now, in all human history. You are one lucky man."

Rather than arguing with him, I say, "Why are you showing me this? Does it have something to do with my case? Do I have a hearing?"

"Oh, no. Well—maybe. I'm not sure. Perhaps. But I was told to show you around."

"By who? Wait—you don't know if there's a hearing? Aren't you the bailiff on duty?"

"Of course I am!" He becomes indignant, as if I have no reason to question him. He floats, his uniform billowing around him. After a second or two, his face brightens. "Maybe you'll find *this* interesting! Follow me!"

Using his arms, he executes a flip and swims down. I consider staying where I am, but I don't want to be here alone. I imitate his flip and follow. We draw close to dark shapes below, which resolve into reefs. We have reached the floor of the ocean. It is dark, with only a faint glow. A closer look reveals that the light comes from creatures on the rocks and the sandy sea floor.

I catch up with Officer Rahab, floating a few inches from the bottom in front of a crusty outcropping about ten feet high.

"How far down *are* we?" I am not sure I want to hear the answer.

"Oh, a mile or so. Not sure. Look at this!"

On the rock was a collection of tiny cones.

"What do they look like, Mr. Adam?"

"I don't know. Tiny trees?"

"Yes! Little Christmas trees! They even glow as if the branches are decorated with lights. So you might not be surprised to hear they are called 'Christmas tree worms.' They're pretty common."

"What are they good for?"

He appears offended again. "Good for? For living their lives. They have no commercial or other value, if that's what you mean. Divers like to take pictures of them. Isn't being beautiful enough?"

Abashed, I mumble that I suppose it is.

"Now, if you want to see some *useless* creatures, take a look over here." He swims to the side of the outcropping and points at the ocean floor. Looking at his feet, I see what looks like someone buried face-up, leaving only the face showing. A deformed and monstrous face. Large, bulging eyes, a spot where a nose might have been, and a mouth that looks like it had been sewn shut. The forehead is mottled and rough, as if the skull was showing through the skin.

"Northern Stargazer. Buries itself here with only that face showing, then electrocutes passing fish and eats them. Purpose? That's it. Want another example? See that thing that looks like a tumbleweed? It's a Shetland Argus. Very brittle, dies easily. No purpose on earth. Or under the sea!" He laughs, but I'm not sure what is so funny.

"However—" he beckons to me, and we swim to the top of an outcropping of rock. "You want to see something with a purpose? Look here."

Above the rock, a bright orange stick floats by. Along its length are ten or twelve translucent bubbles. The top end is a bubble; at the bottom were orange plumes, as if a skinny, upside-down dragon belched fire.

"What is it?"

"It's a colony creature. The top is a gas-filled float. Some of the things attached to the sides are medusae—they work on navigation. The others, the zooids, have various jobs: collecting food, digesting it, reproductive functions, and so on. A little community filled with purpose!"

"But it's one creature?"

"Yes."

"I've never heard of such a thing."

He nods. "Yet it still exists, doesn't it?"

"Listen, how can I find out about my hearing?"

He looks at his watch. "You should be getting back. The judge—"

Something touches my foot and let out a yelp and jerk away. At first, I thought it was an electronic device, but I soon see it is another fish. Its head is transparent, with two eye-like devices inside. They both rotate up, like cameras, to fix on me. As I back away, the lenses turn again—independently of one another—to the side and front again.

Rahab is holding his stomach, laughing.

"What is *that*?"

"A Barreleye. Weird, huh? Transparent head! You can even see its brain."

"It's creepy."

"Ok, Mr. Adam, I need to get back to my desk."

"No, wait—" Without another word, he shoots up toward the surface like a torpedo.

84

I awoke and lay in the bottom of the lifeboat for a few moments before I realized the rain had stopped. It was still overcast, but the diffused light told me that it must be after dawn. The swells were still high, but the wind had lessened, and the chop was down.

I pulled myself up and looked about. Again, I was taken aback at the dire view. No land. No vessels. Nothing but chaotic sea.

I lifted the lid of the bench seat again. The two plastic containers were labeled "water," but they are empty. My heart leaped as I saw a plastic bag with flares inside. But the bag was ripped, and the flares were soggy. Useless.

I glanced at the bow. I looked away.

I took a deep breath and crawled over the middle bench to the forward bench. I felt so weak. Exposure, for sure. Added to the weakness from the davit accident. When was the last time I ate?

Refusing to look further forward than the edge of the bench, I reached over and pulled up the seat lid. Cans. Rusty, old cans of food. I moved them around looking for a can opener, a knife, anything.

Nothing. Just cans.

I dropped back to the deck behind me with a splash. I lay there, trying not to think about Eli's body a few feet away.

I had a lot of knowledge, but it was all worthless. I had a mind for planning and strategizing, but it was all useless. Everyone had abandoned me, ignored me, or been ripped away from me. Even my dysfunctional co-workers of these past few months are gone.

A sob caught in my throat. I had wept a lot in the weeks after I learned that Stella and the kids were dead. At night. In my bunk. Under the pillow.

Now it's only me. On a little boat, on a vast sea, on a large planet, in an immense universe, living in a tiny slice of time.

No ideas.

No plan.

No words.

85

I lift myself up. It takes a lot of effort. With my back propped between the bench and the hull, I hold steady. The position allows me to see over the gunwale. The waves are still high. They sway back and forth; they crash into each other. They move towards my little metal container, lifts it up, then drops it back down. The smaller waves worry against the hull on all sides, like a pack of yapping wolves, causing it to rock and jerk in a pattern that seems random. I clutch the gunwale with one hand and the bench with the other. I jump as thunder roars and lightning crackles, far away and close by.

Motion catches my eye out on the sea. A shape, rising from the water. A black robed figure. Too far away for me to see any details. Yet I can tell he is staring at me. He raises a robed arm and points behind him. Another black shape appears on the horizon. I tense in hope. A ship? Or a whale? Maybe a rogue wave.

The wind blows. I feel a touch of fright again. Fear that has become an old friend. I am soaked through, the rain gear unable to keep me dry in these conditions. They are stiff with salt. I should get up and move about. Maybe even take them off. But it's too cold.

I look back up. The robed figure is gone. The shape near the horizon is rising out of the water, but I cannot tell how far away. No point of reference. Up it comes, breaching the surface like a whale in slow motion. It falls back into the water, creating high waves that speed away from its black body. I count out loud as they race towards me: one-one-thousand, two-one thousand…six before the first wave reaches me. If I have guessed the period between the waves correctly, then the creature is about four miles away.

Which means it is larger than any whale. Far larger.

The head appears again, dives down, and repeats the cycle. Closer and closer with each repetition. Breaching the surface like a black metal missile. Even the *Sea Bull* would not have been safe from this creature. It is Moby Dick writ large, and I am no Captain Ahab. I am nothing.

It comes up, up, up out of the dark foaming water, throwing spray away from its black body like a horse shaking off flies. Shiny silver rivulets flow down its sides.

It pauses at the top of its leap. The calm before the storm. A fermata before the final, cacophonous end.

I am trapped like a fish in a net.

It holds there, unmoving, like a terrible, monstrous caricature of a porpoise, waiting for someone to throw it a fish. But this creature has no playfulness in its soul. I fear to look away; I am afraid to look at it.

As it bends toward me, I see a crown sits on its head—a black crown, made of rock and reef. It opens its mouth as it falls, moving its massive head back and forth, the red and black darkness inside broken by jagged sharp teeth. Water and saliva and bits of seaweed. Pieces of wood.

Whole fish. I smell the foul stench from here. I vomit into my lap.

Its skin is mottled with gray and black and white, broken by scars, cuts, and oozing pustules of yellow-green. Parasitic creatures crawled all over the beast, their carapaces covered with blood and sickness.

Am I dreaming? Maybe this is death. The Grim Reaper in marine form. Repulsive and terrifying. Monstrous, strong, and unassailable. An army of Captain Ahabs could not conquer it.

I am ready. There is nothing left but the chaos of life. I close my eyes and slide under the pool of cold rain and salt water.

86

I sit in the desert.

Cross-legged on sand and dirt. The hot flatness spreads out in all directions, broken only by a dry brown plant here, a sand-blasted boulder there. It is so hot that my skin burns. I have been here for some time. Hours. Since before dawn.

Watching.

The sun rises. Dew forms on the underside of dry leaves and rocks.

Tiny creatures come to life, scrabbling for the smallest of morsels and drops of water. Larger animals roam about, seeking to surprise the smaller creatures.

The sun follows a path—an arc—as if rolling along a track.

Still I sit, watching.

The motion of the creatures halt just before midday. The stillness and heat are suffocating. As the sun resumes its journey, downward now toward the horizon, the beings return. They seek the barest minimum required for life.

The sun begins to set. In the distance, a flock of birds take flight and move off south. As dusk grows, a pack of desert foxes trot by, intent on their tasks.

The stars appear, each on its own track, crossing the blackness as the desert cools.

Still, I sit, watching. For thirty days.

※

I sit in a forest.

Cross-legged on a soft bed of humus and pine needles. The dense woodland spreads in all directions, broken only by a rough boulder here, a small clearing there. The air is cool. I have been here for some time. Hours. Since before dawn.

Watching.

The sun rises. Dew forms on leaves, trunks, grass, and underneath boulders.

The forest comes to life as creatures of all sizes move about, seeking morsels and water. Insects buzz, arachnids crawl. I hear sap coursing through the veins of the trees and bushes; I hear seeds bursting to life in the fertile soil.

Patterns of sunlight, filtered through the canopy above, dance and laugh on the forest floor around me. A floor covered with the detritus of life, decaying and dying so that others may live.

Still I sit, watching.

At midday, the motion of the forest slows. The humidity grows heavy, the creatures grow silent. Flying insects appear for a short time, buzzing and worrying, until the sun begins its trek towards the horizon.

As it begins to set, nocturnals come alive. Worms work the earth below. Nightbirds hoot and hunt. Animals of the darkness prowl.

All grows quiet, waiting for dawn.

I continue sitting. Watching. For four weeks.

❋

I sit high on a mountain.

Cross-legged on an outcropping of rock. Spread below is a valley. In the midst of that valley, on either side of a river, is a sprawling city. I have been here a long time.

Watching.

In the middle of the city are tall structures, offices, churches, and government buildings. Concert halls, restaurants, bus and subway stops. In a concentric circle, farther out, are apartments, stores, and gas stations. Still further lay houses, small businesses, golf courses, and parks. The most distant ring has treatment plants, trailer parks, prisons, and abandoned areas.

The city comes alive before dawn. People appear outside. Vehicles swarm the streets. Tiny creatures crawl about the surface and bowels of the city in seemingly random patterns. As the morning is full, the visible activity slows, but I can still feel the pulse of busyness. At midday, when the sun reaches its apex, the activity increases again. The parks fill with laughing children, attentive teachers, and watching parents. As the sun begins its descent towards dusk, the outside activity decreases.

Streets make a latticework of connections between all areas of the city: rich and poor, big and small, new and old, magnificent and decrepit. Even between so-called barriers—gates, walls, and doorways—people come and go. Communication flows between every point.

As the afternoon wanes, the external activity increases once more. When the sun is gone, lights come on all over the city: industrial lights, street lights, car lights, bike lights, and candles in windows. White, yellow, red, and green. As the night grows longer, most lights wink out, out by one.

Still I watch. Thin, fluorescent threads flow from each person, connecting them with every other person they interacted with that day. Outlining every road they traveled, every mail and email they sent and received, every call and every text message, every electrical signal, and every relationship. It is a dense and complex web, growing within the boundaries of the city, connecting even the most unlikely of persons. When completed, it looks like a meaningless blob of chaotic light. Yet I know that it is a web of order that makes up the lives of those people.

I sit. I watch. For one month.

✻

I sit in space.

Cross-legged on nothing. The stars are spread out above, below, and all around. Misty patches show here and there, which I know are star clusters, nebulas, or even galaxies. Too far for my little eye to resolve into details. Though I cannot see them, I imagine planets of all sizes, orbiting all manner of stars, circling in uncountable galaxies. Moons, asteroids, rings of debris, and comets all following the tracks assigned to them.

Movement catches my attention, but when I look, there is nothing. Only when I look away do I see, peripherally, four dark shapes. One large, one smaller, one tall and spindly, and the last so tiny I almost did not see it. They hang their heads, trudging through the universe, away from me.

I sit. I watch. The chaos of explosion, the order of gravity, the steady march of time.

87

Something nudged my shoulder and I opened my eyes. It was bright. As my eyes adjusted, I saw that it was still overcast, but the clouds were not quite as dark. The swells were still there, but smaller and farther apart. The wind had become a breeze.

I looked beside me. The EPIRB was floating in three inches of water, tapping my shoulder cheerily. The switch I had flipped was in "transmit" position, but the "active" light was not illuminated.

I stood and had to brace myself—not because of the waves, but because I was weak and dizzy. As I steadied myself, I saw a second latch on the far side of the bench. Another storage section. I flipped the latch and opened it.

Clothes. Blankets. A can opener. Water bottles. A hand pump.

❊

After I had opened and devoured a can of fruit cocktail and another of tomato soup (cold), I pumped as much of the water out of the vessel as I could. I stripped off my wet clothes and spread them on the transom to dry. My skin was raw and sickly. It was still a bit cold out. I rubbed my body all over with a dry cloth for ten minutes to get my blood flowing, then put on the dry clothes. They were a bit large, but I had never been so happy with new clothes.

I climbed over to the bow, and, with care, carried Eli's body to the center of the boat. He was already stiff. I stripped his clothes off. Not only had he bashed his head, but there was a deep puncture wound in his side. He was never going to make it. Yet he had pulled me out of the water, told me of our situation, and died. Without a word about his coming doom.

I cleaned the blood from him as best I could, then wrapped his body in a blanket. I arranged his long hair and beard. I placed my hand on his lifeless body.

"Thank you, my friend. I am in your debt."

Wrapping a large tarp around the blanket, I carried him back to the bow and laid him there. As I raised up, I saw that the clouds were beginning to break up. In the distance, blue sky peeked out.

I spent the next few hours checking supplies and organizing them. No radio or batteries. There was a map of the Pacific, which didn't do me any good without a functioning engine. I'd look at it later, though if Eli couldn't get it working, I doubted I could. But I could try. Who knows what might happen?

There was also a small notebook, but no writing implement. It was blank, except for the first page, where someone had written *"non est ad astra mollis e terris via."*

The storm had made a mess of things, so I cleaned the interior, working up a good sweat and a healthy hunger. I opened a can of beans and ate while sitting on the middle bench.

My little world looked pretty good. Clean, organized, and sound. It wasn't much. But it was what I could do.

One small step for one man. After all, it's not a puzzle that I needed to figure out.

I finished eating, rinsed out the can and spoon, and placed them back into the storage bin. I stood amidships, marveling at the expanse of blue sea. The storm's scrubbing had left the world pristine and pure. Calm and orderly.

A school of dolphins appeared, leaping and playing. Their movements seemed random and pointless. But it was clear they were having fun. One detached itself from the group and came towards my boat, leaping just off the bow. One twinkling eye caught mine, as if to say, "Isn't this great?"

I was still laughing when I heard the *chop-chop-chop* of a helicopter.

ACKNOWLEDGMENTS

A heartfelt thanks to my editors and readers Colleen Grimson, Courtney Hancock, Sarah Karr, Karen Stack, Bailee Williams, Swantje Willms, and Linda Zupancic. They spent hours reading drafts and revisions of this manuscript, finding the problems with it and suggesting solutions. I am indebted to them for making this a better story. Of course, any problems that remain are mine alone.

A special thanks to Linda for her insightful comments on themes and continuity, as well as her encouragement to me as a writer. Thanks also to Swantje and Courtney for their attention to typos and tense problems.

Most importantly, I thank my wife, Michele, and my family (Maya, Micah, and Kat), for their encouragement and support in my career of writing. They are my greatest blessings in a blessed life.

I am indebted to many writers and their works in providing excellent resource materials for my research. I won't list them because it would give away what I think the book means, and I don't want to rob readers of their own experience.

For stirring my imagination and love of words, I am indebted to Ernest Hemingway, James Joyce, Robert A. Heinlein, and Orson Scott Card.

The laws mentioned in scene 70 are real laws, still on the books as State or Federal laws, as of this writing.

The creatures referred to in Scene 83 are all real, living creatures, and the descriptions of them are accurate (to the best of my abilities).

Captain J.B. Holland is a legend among a small group of people in Texas.

ABOUT THE AUTHOR

Markus McDowell is a writer, editor, and researcher. He has been writing fiction since he was eight years old, though most of his published works are nonfiction. He has lectured at various universities in the US, Europe, and the UK. He has a Ph.D. from Fuller Theological Seminary and a law degree from the University of London, and is the author of *Praying Through the Bible, Volume 1: Genesis–Joshua* and *Volume 2: Judges–Second Samuel, Prayers of Jewish Women: Studies of Patterns of Prayer in the Second Temple Period*, and *Jurisprudence & Legal Theory for Law Students*. This is his first novel.

If you wish to receive notice of publication of other books and articles by Markus McDowell, visit the websites below:

- Mailing list http://eepurl.com/bGVLrL

- Facebook https://www.facebook.com/MarkusMcDowellAuthor/

- Website www.markusmcdowell.com

22571310R00179

Printed in Great Britain
by Amazon